CW00833069

INSIDE OUTSIDE

FAYE ARCAND

Blue Robin Books

*Dedicated to my husband Michael.
My number one fan. Thanks for
always believing in my dream.*

Part One

Chapter One

LESLIE

The world, like my brain, is in constant motion. Thoughts whirl endlessly in loops both high and low. When this whole thing started, I was feeling pretty good—not great, but good... by the time I got home, my brain ached with doubt and self-loathing.

It was a Tuesday night. Probably near ten o'clock. My favorite time to shop. At that time of night, I didn't need to dodge abandoned carts left by moms who wandered aimlessly from shelf to shelf to read labels. I'm not sure who they were trying to impress, but same shit, different jar. I used to be one of those people—a label reader. I'd only buy organic and cringed at the thought of buying something with an expiry date within the same calendar year. Shopping later in the day meant having the aisles to myself and freedom from judgment. I didn't have to hide my cupcakes behind a box of tampons or buy a bag of lettuce—to impress who knows who — that would later be tossed. Camouflage doesn't last forever. I learned that the hard way.

On that Tuesday night, I raced through the aisles, my head down as I filled my cart with chips, cookies, snack cakes, and wine. I passed by a mirror and automatically tugged my over-sized hoodie over my bulky track pants to remain shapeless and concealed. Heck, for all anyone knew, I was an escaped princess in disguise as I shopped for my insatiable young lover. A similar plot twist in my last romance novel. Readers loved her real curves and take-charge attitude, and I enjoyed writing her. Even now, my mind swirled with ideas of a sequel—her lover would die, and she'd meet the twin brother—or maybe the twin sister.

A giggle escaped me as I steered the cart to the dairy aisle in search of ice cream.

Then it happened.

"Shit." I spat as my feet froze to the slick, shiny floor. "Shit. Shit. Shit." Blood rushed to my head, and I dove over to the frozen fruit section, opened the glass door, and stepped behind it.

The warm store air mingled with sub-zero temperatures, and the glass immediately fogged up. I wiped a tiny window to peek through and studied the situation before me.

Why is he here? Hell, he never did the grocery shopping when we were married. Why would he do it now? I studied how his hair barely grazed his jacket collar. A jacket I gave him for our anniversary a couple of years ago. Does he remember that day? The special night, the love ... does he think of ...

There. That's why he's here. His new wife emerged from behind the large display, and I pushed myself farther into the freezer. They stood side-by-side, the baby strapped across her ample chest as she swayed back and forth. She wore body-hugging, sleek, peek-a-boo yoga gear, her hair perfectly coiffed.

Not a strand out of place. She smiled and touched Phillip's chest. The simple action radiated an energy that resounded even to where I stood in my hiding spot over thirty feet away.

I want to be her. She's everything I'm not and never could be. And, the baby...

My gut tightened in a mangled knot as I saw the happy little family. It wasn't mine and knew it never would be. Memories of Phillip engulfed me as I gawked at the seemingly perfect couple like they were celebrities. *It's not fair. The dream was mine. I'm supposed to hate him. I do. No, that's a lie. I miss him so much I ache.*

At that point, he laughed. I wanted to hear what was said, but I dared not move. I wiped the glass in front of my eyes again in time to see him turn toward me as another customer nudged me.

"Hey lady, I need blueberries," the guy said. "Can I get in there?"

I grabbed a bag and shoved the berries in his direction as I watched Phillip and his new family turn and amble up the aisle. In his arms he held a bag of diapers. A lump filled my throat. The pain stabbed deep into my soul as I gulped the cold air. Spasms raced the length of my body as I fought to contain the bulging agony that threatened to burst out of me.

"Lady, these are the wrong ones," the guy said behind me. "Seriously, like, are you okay? Do you need a doctor?"

My hands shook, but I managed to grasp the cart's handle and back away from the freezer. The customer gaped at me as I inched around the corner and tucked in behind a nearby pillar. I hoped I resembled a light-footed ninja rather than a gasping chubby lady avoiding her ex. I continued my duck and peek until I reached the front. My heart raced as though I'd run a marathon, but I continued to the self-checkout.

A tiny trickle of sweat traveled from under my breast over

my huge, rounded, distended belly and hit the waistband. If I stay here much longer, I'll be in a fucking puddle of tears and sweat. Yup, all over the floor to be walked upon, avoided, or heaven forbid, ignored altogether.

A cashier with thick glasses and a nasty overbite watched me. *Why is she staring at me? Hasn't she ever seen a fat girl in the self-checkout line? Yup, judgmental people like you and Phillip push me to the edge. I still needed to make it to my car. What if they're in the parking lot? Breastfeeding or making out in the backseat? Do they still make out?*

My brain wouldn't stop. It went to sick and twisted corners I tried to block it out. A deep, jagged breath of frustration and torment rose in my chest. It clawed at the soft, pliable surface and begged to be released. Instead, I tucked my chin as far down into my hoodie as I could, swallowed hard against the searing agony in my throat, and bolted to my Jeep. I locked the doors, tore open a box of sticky, gooey snack cakes, and shoved a whole one in my mouth. Crumbs erupted everywhere, but it didn't matter because even before I finished chewing, the next clear cellophane package was ripped open.

The binge lasted two days. Flecks of strawberry icing stuck to my cheeks to resemble pockmarks, crumbs wedged into every orifice, and my clothing bore the stains of ketchup, ice cream, and grease. A mirror would show me as a street junkie. I couldn't physically move. Exhausted, I wanted to die. I wasn't sure who I hated more, myself or Phillip. It didn't matter, anyway. Nothing did. Nothing could fix me or the situation. The binge changed nothing, but it provided an ugly numbness that reminded me of my need to decipher the good from the bad.

Why do I do that to myself?

It was almost eight o'clock and I was still in a stupor as I stumbled into my giant round nesting chair and stared out the window. Why do I do that to myself? My foggy brain even dulled my sight. Nothing was sharp or focused. Everything around me moved in slow motion and I had to be careful not to spill the full fat latte that was delivered to the door just minutes before.

With my latte in hand, I grabbed my notepad and pen and tucked in under a blanket to watch the morning activity of the small, scruffy triangular park across from my townhouse.

It was actually a tromped-down section of grass and worn patches that led to a gravel path going God knows where. Was it a park? Did it have a name? There were no swings, slides, or picnic grounds. It was more like a neglected green space with a trio of struggling cedar trees and a couple of spindly pines used to shield and soften the area between the street and whatever lay behind. A lone gray bench with a dedication plaque in the center backrest, sat left of the trail and filled the small space.

If you drove down the four-lane highway between the park and the townhouse, you'd probably miss the park completely. But living close, I was hyper-aware of my surroundings for fear someone would cross over and pitch a tent on my small, mani-cured lawn that bordered the polished rock path to the front door. The shabby area with its weeds and strewn trash regis-tered in our minds when Phillip and I bought the place eight years before. The realtor had assured us the entire area was about to be rezoned. But that never happened, and it faded into the daily ignored background.

I pulled my blanket closer and concentrated on the buttery light cast by the late summer sun to welcome the day.

The guy I dubbed Prince, because every girl deserves a prince in her life. He always arrived before anyone else with his overflowing shopping cart to dig through the trash for cans and bottles. His behavior was predictable and compelling. With his plastic poncho and filthy clothes, he showed up every morning.

Unlike some guys I know, his behavior was predictable and compelling.

He stuffed his finds into a stretched-out black plastic trash bag hanging precariously from the side of his cart. It was like a massive, lumpy bag of Santa coal.

Once he was done, he'd sit on the bench with one arm stretched along the top, his foot propped on his knee, eat a sandwich, and then stand up to lean into his cart as he pushed it wherever he went for the day. It was like clockwork.

Over time, the morning strangers became familiar and welcome. There was a sense of accepted order and deliberateness to their actions, as if they all had somewhere to go and something to do. I'm not sure if they rolled into my life or me into theirs, but either way, they became my friends when I most needed someone.

"Good morning, Prince." I said as I stood before the window.

The city bus huffed to a stop, and a tiny elderly woman alit as she had done the day before—Queenie, I called her. She had an air and posture of a fine British upper-class lady. She stopped briefly to adjust the sleeves of her coat, tugging each down from the cuff, and then squared her shoulders before she walked with a demeanor of purpose and confidence in the same direction she walked every weekday morning. As I watched her, a prickle of envy skittered over me. Such a slight woman, yet she appeared steadfast and strong. Once, many years ago, I vowed to be strong and fearless, but promises sometimes get lost in the fight for survival, especially when there's a secretive perch to view the outside world and you never have to let anyone in.

I shook my head and studied my coffee. Now lukewarm, it appeared thick and chalky. The school bus, with its bright flashing red lights, caught my eye as I swirled the contents of my cup. School was back in session. A crowd of young people congregated next to the green space and mingled farther back on the fringes. Prince sat down and propped up his foot as the bus pulled to a stop in front of all the students. The bus blocked the view, but as it pulled away, Prince stood to leave, and a woman pushing a stroller came over the knoll into view.

The woman, who walked with a pronounced limp, also came through every morning. Her gait reminded me of a child's toy with different-sized wheels as she listed from side to side. Up down, up down... It was like clockwork and she was always the last one to arrive in the morning before the rush calmed.

"Good morning, Limpy-Mommy," I said to the window.

The day had officially started.

Chapter Two

SELENA

Where the fuck are my sneakers? I combed through the room I
shared with my two younger sisters. There was no way to call it
a bedroom, as it was one grimy mattress on the floor for the
three of us, but still, things went missing. I knew I'd left my
shoes at the door of the room, so I shoved everything aside in
my search, but came up empty.

I didn't need this crap on my first day at a new school.
Everyone was up. Mom worked late, taking her morning shift
off. If no one knew better, they'd think it was sweet how
everyone was gathered in the kitchen excited and anxious for
the first day of school, but the Hallmark moment was pure bullshit. God, I couldn't wait for this year to be over. At least then I
could call my own shots.

"Mom," I called on the way to the kitchen. "My shoes have
disappeared. I can't find them anywhere."

"Well, Selena, just come eat something. I'm sure they'll turn up."

"I want my fucking shoes." I glanced over to where Sofia was shoving a fried potato in her tiny mouth, and Victoria picked at the soft center of a piece of toast. Mom flitted about as her boyfriend, Gilbert, sipped a beer.

"Don't talk to your mother like that," Gilbert said as he leaped to his feet. The chair flew across the worn tiles and smacked into the wall. The jarring eruption sent defiling waves rippling through the room to silence and still us all.

"Not a worry," Mom said as she wrung her hands. "Let's get back to eating so the girls can get to school."

Gilbert strode over and stroked Victoria's hair. She didn't look up as he let his hand linger, then fall to her shoulder, where he kneaded the area. I sensed the challenge and wanted to gouge out his eyes and wipe that sarcastic grin right off the face of the Earth. The whole thing was fucked up. Hell, Vic was starting grade seven and shouldn't have to put up with such shit. The way Mom pandered to the asshole and ignored everything else was beyond any common sense.

"Sofia, Vic," I said, "as soon as I find my shoes, we're leaving, so make sure you're ready. Come help me look."

Gilbert lit a cigarette and took a long pull as he stared at me through slitted eyes. The smoke wafted lazily from between his lips. Mom sidled in beside him and took a drag as the girls scrambled in search of my shoes. I watched Mom as the heavy stench of lard from the frying pan mingled with the smoke as Gilbert cracked another beer.

"I found them," Sofia shouted. "And they are stah-ink-keeeeeeeeee." She pinched her nose as she showed me.

There, under a threadbare mat on the front step, were my sneakers. Both smeared on the outside and stuffed to the toes with dog shit. There was no way I'd cry. I knew. I wasn't stupid. It was Gilbert. My only shoes now unusable.

"We'll boil them in vinegar," Mom said. "That might save them."

"How am I supposed to go to school today? I can't go barefoot."

Mom scooted into the bedroom she shared with Gilbert and came back dangling a pair of high black faux leather boots. It's not like there was much choice. Believe me, if I could've gotten away without shoes, I would've.

"The boots suit you," Mom said. "You look like a model." She didn't get it, but Gilbert sure did as he stared at me through glazed eyes with the start of a grin on his face.

Bastard.

I shuffled along like a teenage hooker down the back alley with my two little sisters in tow. Their school was a block from my bus stop. I left them and hobbled over to where the other students waited.

I wanted the ground beneath me to open up and swallow me. I didn't want to be in this place or near these people. All this fake-ass crap made me want to hurl. *Just one more year. I can do this. I have to do this.*

At the bus stop, I ignored the burn in my squished toes and adopted a face of boredom and cool detachment. No smile, no raised brows, and definitely no eye contact. As far as everyone else knew, I had planned my wardrobe weeks before, like everyone else with their back-to-school shopping. They didn't know the boots were two sizes too small, squished my toes to the point of blistering pain, and a safety pin held the zipper in place.

At the group's edge, I shifted from one foot to another as pain crept into my ankle and calf. To the untrained eye, it appeared like people stood all over the place, but I immediately recognized the small groups and the order of things. Nervous energy buzzed through the crowd when the school bus arrived. I stayed near the edge and out of the way. The crowds' chatter filled my head with snippets of overheard conversations.

"Jennifer went to France this summer," one said.

"She told me she got really drunk," another said.

"I heard Zach hooked up with Alison."

This brought squeals from the small group as the bus door swooshed open for boarding.

A girl with long blonde hair bumped me from behind. I stepped aside to let her pass. It's the same everywhere, the unspoken rule says popular and pretty are first on and first off the bus, and new students were obviously low-life losers, like me, who got on last, and no one cared whether we got off.

Last year I changed schools three times, then two weeks ago, plans changed again, and we moved in the middle of the night to avoid the landlord. All five of us squeezed into a two-bedroom bungalow just beyond the hill. It was a neighborhood where the police knew the players and didn't show until someone was dead or got chased into the rat-infested pit. It was a stark contrast across the four-lane highway where the bus picked us up. There stood million-dollar townhomes with ornately carved front doors, wall-to-wall windows, and symmetrically perfect trees and shrubs lined the block. It obviously reflected the people who lived in the buildings. I'm sure it housed Seattle's finest, richest, and most brilliant people who lacked for nothing.

I boarded the bus and took the last seat, or what little remained of it, beside a fat girl with flaming red hair and angry pimples everywhere. She swung her chubby legs into the aisle, and I wedged between her and the seat back in front of me. I didn't want to put my butt in the redhead's face, so I leaned forward as I squeezed past.

"Hey, what are you doing?" the student in the seat directly in front screeched as she whacked at my bag. "Jesus Christ, you're gonna rip out all my hair."

"Sorry." I pulled the bag tighter to my body.

All eyes were on me. I wanted to disappear into my threadbare jeans and hooker boots. Instead, I squeezed my butt between the bus wall and the girl's leg, then pressed myself as close to the side of the bus as possible. The window, caked and streaked with grime, offered little in the way of a view past the inner sanctum, but I saw some homeless guy pull something out of a plastic bag as the bus jerked into motion. Heat from the red head's soft pudding body pressing against mine made me sweat. The air filled with the vague sweet scent of vanilla tinged with weed as the back-riders sucked on their glossy vape pens, blowing the clouds to the floor and behind the seats. I wanted to scream as I listened to the drivel and giggles. Finally, the bus slammed to a stop, and the driver swung the door open. My legs bounced in anticipation of getting off.

I stood when the bus was nearly empty and stepped outside into the crisp air. My head cleared immediately as the crowd dispersed to leave one person standing alone, waiting.

"Hi." I tucked myself under his arm and slipped my hand into his back pocket. "Fancy meeting you here."

"I'm glad you finally decided to join me," he said, draping his arm around my neck and kissing the top of my head while we walked toward the school's front door.

"I had very little choice, believe me," I laughed. "Perhaps spontaneous escapes under the cover of night has its advantages, like finally ending up in the same school catchment, right?"

My cheap-ass boots clicked against the concrete steps as Chad and I entered the school to begin our senior year.

.   .   .

Chad and I had hooked up six weeks ago at a party in my old neighborhood. We were both single and lonely. Hey, it's life. I suppose if I analyzed the whole thing, it was fun and came with benefits that were very good and often excellent. I didn't mean it to be anything serious; it was something to do to kill time and actually feel good for a while. Hell, we came from different worlds, but who am I to question destiny?

"Selena?" The way he said my name with a slight raspy undertone sent shivers. He had all of my attention by his mere presence. He placed his hand on my hip. "Hey, want to have a coffee after school?"

"No, I can't. No. I really have to get home to my sisters," I stammered as his thumb grazed the front of my hip. I forced myself to take a deep breath as I ached to fall into him and feel him. "My sisters ..."

He leaned forward with his entire body and nibbled my bottom lip. "It's just coffee." He breathed each word into my neck.

All I could do was nod. *My sisters will be fine for an hour. Yeah, I'm sure they'll be okay. Wouldn't they?*

"Meet me at Java Jenny's at one," he said as he waved his hand without glancing back.

The first half-day of school was uneventful. No one acknowledged me or introduced themselves. It was the same at every school. Cliques, loners, and geeks knew their place, and I was invisible, which suited me fine. Some shot me sideways glances when I was with Chad, but they stayed silent.

The coffee shop was a couple of blocks away, but by the time I got there, my feet were on fire and a sharp pain shot up my legs every time I moved. My toes were in the vice grip of my boots, and any weight I put on the ball of my foot pushed the bruising deeper. I entered the coffee shop and spotted Chad immediately in the line. He was an inch or two taller than me. His jeans hugged his butt perfectly, and his crazy mop of curls was contained in a tight knot on top of his head.

Oh my God, a few nights ago, his hair tinged with sweat tickled my face as he leaned in to kiss me. My heart threatened to pound right out of my chest as I pictured myself laying beneath him as I ran my fingers through his hair and pulled him closer.

"Hey, Selena, what can I get you?"

"Hey," I stammered as my thoughts tumbled back into place. "I'll have a large, sugar-free vanilla latte, non-fat soy."

"I better write this down." The line moved up one. "Here, say it into my phone."

He held his phone to my mouth as I leaned closer to him and repeated my order. His toothy grin made me forget my feet for a second. I turned and scanned the seating area. Many people worked on their computers or talked on their phones as they sipped their coffees. Some, deep in conversation, hunched forward over the small round wooden tables as they talked. I tucked into the only spot left, right in front of the restroom doors. I pulled out the straight-backed chair and lowered myself into the seat, stifling a moan of relief as I stretched my legs under the table.

"Here you go." Chad set the large steaming coffee in front of me.

"Thanks. I need to tell you that I can't stay. I have to get home for my little sisters." I dug in my purse and held out a five-dollar bill.

"You get the next one." He pushed the bill away.

"Thanks." I shoved it back into my purse, relieved since it was the last of my money.

It had become a running joke—me getting the next one.

Chad never let me. When we talked, it was usually about music or our fantasies of getting away from our families, but there was one time when things got personal, and I told him about life at home. He knew about the lack of funds, though he never once brought it up.

I stirred my latte as he hung his jacket over the back of his chair.

We sipped in silence. The morning fiasco was still eating at me. *Gilbert is such a fucking bastard. I wish he'd leave. Get out of our lives and dick right off.* The tension of having him in the house distracted me from everything.

"You okay?" Chad asked as he stood up.

"Yeah, I guess. Listen, I should go. There's crap at home and—"

"The crap isn't going anywhere. I'll be right back."

Chad entered the men's room when some bright red block letters by the till caught my eye.

Part-time positions available. Apply to manager.

I hobbled to the front with as much composure as I could muster with my sore feet.

"Hi, I'd like to apply for the part-time job."

The Java Jenny girl gave me the link to the website, and I returned to the table to complete it. I had to leave most of it blank, but I filled in my name and phone number, then wrote: I can work weekends and evenings. I learn fast and will work hard.

How am I going to work evenings when Mom's on a split shift? And weekends? Shit, Mom is at the diner the entire weekend. Should I stay home? How will I pay for my phone? The girls must almost be out of school. Shit. I shouldn't be here.

Chad returned as I hit enter. I'd make it work. I had to.

"I have to go. Sorry." I checked the time on my phone and gulped the last of my coffee. "You know how it is, right?"

"Yeah, sure. I thought maybe we could, you know... go somewhere."

"No fairrrrr," I whined as I studied his beautiful full lips. "Fuckkkkkkk, you make it so hard to leave." I pushed myself to stand and pressed my head into the nook of his neck. "I wouldn't if I didn't have to. You know that, right?"

"Come on, I'll walk you to the bus stop."

It was all I could do not to rip my boots off, but I still noticed he didn't answer my question. I'm sure I looked like a complete dork who walked like a duck. I had to keep my knees bent to force a spring into the next step and lessen the weight on my feet.

He reached to take my arm when a rock stabbed through the bottom of my boot, causing my ankle to buckle. "You okay?"

"Yeah, I'll be fine." I let him hold me as I wobbled along beside him.

We stood to the side of a bus stop where a large photograph of a young, smiling couple approached the entrance to the Space Needle. The sign said: Stay Home and Take in the View. Someone had drawn devil horns and beards on both models. Paper coffee cups and cigarette butts littered the area, and the Plexiglass shelter had graffiti scrawled across it in red pen and swear words were etched into the wooden bench seat.

"You don't have to wait. I'm not sure how long it'll be."

"Don't be silly. A gentleman doesn't leave a lady after sharing coffee." He winked at me.

I couldn't help but smile.

The bus finally pulled up, and the accordion doors slapped open in front of me. I stood back and let everyone else get on as I turned to Chad.

"See you tomorrow." I quickly hugged him, and brushed

my lips against his. Oh, how I wanted to grab him and love him, but now was not the time. Home. I needed to get home.

I took the first seat and waved out the window. As soon as he was out of sight, I unzipped the boots and freed my feet. A woman across the way stared at me and clucked her tongue, but I didn't care. Bitchy Karen, you got me, didn't you? So stupid and petty. Get a life. There were more important things to be worried about. Like the time. It was past three-thirty, and I was over a half-hour late in getting home. Shit. Shit. Shit. He'd be there alone with the girls.

Oh my God, what the hell was I thinking? Stupid. The first day of school was a half-day, and I should've been home an hour ago. I didn't make any arrangements for the girls. I needed to hurry. If anything happened, I'd die.

My nerves were frayed by the time the bus slowed for my stop. I shuffled to the door and hung on to the pole until it stopped. I tip-toed down the steps of the bus and perched on the edge of the bench as I forced my swollen feet back into the narrow opening of the boots. I didn't bother zipping them up. A new anxious energy trembled through me, urging me to hurry—to get home. The girl's school let out at noon. They'd be home by now, and I needed to be there. It was all on me. I stood at the pedestrian light as my swollen feet pulsed in time with my racing heart. A shiny Jeep, the color of a glistening black jelly-bean, stopped. The driver wore a bright pumpkin-orange scarf which made me think of Halloween. I dashed across the cross-walk as fast as I could with the boot tops flapping and forced myself forward as the boot heels sank into the deep pebble path.

I needed to hurry. I needed to save my sisters.

Chapter Three

LESLIE

I settled in by the window with my laptop to write, but before long, my eyes grew heavy, and I drifted off to sleep in that lovely way of not trying. No looped thoughts, just a merciful quiet. Peace.

A thwack on the front door startled me awake. It wasn't a regular knock but more like a slap. Prince? My fuzzy brain chuckled. Maybe he found me.

I uncurled myself from the cushion's deep comfort and shuffled toward the stairs.

Thwack. Thwack. Thwack.

"I'm coming. I'm coming." I padded down the steps, stretching and pumping my arms to get the blood moving again. Through the peephole, there was a distorted figure of a man I didn't recognize. The huge bald head continued into a long face covered with a bushy beard. Who the hell is that? With my hand on the doorknob, I peeked out in time to see his hand come barreling down on the door. I could tell he didn't want to take no for an answer.

"Who is it?"

"I'm looking for Leslie Richter."

"What do you want?"

"My name is Franklin, and I have a delivery from McAfee Publishing."

Okay, that made sense. I turned the deadbolt and pulled open the door.

"Leslie Richter?" he asked politely, with his hands crossed over a package he held in front of him.

I nodded.

"Good," he said, as his stance and demeanor changed to one of contempt and boredom. "Consider yourself served."

He shoved a fat envelope in my direction, dropped it, and left. It fell right between my bare feet. I gawked at the offensive package. I wanted to kick it straight back in the guy's face, but he was already on the sidewalk, headed for an illegally parked rusty blue sedan.

"Asshole," I said. I picked up the envelope and slammed and dead-bolted the door. "Who are Westin, Pearson, and Zubliski?" I tore the end off the envelope and pulled out the thick contents. I was subpoenaed to testify for something. Typed in bold at the top of the papers listed my ex-husband as the plaintiff. He was suing me for defamation of character, slander, and reversal of spousal support. I flipped through the papers.

"What the—? Oh my God, I don't believe it. He's the one who cheated on me. Defamation? What a jerk."

The blood surged through my veins with an intensity worthy of a comic book hero. I was ready to burst out and fly with my fist aimed straight at his gut. Stunned. I'm stunned. There's no other word for it. Well, he better get himself ready because I'm done being a pushover. I'm ready for a good fight.

"I can't believe he'd sue me. Me!" With a renewed sense of energy, I flew up the stairs two at a time to get showered and dressed. "The nerve. I need to talk to Max."

Max wasn't just my lawyer; he was my friend and confidant. We'd known each other for ten years, and he knew every nook and cranny of my soul. I had no secrets from Max and trusted him with my life. When we first met, there was an aura of instant trust, like being cocooned against the negativity of the world. He was older by at least ten years, and his poise and slight twang in his voice were beyond attractive. With his goatee, he reminded me of a young Colonel Sanders who lifted weights and filled out a suit in a way no chicken guy ever could.

"What do you mean I have to go to court?" I stood before him with hands on my hips. "Max, you're the best lawyer in town. You know these allegations are a ridiculous waste of time."

"Les, I'm afraid this is a court order, and it's my duty as your lawyer to inform you that you must attend court as directed. I'm going to draft some documents to countersue, so try to relax. By the time we're done with him, he'll wish he'd never heard your name."

"What are you going to do, Max? I don't want to fight anymore. I need to get on with my life. What's this whole thing about, anyway?"

"He's accusing you of putting up derogatory pictures of him on Facebook after the two of you first split."

"What? That's almost a year ago now. And I only left them up for a day or two before deleting them."

"Come on, Les, you know nothing is ever deleted. Someone, and my guess is it's Phillip's lawyer, has a copy somewhere. He's also suing you for slander, which is basically the same as defamation, but it's verbal. What did you say about him and to who?"

"How the hell am I supposed to know? I said a lot of things."

"Well, the one thing about slander is the statements need to be false. You may have said mean things about him, but if it was factual, then there's no slander. Did you go around spreading false information about Phillip?"

"Absolutely not. I told everyone how much of a complete and utter prick he was, and it's the truth. I'd get on the stand and swear to that under oath."

"Okay, I believe you." Max reached for some papers on his desk. "Here," he scanned his notes, "the third thing, and the one I believe is the actual crux of this lawsuit, is money. The other things are fluff and distraction."

"You're probably right. He called me last week telling me the new missus doesn't like the idea of him paying spousal support. She says I'm a famous writer, and they shouldn't have to support me."

"He called you?"

"Yes, a few days ago. He sounded pretty stressed out. The baby was screaming in the background—it sounded pretty tense. I told him to go fuck himself and hung up."

"Well, thank God you didn't get snarky with him." Max shook his head and smiled at me from across the desk. "I'm going to add harassment to the list of countersuits. You're not to answer any unknown calls and definitely none from him. Has he paid support owing?"

"I didn't even realize at first because I don't regularly check the balance of my accounts. After the subpoena came, I checked online, and there hasn't been a deposit for the last couple of months."

"Okay." Max made some notes. "What did you mean when you said he sounded tense?"

"I lived with Phillip for a long time. I could tell by the sound of his voice he was tired. It was a cross between exhaustion and exasperation." I studied the stack of papers in front of Max. "The tone in his voice was the same as when his father died. He sounded unusually sad and broken."

"That, my dear, is not your problem." Max reached across and squeezed my hand. "I've seen what this divorce has done to you, and that's our concern. You're not the same person. You're ... I don't know, the bitter ex-wife."

"Wha—?" It was like he'd smacked me across the face. "I know what you're saying when you use those words, but—" My eyes burned as I fought to reconcile his words. "Max, my husband got another woman pregnant while we were undergoing fertility treatments. If that doesn't spell out asshole, I don't know what does."

"Leslie, I know, but ..."

"Don't, Max. Please don't. Don't tell me I'm bitter and angry like a dried-up old prune. I ..." I pointed at my chest. "I needed him to see me. I'm not the bad guy here. People tell me all the time how nice I am." My voice was screechy, but I couldn't stop. "Did you hear me, Max? I'm nice. Tell me you know I'm nice." Suddenly, all energy drained from me, and the fight in me dissolved. I slumped back in the chair and eyed Max. "I'm nice. I know I am."

"Leslie, what Phillip did to you was unfathomable. It was unfair, unjust, and downright nasty, but it shouldn't define you. It's a reflection on him." Max stepped around the desk and stood beside me. "You have become the bitter ex-wife, though, and it's not very pretty. I'm telling you the truth because I love you. You're my friend. Les, it needs to be reined in, and you need to dig deep and bring back the Leslie we all know and love." He looked me straight in the eye. "Les, they're going to have witnesses lined up to say, even reluctantly, how nasty you've been."

"Isn't that slander?"

"It's not if it's true. And, believe me, they can and they will." Max leaned against the edge of the desk in front of my chair. "They're looking for a fight." He pulled his fingers through his white beard as he talked. "I'll find out exactly what they have on you and what they're looking for."

"I just want it all to end. I'm full of rage—I can feel it boil inside me. Max ... " I peeked up at him and lowered my voice. "I imagine them together with their baby. The baby I couldn't have. They laugh, smile, and remind themselves how much of a joke I am. It's all I can think about." I focused on my hands and continued. "I haven't written a decent chapter in months. My agent and editor are threatening to drop my contract. Max I can't ever have a baby—I can't create anything. I'm a barren, sterile, empty vessel of a person."

I couldn't believe I'd actually said it. The words floated out of me like a noxious clinging stench, mocking and ugly. There was no escape from reality. Everything I said was true. I brought my feet up on the chair and hugged my legs. "I can't do this... I can't..."

"I'm sorry this is happening, Les." Max kneeled beside me. "I really am. You deserve better." He put a finger under my chin and raised my face to his. "We'll take care of this." He nodded as he spoke. "Trust me. I'm with you. I'm not going anywhere."

I gave him a quick hug, then pulled away. He always took care of things. I grabbed a tissue and wiped my runny nose. He was right. The attitude and nastiness needed to stop.

"Why don't you go home?" He placed his hand on my shoulder. "I'll get to work on this file and see what we can do. You concentrate on getting back to your regular self. You're a lot stronger than you think." He rubbed my back and stood to his full height before making his way back behind his desk.

"I feel like such an idiot right now." I grabbed another tissue. "Things need to change. I've known that for a long time, and I've done it before. I'll do it again."

"Your secrets are safe with me," he said as he handed me a tissue box. "I also know you're a strong and capable woman. When you're done with all this stuff that's mired you down, you'll be ready to take on the world."

"Thanks, Max." Tears escaped down my cheeks, and I used my shirt sleeve to wipe them away. "I'm so grateful, Max. I promise, I'll get my shit together... I have to..."

"I'll call you when I've got some answers."

I nodded and stood to leave. A sharp thrust from my lower gut went high into my chest. I opened my mouth to say something, but nothing came out. Secrets. Max mentioned secrets. I wasn't sure I'd ever be okay.

I pulled the Jeep into the private garage at the back of the building. When Phillip and I first toured the house, I loved the idea of walking straight from the parking garage into the foyer of our own house. Today, memories of when Phillip scooped me up and carried me over this threshold overwhelmed me.

We'd already been married over two years by then, but the townhouse purchase was something to celebrate. He carried me inside, and as he walked, he kissed me with an eagerness and heat that made us one. Once through the door, he kicked it closed with his foot and laid me down on the icy tile floor only to warm me with his body. He was so gentle. His feather touches radiated up and down my body, caressing me like a fragile flower meant to be stroked and cherished. We gave each other what we both needed. Even now, I could still see him there, by the door, and hear his voice in the walls. I'd believed all his declarations of love and devotion. Even in the end, when wicked whispers made their way to me, I still believed.

Now here I was, alone, angry, and fucking exhausted. I sat on the bottom step and studied the floor by the front door. The passion was like a million years ago.

He said he'd love me forever. I told him I'd give him a house full of kids.

We both lied.

I don't know how I ended up on the floor or how long I'd been there. A raw, numbing cold radiated from the tiles into my already chilled body. My phone vibrated on the floor—shivering, just like me. Max's name and picture appeared on the screen, and I stared at it. The dampness of my recent tears kept me still. I'd already humiliated myself enough today. Enough was enough.

The phone stopped, and soon pinged with the alert of a waiting message.

I rolled onto my belly and pushed myself into a crouched position. I covered my face with my hands and rubbed vigorously, hoping to renew some sense in my brain. Everything was off-kilter—like all the junk food was stuck in an enormous toxic wad in the center of my gut. I grabbed the banister and pulled myself up the stairs from the foyer to the main level. The entire house was dark as I climbed the next flight of stairs to my bedroom. I crawled into the unmade bed and pulled the covers around me. This day needed to end, but my mind wouldn't stop.

He called me bitter.

I'd made such a fool of myself in front of Max. He said I'd changed. Said I talked too much. He probably wanted to call me vulgar but was afraid to. Had other people noticed, too? Was I different?

Oh yes... Max called earlier. Maybe Phillip canceled the case. Maybe he loves me and wants to come home. Stop it. He's gone. He's with someone who could give him a baby.

"Stop it." I sat up, shook my head, and felt around for the TV remote.

My mind wouldn't stop, though. Maybe Phillip still secretly loved me. I pulled the blanket and heard the remote drop off the end of the bed.

"Shit." I forced myself up. The batteries had popped out and rolled in opposite directions on the hardwood floor. One surfaced immediately beside the dresser's leg. I couldn't find the other until I looked under the bed. There it was, right in the center beside a large dust bunny. I'd have to get the broom to knock it out. I plopped myself on the floor and threw the remote under the bed.

"There, now you're all together. I didn't want you, anyway."

Chapter Four

SELENA

My lungs hurt as much as my bare feet. I fought to ignore the constant stabbing of jagged rocks and stray pieces of fucking broken glass. I thought if I sprinted as fast as I could, it would lighten my step, but it didn't help. When I finally neared the house, I could see the TV's flickering light through the threadbare sheet used to cover the front window. Gilbert wasn't handy except for plugging into other people's cable and Wi-Fi.

We live more than halfway down the narrow lane of what I could only call shacks. The lane has two deep ruts and sharp jutting rocks. A person could easily break a neck around here, and I wasn't sure anyone would come running.

I had the house in view and moved as quickly as my aching feet would allow. There were two weather-beaten gray wooden steps leading up to the warped front door. I tiptoed to avoid slivers and rusty nails. I neared the once-white door, the surface engrained with oily grime and grunge. Above the handle was a smudged boot print where someone had kicked it. I turned the knob. It was locked.

"Shit."

I wanted to walk in unannounced, but now had to knock. I could hear the raised volume of the television. Canned laughter filtered through the thin walls and door to fill the air with false mirth.

Sofia answered the door immediately. Her wispy hair, full of static, stood up and flitted through the air. She wiped the fly-away strands from her face with both of her still dimpled hands and smiled up at me.

"Hi, Selena. We were playing a game. Do you want to play?"

"No, but you can tell me where your shirt is." I glanced across the room and saw Victoria pulling her shirt over her head. At first, she wouldn't make eye contact, then she folded her arms and glared at me. My heart skipped, and my stomach sank as I surveyed the situation.

"Gilbert said I didn't have to wear one." Sofia's eyes were wide as she looked from me to him.

"Well, if it ain't the world's princess finally home. Yer mama ain't gonna be none too happy to find you're out flitting around. I bet it's a boy. It's always a boy, ain't it?"

"Victoria, Sofia, go to your room. I'll fix you a snack in a minute." I kept one eye on him sitting in his brown cracked vinyl recliner with his long skinny legs propped in the air.

"Are you mad, Selena? We were just playing."

"Come on, baby." Victoria pushed Sofia toward their bedroom.

"I'm not mad." I gazed down at the girls and smiled. "Sorry I'm late. I want to hear all about your new school and your teachers." I shooed them into the bedroom and hobbled over to Gilbert. As I got closer, the stench of dirty feet and body odor filled my every breath. Shirtless, he scratched his hairy belly as I got closer.

"You're lookin' a wee bit ornery, princess."

"Stay. The. Fuck. Away. From. My. Sisters. Is that clear?"

In my anger, I stepped closer. I wanted to pound my finger into his chest to drive the point home. Before I knew it, he reached out, took a handful of my hair, and pulled me down against him. The dampness of his hairy flesh pressed against my cheek, and my legs gave out from under me. As I fell forward, he pulled until my hair suspended me.

"Don'tchu ever threaten me, ya lil bitch. This is my house, and the likes o' you ain't gonna tell me what I can an' can't do. Is that clear?" He slammed the recliner down, stood, pulled me higher by the hair, then tossed me across the room.

"Don't you ever touch them, or I'll kill you myself," I hissed.

He made like he was going to come after me, so I skootched across the bare linoleum floor to put as much distance between him and me as possible.

"Off you go now, pretty lil princess." He laughed as I left the room.

Chapter Five

THEN

LESLIE

At the age of fourteen, Mother finally allowed me to attend public school. I couldn't believe it was actually happening but there it was. Right in front of me. Pine Hills High School, or PHHS, as the students called it. Never in my entire life had such intensity surged through my body to arouse my pulse. It skittered in time with my tapping toes. My stomach growled, not from hunger but from the anticipation of a new life, free and thought provoking. This—this beautiful red-brick building held promise and wonder within, and I was going to be a part of it all.

Mother was dead set against me ever going to public school. She said terrorists or worse—other psycho students with a vendetta against the world—could strike at any time.

"Homeschooling is better and safer," she said. "Those other kids are mean and nasty."

"Mother," I begged, "I'll be the best daughter ever. Terrorists don't bomb schools in Nebraska. They go for big cities. I promise to be good and make you proud."

I'm not sure why, but she finally gave into my pleading. Maybe she was tired of my constant asking or all the promises and assurances I made, but it was worth it to be normal for a change.

My dream stood before me. The tall doors beckoned, and I never wanted to forget this—my first day. Red cinder block framed the doors, making them stand out like two tall narrow eyes overlooking the comings and goings of all who passed there. The school's name above the doors had the H's in Hills and High dipping in scroll to resemble raised eyebrows. I stared at it and wondered if the designers meant for it to resemble eyes. It was clever.

Students buzzed around the grounds—some sprinted and leaped over things to get where they were going, while others sauntered and chatted. The liveliness ricocheted amongst the students as they greeted old friends as if they hadn't seen each other in years. Everyone appeared to know each other, and Mother had warned me they wouldn't be open to making new friends, but I didn't care. I was here, and that's what mattered.

The previous week, we'd come to the school to register and get a quick tour. They showed me my homeroom class and the nearest bathroom. The friendly lady in the office gave me a school map showing all the classrooms and exits. I studied it every night until my eyes burned, and I could no longer see the black lines.

The five-minute warning bell rang, but I didn't move. I wanted to drink in the entire experience so I could play it back in my mind later, but the throng of students all headed in the same direction swept me along with them. They pulled me into the crowd, and I shuffled along. It reminded me of cattle led to slaughter, where they all crowded to get through gates that separated them into different sizes, classes, and chutes, but this was different—I was sure of it.

"What the hell are you wearing?" A boy stared at me. He stood close enough that the heat of his breath brushed my cheek. I didn't turn, but lowered my head and saw his toe poking through his shoe.

"Holy shit, she looks like one of them farmer girls," another boy shouted over my shoulder. I cringed at his closeness. The lingering stench of his fermented breath, laced with sour milk, hung in the air. "She probably milks cows and plucks chickens."

The boy who started it sneered at me and pinched his nose with his fingers. There was dirt embedded into the folds of his neck, and I could see he'd chewed his fingernails down to the quick.

"She smells like shit, too," he declared. Nearby kids laughed while others rolled their eyes and pushed ahead into the school. "Hey farm girl, do you want to play in the barn with me? We could make a little hay?" The boy thrust his hips forward a few times and stuck out his white-coated tongue.

"Enough." The voice of an adult interjected. "Timothy, see me in my office at lunch break, please. Come on now." She encouraged everyone forward through the doors. "Classes will start in a few minutes."

I inched forward into the school. The magic had faded, but I wouldn't let those heathens ruin my day. Mother had made me wear a kerchief on my head. I meant to take it off, but in my excitement, I forgot it was there. I reached up, dragged it off, and stuffed it in my pocket. Most everyone else was in faded blue jeans, short skirts, T-shirts, or sports clothes. One girl about my age wore a skirt so short that it made me blush. Her long brown hair had black streaks and cascaded around her face like a fountain's waterfall from the ponytail on the top of her head. I didn't want to stare, yet I couldn't help but watch her. She moved like a dancer, with pointed toes and delicate refinement. Her head held high—proud and strong—and her back was perfectly straight. She was the most beautiful girl I think I'd ever seen in real life. I scrutinized my dark brown corduroy mid-calf skirt, black stockings, and thick rubber-soled sensible shoes and realized I did, in fact, resemble a farm girl.

Heat rose in my cheeks as I realized how much I stood out for the wrong reasons. As I raised my eyes, a boy who was more like a full-grown man brushed by me. His sandy blond hair hung halfway down his back, a full beard of red-blond covered his face, and his jeans hung loosely over his hips with a dangling tie at the waist. His white button-up shirt gaped open to show a bare muscular chest. He smelled new and delicious and made my heart skip in a way it never had before. I stared after him as he made his way down the crowded hallway. I wondered if he knew the dancer girl.

I found my homeroom and slipped into the first empty seat at the back of the class. The jittery feeling returned as the male teacher waited at the front. My toe tapped in anticipation, and my palms broke into a sticky sweat. I barely heard anything as blood coursed through me like a vacuum cleaner going full blast. I took a deep breath. They all had a pen and paper on their desk. I did the same.

"Class, my name is Mr. Dexter, and I'll be your homeroom teacher for the next week until we're all settled. While I recognize many of you, there are some unfamiliar faces in the crowd, so we're going to do roll call."

The teacher called names, and students raised their hands and said, "Here."

I'd read about this and practiced in front of the bathroom mirror. The teacher went alphabetically down the list. I listened carefully to keep track of when my name would come up.

"George Latimer?"

"Here." A hand next to me went up.

"Leslie Matheson?"

That's me. I froze. I forgot what to do. Was I supposed to stand? A bead of sweat trickled down the center of my back.

"Leslie Matheson? Are you here?"

"Yes. I'm right here." I bounced in the seat and held my hand up as high as I could. My blue and white checkered kerchief slipped from my pocket and fluttered to the floor as my hip hit the desk, sending my pencil flying. I wanted to die. If God were merciful, he would have immediately shot me through the heart with an errant lightning bolt and put an end to my misery.

"Thank you, Leslie. It's nice to meet you."

I sat back down and swept the kerchief up with my hand. I shoved it deeper into my pocket and tried not to make eye contact with anyone.

"Moooo, Moooo, Moooo ..." echoed off the walls and mixed in with the growing laughter of the class. I slumped farther into my desk and dug my nails into the soft flesh of my hand. Maybe this dream of public high school wasn't the best idea.

Chapter Six

NOW

LESLIE

The morning after seeing Max, I got up earlier than usual to watch the street come alive. I made a cup of tea and settled in my chair with the cat, who immediately curled into my side and licked her paw.

A street sweeper bumped and skittered along the sidewalk edge as an orange mangey cat walked effortlessly along the narrow back of the park bench, leaped down, and disappeared behind the cedar trees. I hugged my hot cup and sipped. Prince appeared with his cumbersome shopping cart. His body was nearly horizontal to the ground as he leaned all his weight into the cart to move it.

The calm of predictable routine fell over me like a cozy Christmas sweater, keeping me warm and safe. Though I was alone, these strangers had become family. They didn't know how important they'd become to my daily survival. Seeing the little routines play out every morning with Prince, Queenie, Limpy-Mommy, and the pretty student—now dubbed Damsel because there was a glow of youth and vitality to her. I had become a part of something solid and predictable.

I reached for the binoculars I'd ordered online and held them up to inspect the scene. At first, there was nothing. The entire area appeared blurry and jumpy until I blew out all my air and stilled my hands.

There she was, running for the bus. I bounced in my seat in unison with her long legs as I watched her long dark hair swing from side to side and her arms pumping wildly with the motion of her legs.

"Hurry! Hurry! Hurry!" I shouted at the window. "You can do it, Damsel. Hurry!"

I held my breath as the young girl disappeared behind the bus, only to have the bus pull away from the stop with her still standing there. Surely the driver had seen her. Why wouldn't he let her on the bus?

I wanted to rush over, rub her back, and soothe her, but she didn't even know I existed. Her long, slim face resembled an under-fed fashion model, with large dark eyes and low bowed brows to frame her face, giving her a bit of a mournful look. Her sunken cheeks made her cheekbones pop and complemented the straight nose, sharp chin, and long jawline, leading to full sensual lips. The running added a healthy pink glow, which gave her a girl-next-door vibe. I wish I could've been that self-assured at her age. Hell, I was a mess.

I lowered the binoculars and shook my head.

I have no family. These people are strangers. Hell, they're vagrants. I need to write instead of watching a bunch of strangers do the same thing over and over. Shit, I have a job to do and deadlines to meet. Those people could cross the street and rob me. I seriously have to pull myself together. I'm such a fucking loser.

I watched as Damsel stepped close to the main road and stuck out her thumb.

"Oh, that's not a good idea," I said. The binoculars clunked to the floor as I leaped to my feet. "Don't be stupid." I wanted to knock on the window to get her attention, to tell her to wait for the next bus, but I knew she'd never hear me. The floor-to-ceiling, triple-paned window provided soundproofing with its extra thick glass and was mirrored on the exterior. No one could see or hear me, no matter how much I shouted.

In less than a minute, a red minivan pulled up, and I watched as the girl leaned over and talked to the driver through the passenger window.

"Don't do it. Don't get in. Don't ..."

But she did. I glanced at the male driver. He looked normal enough, but the bottom of my stomach still lurched. The vehicle merged back into traffic and disappeared in an instant.

"I should've gotten the license plate. Damn it, this is how these young girls end up splashed all over the front page of the morning news."

Chapter Seven

SELENA

Thursdays... Shit, I hate them. Mom gets up before the moon exits the sky to do the breakfast shift and isn't around to get the girls off to school.

It wouldn't be a big deal, except there was no way I could leave them alone with Gilbert and trust they'd actually make it to school. The girls were always slow to get ready.

"Come on, Victoria." I'd pull her arm to rouse her. "We need to get going soon."

"I don't want to go to school today," she mumbled. "Leave me alone."

"I'm not leaving you here." I yanked her to the floor and forced her to sit up. "Now, get dressed."

"Stop it. You're not being fair," Victoria squealed as she slapped the air.

"Listen to me." I got in her face. "There's no way I'm leaving you alone here with him. I'll take you to school in your pajamas if you don't get up and get dressed right now." Everything was a fight.

I gave Sofia and Victoria half a grilled cheese sandwich Mom had rescued from the restaurant. Mom always made sure if someone didn't touch their sandwich, or pie, or whatever, she'd save it from the garbage if she could. Sometimes we had spaghetti and fish and chips on the same night.

That morning, it took the girls forever to get dressed and ready. The elementary school was about a half-mile away from the house, right at the end of the lane. It was another minute or two over the hill to my bus stop.

The girls ate their grilled cheese on the way to school and dragged their feet, making me crazy. I dropped them at the fence, then waited as long as I could to be sure they were safe before I raced for my bus.

I knew I was late, but the deep, round pebbles sucked my feet deeper with each step. I had my sneakers back—thanks to Mom, who'd hosed them out, boiled them and poured bleach over them.

I swung my arms quickly and broke into a full run to arrive as the bus pulled away from the curb. I huffed and puffed from all the running and couldn't chase the bus. Damn, I needed to get to school. It was important to finish this year out. I pulled the faded pink scrunchy from my wrist, tied up my hair, and stuck out my thumb.

A red minivan pulled over right away.

"Do you need a ride?"

"Yes, I missed my school bus. I need a lift to Washington Heights on the corner of Shell and Green."

"Sure. Not a problem." He pushed a button to unlock the door. "Jump in."

"Thanks." I brushed a stray Cheerio onto the floor before getting in.

"Not to worry. A pretty girl like you could get into trouble hitchhiking," he added as he pulled back into traffic.

I hugged my backpack to my lap and held onto the door handle.

"Are you sure you're a high school student?" He stopped at a red light, turned to me, and let his eyes travel from the top of my body to the bottom. "You're beautiful. And ... exotic and sultry." He stared at my breasts as the traffic moved again. I hugged my backpack tighter and leaned against the passenger door as he continued to drive. "You don't want to go to school, do you? We can climb in the back and have a little fun. What do you say?"

"No, thanks." I kept my face forward and watched his hands from the corner of my eye. My gut churned, and I thought I might throw up all over him. "I need to get to school—that's it. Like I said, I missed the bus."

"I'd make it worth your while. You could go buy yourself something pretty." He reached into his suit jacket and took out his wallet. "I think you'd like what I have to offer."

I didn't move a muscle as I kept my gaze glued to the front window. There was still at least another mile to the school, and I wanted this lousy excuse for a human being to get me as close to there as possible.

"I have some special toys in the back," he whispered. "Come on, let's go play."

His hand inched across the seat toward my leg, and a shiver of revulsion raced through me.

"Not my thing. You can let me out here, and I won't tell the cops."

His head snapped back as though I'd slapped him. He swerved to the side and slammed on his brakes.

"Get out, bitch."

"Tell your wife I say hi." I nodded toward the ring on his

finger. "And the only thing I see in the back is a baby car seat, you sick bastard." I pulled the handle and pushed hard on the door. My school bag got sucked back into the van as he sped away, but I hung on, and it came loose just in time as he sped up.

"Asshole. Why can't people be normal? A simple ride. That's all I wanted." I breathed a sigh of relief when I saw other students still strolling toward the school and hanging out in the parking lot. I was closer than I realized.

No one cared, though. Over by the outdoor basketball court, a small group of girls talked to a teacher. Two of them sucked on vape pens and laughed, while one leaned in and pressed her ample chest against the teacher's arm. On the other side, a couple was making out. Past the couple, a tall, lanky boy wore a T-shirt with a picture of a gun dripping blood on the front. Nothing was normal. This town was seriously fucked-up. This school was worse than the inner-city school I attended before. At least there, I knew what to expect, but here the ultra-wealthy mixed with the dirt poor, and most times, I couldn't tell which was which.

According to my phone, I still had seven minutes before the first bell. I had made good time in the pervert's car and lived to tell about it. I pushed the door to the bathroom open and entered a stall. With the door locked, I sat down and rolled the toilet paper around my finger to make another roll. It didn't always work because the paper sometimes came off one square at a time, but this one was flying off the roll. I'd be able to supply myself and the girls with real toilet paper all year. I secured the finger roll with an elastic band and put it in my bag. It was then I noticed the telltale smudge in my panties. Damn. I only had a few minutes before class. I grabbed my bag, raced to the office, and requested to see the school nurse.

"Fill out this form, list your symptoms, and I'll see if she's available," the secretary said.

"You don't understand. I'm not sick."

"Then what do you want?" She tilted her head and raised a brow.

"I got my period, and I don't have any pads," I said to the secretary.

"Okay. Give me a minute, and I'll see if the nurse is available."

"Well, how's that for timing? I'm right here." A short, round woman waddled up behind the secretary. "I'm the school nurse. Is there anything I can help you with?"

"This girl needs some hygiene supplies."

"Send her back to my office immediately," the older woman said as she put her pudgy hand on the secretary's arm.

"Yes, ma'am." The secretary turned back to me and nodded. "Go to the door." She put her hand under the counter and pushed a button to release the lock with a buzz. I opened the door with a hard shove, and not knowing where to go, I waited. It was a busy place. Multiple phones rang, teachers chatted as they stood by the copy machine, and doors opened and closed every few seconds.

"Over here, dear," a voice called. "Come on, then. My office is down here. Why don't you take a seat and tell me about yourself."

"My name is Selena Henderson, and I'm a senior. Sorry to bother you with this, but I don't want to be late for class. I just need a pad or tampon. I don't have any money with me. Thanks for your help."

"Not to worry." She blinked repeatedly. It was like her entire face collapsed around her nose every time she blinked. "I've got some hygiene products in the cupboard here. Do you need some just for today?"

"If it's okay, I need some for a few days." I stared at the floor. "My mom hasn't been paid yet, and ..."

"Don't worry, dear. You don't need to explain." She blinked, and her face contorted again. "Here's enough for the week. I have a feeling we may get to know each other. My name is Mrs. Bonder, and I'm the school nurse. If there's anything I can do, or if you have any problems, you come see me. Understand?"

I nodded and accepted the bag of supplies.

"Thank you. Sorry to be a bother."

"You're no bother, dear." She blinked again. "You best get to class now."

I folded the bag in two and shoved it to the bottom of my school bag.

"Can I also make a report about a creepy guy in a red van?" I asked.

Mrs. Bonder listened to my story and noted the information. "I'll report it to the principal, and he'll alert the police. Without specifics like the man's name or license plate, not much will happen, but it'll be on record."

I left for classes feeling like the day was already getting better.

Later, in physics class, my phone vibrated. I checked to make sure the teacher wasn't watching before I read the message.

Hi Selena.
We got your application. Would you be available
for an interview at 3:30 today?
Training will start tomorrow.
Please let me know asap. Mindy, Mgr. Java Jenny.

I hesitated for a second as I thought about the girls. If I

worked weekends and after school, how would I keep them safe? My fingers itched at the keyboard until I texted back:

Hi Mindy. Yes. Thank you, I'll be there.
See you at three-thirty. Selena.

I clasped my phone and stared at the message. I'd figure out something with the girls because I needed the job.

"Selena, please bring me your phone," the teacher said. "You can have it back at the end of class."

Damn, I'd forgotten where I was for a second. I handed her my phone.

"Is there any way you can start today?" Mindy, the manager, asked after the interview. "I had two staff call in sick."

This was a tough call. Did Mom say she'd be home after school? I'm sure she said she'd be home at three today.

I convinced myself Mom was home, though I wasn't sure. He wouldn't try anything when I was expected to walk in any minute, and yeah, Mom said three o'clock ... I was pretty sure.

"Yeah, sure, today is great," I said.

The shop was busy as I wiped tables and gathered cups. The manager locked the door at nine—I'd been there for over five hours and loved it.

"Great job, Selena," Mindy said. "Thanks for starting right away."

"No problem. I ah ... I ..."

"Oh my god, you're not going to quit already, are you?"

"No, but I have two little sisters, and I can't leave them at home alone on Saturdays. Sorry, I should have told you."

"How old are they?" the manager asked as she lowered all the window blinds.

"Eight and eleven."

"I suppose you could bring them and leave them in the back if you're sure they won't set the place on fire, or destroy the building. Do you have an iPad or something they can watch?"

"No, but they can use my phone, and they can bring their coloring books and stuff." I twisted and untwisted the rag around my hand as I stood before my new boss. I was afraid my voice would crack as a sense of relief flooded me. "Thank you for understanding."

"You know, Selena, I admire your upfront honesty. I'm glad you told me about your sisters. Don't play games with me, and I'll always be straight up with you. Deal?"

"Yes, it's a deal. Thank you."

"Okay, go clock out. I think your guy's been waiting out there long enough."

"My guy? What guy?"

Mindy shrugged and cocked her head toward the locked door. "Well, he's not mine, so if you need me to, I'll call the police."

I smiled as I saw Chad sitting on the concrete planter outside the store. "No, I know him. It's all good."

"I scheduled you for Saturday and Sunday, nine to three. Does that work?"

"It sure does." I took off my apron. "And I'll make sure the girls have lots to keep them busy." I paused. "Thanks again."

"Go! Before I make you scrub the floor. And don't be late."

As soon as the door opened, Chad pushed himself to a standing position and came toward me. My heart raced faster than it ever had, and the tiny hairs on the back of my neck stood. My face flooded with warmth, and I'm sure it was beet red.

"Hi. Hope you don't mind that I waited for you."

"No, it's good to see you. How'd you know I was here?"

"Well, people are talking," Chad said. We walked side by side toward the bus. "It's complicated. I've gone to school with these guys since kindergarten, and you're new to the school."

"And ..."

"Um, they're asking some questions, like where did I find you, and how did I get so lucky?"

"Really?" I had no other words. I didn't know how to read this guy. It started as a quick hookup, but we'd connected, and it worked—we worked. This guy knocked me off balance, and I wasn't sure if it was one hundred percent real. *Is it all in my head, or is he a great actor? I don't even know him. Guys like this aren't normally single. Why me? Is he after something? I have nothing ...*

"This is my bus. I have to go."

"Okay. See you tomorrow."

He kissed me with his whole body, then watched me climb the three steps onto the bus. Breathless, I glanced out to where he stood with his hands shoved deep in his jeans' pockets. My heart fluttered.

I smiled.

He smiled back.

Chapter Eight

NOW

LESLIE

The morning brightness from the large window seeped into my consciousness and forced me awake. It was Friday morning. Sometime last night, I'd crawled into my chair and covered myself with a nearby throw. Every muscle, tight and knotted, protested as I rose in a sudden panic. Will the girl show up, or is she dead? There was no sign of life anywhere. I pushed my face as close to the window as possible, leaving greasy streaks on the clean glass. Where was everyone? A heaviness took over my body as my mind failed to comprehend the scene. The world disappeared. Then I saw him. Actually, his cart came into sight first, and a flood of relief washed over me. My breathing barely registered as my head floated in confusion.

Without thinking, I reached for the soft flesh under my upper arm and pinched it over and over as I waited.

"Please ... Please... Please..." The small park filled slowly. One student, then two, three, four. "Phew, there she is. The guy who picked her up could've been a real psycho. I wonder if she realizes how lucky she is?"

In my life, I'd learned and adapted to survive. For my sanity, I knew I couldn't let a similar scene play out again. I needed to pay more attention and stop being such a lazy cow who stood by idly as a young girl stepped into danger. What if the young girl's picture splashed across the television with me as the only witness? I wouldn't let it happen again. I needed to pay extra attention and be ready for anything.

I figured that if in the future I started getting up at six-thirty, I'd be able to gauge each morning situation as it arose and I wouldn't miss anything. I'd be dressed, have the car keys at hand and be ready to spring into action immediately if necessary.

I rubbed my tender arm and examined the recently bruised flesh. The pinch of reality, I called it. It kept me from going over the edge in the what-if game. Having Damsel out there and possibly in harm's way had taken me back down a dark path and taught me a lesson. I should've known better. It's my fault, but she's alive.

Chapter Nine

SELENA

Mice skittered and scratched inside the walls of our bedroom. As I laid on the floor, it was like they talked to me—we all wanted to escape the trap we found ourselves in. Mom had always told me getting my education was the way out, but no matter what I did, barriers blocked me at every turn. It didn't seem too much to ask. Finish school and work full-time... The idea of having a full paycheck and a safe place for me, Mom, and the girls was all I ever wanted. For years, I've seen Mom scratch out a living, but I could work my way up to be a manager one day and make decent money.

Mom had already left for the early shift at the diner about twenty minutes ago, and though she always tried to be quiet, it didn't matter because I'd set my alarm to vibrate and listened for her. When I woke up, the first thing I did was make sure both girls were beside me. A few months back, at our old house, I woke to find Victoria gone and Gilbert standing in the doorway watching me and Sofia sleep. Panic hovered above, ready to take hold, when Vic returned from the bathroom and snuggled in sleepily beside me. He stood and watched every move. After, I refused to sleep if Mom wasn't in the house. Fucking bastard.

Thursday mornings were tough, and twice I'd missed the bus. Getting the girls up and out the door in a timely fashion took threats, promises, and sometimes downright dragging. I tried to talk to Mom about Gilbert, but something wasn't right with her lately. She was distracted and distant. She didn't ignore me, but I wasn't sure she actually heard everything I said either.

She'd promised on her life five years ago that she'd never let us slip into the system again. She met Gilbert when he was a customer at her last job. In the beginning, we thought he was okay, but he moved in pretty fast, and everything changed. Now, something about Mom and her current mood worried me. *Shit, I hope she's not drinking again. She's the only income we have.* Mom says Gilbert keeps his veteran's pension for himself. *Says he shouldn't have to pay for a bunch of kids who aren't his. Mom says he pays the rent and helps with the girls, but he's still a first-class jerk. I don't know why Mom can't see that. Oh man, I hope she's not drinking—the last time she went on a bender, it was a nightmare. The three of us got separated—thrown into the foster system.*

I heard Mom leave, so I tiptoed to the bathroom. I had to hold the door closed with my foot because it would creep open an inch at a time.

I returned to the bedroom and stepped over the girls on the mattress. "Come on, you need to get ready." They rolled to the center but showed no sign of being awake. "Victoria. Sofia." I shook each of them. "Come on, you two, it's time to get up. We're going to be late."

I unfolded my clean jeans and held them before me.

"What the ..." Someone had slashed them diagonally from the hip to the inner thigh on one side and right down the side seam on the other. "Fucking asshole." I grabbed my other jeans, and they were all the same. I knew it was him. He was the one home all day and did whatever he wanted. I suspected he was the one who had filled my shoes with shit, too, and knew I'd have to wear those hooker boots.

"I don't wanna go to school today," Victoria said from under the blanket. "I'll stay home with Gilbert."

"You're not staying home with him. Mom's working and I have to go to school. Come on."

"I don't feel good," Sofia mumbled. "Victoria kicked me."

"Seriously, you two, get up and get dressed before I haul you out of there myself. I'm not in the mood for games this morning."

It wasn't the girls' fault. I didn't want to get out of bed either, but there was no choice. I slipped into the slashed jeans. Fuck. All I could see was skin. I checked my one pair of sweats and saw they too had been hacked completely through and were now trash.

I wanted to pounce on him with open claws and leave him in a heap of shredded flesh, like he'd left my clothes. It's like living in a hellhole with a skanky bastard who always peeks around corners as he licks his lips like a wild animal sizing up his prey. We needed to get out, which meant convincing Mom. I hated my life; unlike my sisters, I was acutely aware of the lurking dangers.

"Victoria and Sofia, stop bickering and get your shoes on." They gathered at the front door as I glanced to where Gilbert sat in the recliner chair, already drinking a beer—watching every move. It was 7:52 when I pushed the girls out the door and pulled them along in an effort not to be late.

"Nice jeans." He raised his beer in the air. "Cheers to a bit of skin." He took a long drink as I slammed the door.

"You're going too fast. Selena, slow down," Sofia cried.

"This is stupid. I want to go back and watch TV with Gilbert," Victoria said. "He told me I could watch whatever I wanted." Then she stopped dead in her tracks.

I walked with Sofia in tow and glared back at Victoria, who stood rooted, with her arms crossed and lips pressed together.

"If Vicky isn't going, I'm not either."

I took a deep breath and walked back to Victoria.

"Victoria, you're fuckin' pissing me off. We all need to get to school, yet here we stand in the middle of an alleyway."

Sofia held my hand as I crouched down and looked Victoria in the eye. I tucked her hair behind her ear and stroked her cheek. She turned away.

"I think this goes beyond watching TV all day. What's going on?"

"Nothing." She stuck out her bottom lip and furrowed her brow. "And don't touch me. I'm not a baby."

"Remember I told you; sisters can't have secrets." I held my breath and waited.

"It's the golden rule, Vicky," Sofia chimed in.

Waiting was hard. It was all I could do not to yank Victoria kicking and screaming down the narrow alley. I clung to the clammy warmth of Sofia's hand in mine, and the air thinned around us—even the birds stopped singing. I had to let her tell me. Vic was stubborn, and I knew she wouldn't be pushed. Please, please don't let it be what I think. I'm not strong enough for all of this.

"Come on, Vic, I told you my secret about Chad. It was a pretty big one, don't you think?" I watched Victoria's face soften and could almost hear the wheels turning as she contemplated the consequences of telling.

"He said I'd get in trouble if I told you."

"Who?"

"Gilbert."

"Okay." I held my breath and fought to keep my voice calm. "I don't think you should tell me. I don't want you to get in trouble." I shifted my stance away and stroked Victoria's cheek again. Heat radiated from her velvety skin. She was eleven going on twenty. With her angelic face, dark blond hair, and budding young body, she definitely got the boys' attention, but it was Gilbert who worried me.

"You don't want me to tell you? Are you sure?" Victoria asked, wide-eyed. She stepped back and kicked a pebble.

"Yes, I'm sure. I would like you to tell Sofia, though, and I'll turn away and listen. That way, you're not telling me. What do you think?"

"Yeah, I guess so."

The dryness in my throat choked me as I tried to swallow a loud sigh. With Sofia's small hand still tucked into mine, I turned away.

"Gilbert said if I stayed home, I could watch TV and have ice cream."

"I want to stay home, too," Sofia said.

"Anything else?" I shifted in order to see Victoria.

"He said ... he told me ..."

Wait. Breathe. She'll tell me. Oh my god, I think I'm going to explode. Breathe. Breathe.

"Gilbert told me he wanted to take pictures of me, so I'd be a famous model and get rich. He said it was a surprise, and I'd get in trouble if I told anyone. He thinks I'm sexy."

"Did he use that word?" I cringed at the thought and fought back the rising bile in my blocked throat.

"Yeah," Victoria nodded. "He said being sexy was a gift. He was nice."

"Vic, has he taken any pictures yet?" My voice sounded high-pitched and hysterical to my ears. The bile continued its upward push in my throat.

"No. It was supposed to be today. He said I had the prettiest smile he'd ever seen. Now, you've ruined the whole thing."

I heard nothing past "No." I let out a long sigh and turned back to Victoria.

"Thanks for letting me overhear your secret. I'll take you for ice cream as soon as I can, okay?"

"Me too?" Sofia asked.

"Yes, both of you." I turned to Victoria. "I didn't know you wanted to be a model. You always told me you hated having your picture taken. What changed your mind?"

"You don't know anything about me," Victoria challenged. "You think you're the boss, and we should listen to you because you're older. I'm not stupid, you know."

"I didn't say you were stupid. It's just—"

"I was going to get rich," Victoria cut me off. "He said he could sell the pictures on the internet for lots of money. It's only pictures, and you've ruined everything. I want to take care of Mom ..." Her voice faded off.

"Vic, I need you to know Gilbert is not your friend." I grabbed her shoulder to make sure she listened. "He's an asshole who wants to use you for bad stuff. Promise me you'll both stay away from him. If you want ice cream, I'll get it for you. If he tells you not to tell, you come tell me immediately." I looked back and forth between the two young girls. "Promise me."

Victoria glared at me, and Sofia cried.

I bent down again and pulled her close.

"What's the matter, sweetie? Tell me."

"Teacher says we should stay away from bad people. You said Gilbert is bad."

"Your teacher is right. If me or Mom aren't home, then you stay together in your room. Gilbert is a creep, and I don't want him anywhere near either of you. Come on, if we're lucky, we can get you two to school before the first bell goes."

I wiped Sofia's tears and hugged her tight.

"You okay, Vic?"

"Whatever. You don't care, anyway. You want things your way. Maybe I do want to be a model."

"We'll talk more about this, but for now, please trust me."

I took the girls' hands and slowly jogged between them to their school.

After dropping them off, I glanced at my phone and sprinted with my school bag bouncing on my back, hoping the bus would be late today, but as I got on the pebble path, it pulled away.

"Damn."

I slowed and made my way to the bus stop. Other than the homeless guy sitting on the bench, the area was deserted.

I wonder how much he makes from bottle picking. I could do that at night, then I'd always be home. Gilbert, the bastard, wanted to take pictures. It doesn't even seem real. I need to talk to Mom again. Between her wages and mine, we can survive without him around.

It was all I could do not to race home and do physical harm to that poor excuse of a human being. The conversation stabbed my heart as truth stared me squarely in the face. I needed to talk to Mom. She'd be home for the girls at two o'clock, so it'd have to wait for later. The girls are safe right now. I'll deal with it tonight. Getting to school was the priority right now. I set my backpack down, removed my jacket, and tied it around my waist, hoping to hide the rips in my jeans.

As I walked to the road's edge, the homeless guy pushed his cart toward the sidewalk, and I stuck out my thumb. A red minivan slowed and pulled up in front of me. It was the same perv who picked me up a couple of weeks ago. I stepped back until he recognized me and sped away, nearly hitting another vehicle. I stuck my thumb out again. Lots of cars slowed down, and I thought they were going to stop only to have them speed up. Finally, a black Jeep pulled over and the window lowered.

"Do you need a ride?"

"Yes, I missed the school bus. I need to get to Washington Heights High School on the corner of Shell and Green Ave."

"Jump in. I'm headed that way. I can drop you off."

"Thank you."

"No worries. You have to be so careful these days. My name is Leslie, by the way."

Chapter Ten

THEN

LESLIE

The first few days of school took some getting used to. No one knew I was alive. It was like I was invisible. I dreamed of a kindred spirit, a lifelong friend. I'd read dozens of wonderful stories about girls who giggled together and discussed their dreams and first kisses—I wanted it more than anything.

Mother always told me things come to those who wait. I bided my time, and after a month, when I was near to losing my faith, a beautiful and unexpected kinship unfolded in my life. It happened by accident, and while I was glad it did, the picture didn't quite match the one of two girlfriends exchanging laughs. It was different. Very different. And for me, terrifying.

I walked down the hall toward class, same as always, when he slammed right into me.

"Whoa, sorry." He jumped back. "I didn't see you."

I didn't say a word. He went his way, and I went mine. Then the next day, the same thing happened, but I moved out of his way this time. He glanced up at me.

"Hi. My name's Johnny," he said with a wide grin.

"Oh, I ... I'm Leslie," I whispered after checking behind me to ensure he wasn't talking to someone else.

"Nice to meet you, Leslie."

His eyes sparkled when he spoke, and his small dimples in the center of each cheek teased. "We need to stop meeting like this. Someone's going to get hurt." He laughed at his own bad joke.

All I could do was nod.

Every day for the next week, we met and avoided the near collision. I got braver as I let him get closer and closer before stepping aside. It was a flirtatious game that gave me such a thrill I couldn't sleep at night. All I could do was wait for the next day.

"Oops, you're slow this morning," he said as he bumped my shoulder. The vibration from his touch gained momentum like a fast-moving tsunami and quivered through my body, sending pulsating shivers to places I didn't know shivers could travel.

"Sorry, it's Monday, and I was up studying all night. I guess I'm moving slower this morning."

"Well, Leslie, I think we have to stop meeting like this and get to know each other better. What do you say?"

"Um, well, I guess." I wondered if he could hear my heart thumping against the inside of my chest. It echoed endlessly between my ears, obscuring everything else around me.

"Tell you what." He took my hand in his, leaned closer, and peered into my eyes. "Meet me at the basketball courts behind the school at three-thirty. Then we can go for a walk or sit down and actually talk."

I nodded my agreement, so he dropped my hand, grinned, and continued down the hall. I couldn't speak as I strolled on autopilot toward my next class. My hand tingled from his touch, and I knew I'd never be the same again.

We met that afternoon by the basketball court where we talked for hours about teachers, classes, and ourselves. I mostly listened. I knew I had nothing interesting to talk about, but he didn't seem to care or notice. After that day, we met nightly. It was easy to slip out to meet him as Mother worked most evenings at the hospital.

"Do you always call your mom, Mother?" he asked me on the third evening.

"Yes, I've always called her Mother." I could tell from the slight twist of his lips that he thought I was weird. "I've never thought about it. It's always been her and me. I've been home-schooled until now."

"It seems sort of, I don't know, formal." He shifted his weight toward me. "Didn't you play with other kids?"

"Of course, I did. I had a friend once. Her name was Sarah ... or Sadie—I can't remember exactly. She was older than me, though, and moved away soon after we met." I hid my face in my hands. "I'm weird, aren't I?"

He raised his eyebrows and tilted his head. He knew I wasn't normal. It didn't take him long to figure it out—a lot faster than me, as a matter of fact. I didn't figure it out until I started going to the library to read and watch things Mother never intended me to see.

"When we lived in a different town, we went to church every Sunday, and I saw people there," I squeaked.

"That's not normal, Les." Johnny turned and pushed the

hair off my face. "It's like you don't even know about reality—like what real kids do and stuff."

"I do know." I peeked up at him through the stray strands lingering over my eyes. "I've read a lot of books, and I watch people and I'm a quick learner." The place where he'd touched my forehead to move my hair warmed, and I wanted to nudge him like a purring cat prodding for more strokes. I wrung my hands and stared at my fingers. "Do you still want to be my friend?" I asked after a long silence.

Johnny studied me. His eyes swept from the top of my head to the bottom of my rubber-soled shoes. I waited as heat built inside the center of me and pulsed outward. It crept under my skin, leaving a trail of lingering tickles like a featherlight caress. Every time Johnny moved, a seismic bolt of feverish heat raced through my body to numb my brain and brush the feather along the entire length of my skin. He put his finger under my chin and raised my face. His fingers smelled of stale cigarettes and onions as they stroked the delicate and sensitive skin along my jawline. It made my mouth water, and the burning surged through me as I allowed him to direct my face upward.

"The answer is yes."

I couldn't remember the question. What was the question? A long sigh of breath escaped my mouth as he removed his finger. I didn't move. I didn't speak. I waited. He was right. I knew nothing about what normal kids do or say. I was like a toddler on a new playground, eager to participate, but left on the fringes to figure out the rules.

"Come on, we better get going before it rains." Johnny stood and offered his hand.

He pulled me up with ease, then shoved his hands farther into the depths of his pockets and walked ahead of me. I fell in step beside him and fought to match his pace.

"Are you okay, Johnny? Did I do something wrong?" With

every word out of my mouth, his pace quickened. I was afraid if I said anything else, he'd break into a full run. The soft damp earth on the road's edge sucked at the rubber soles of my shoes, making it hard to keep up. I side-stepped a murky puddle and caught my foot on the broken edge. It happened fast. There was no slow motion for me as Johnny stepped in front of me to break my fall.

"You need to be more careful." He searched my face, then pushed himself back and rubbed his hands over his eyes. With a deep breath, he dug in his shirt pocket, pulled out a cigarette, and lit it. He took a deep, long drag and let the smoke waft lazily out of his nose and mouth. "You're different, and different isn't always a good thing, but I told you I'd be your friend." He pointed at me with the lit end of the cigarette. "We'll stay friends. Okay?"

"Okay." I wanted to jump up and down and do a cartwheel, but I forced myself to remain calm and not be too different because, like he said, different wasn't necessarily a good thing.

I learned to cope at school and not do anything stupid to compromise my friendship with Johnny. The rules were unwritten, but with some intrinsic radar, I understood being together outside of school was a completely separate existence from the classrooms, hallways, and cafeteria.

Johnny and I would pass each other in the hall, and he'd ignore me if he were with his buddies. I no longer got teased the way I did when I first started school, but only because an obese boy with a patch over one eye and a pronounced limp joined the school and was more of a target than I was. They'd call him Pirate Blue Blubber as they pretended to sword fight and make him walk the gangplank. He was even more different from me, poor guy.

A whole week had passed since Johnny had agreed to still be my friend, and yet we hadn't met once. Mother was on day shift, which meant I needed to be home every evening and couldn't sneak away to be with him. I did my chores and stayed in my room to read the latest romance book I'd borrowed from the library. I kept it stuffed deep beneath my mattress to hide it.

Oh, how I missed Johnny.

We stopped at the storefront windows and made fun of the ridiculous fashion and outrageous prices. He jostled for a front view, pushing my body with his hip. At first, I lost my footing, but then leaned into him with my full weight to move him out of my way. I braced my rubber-soled shoes against the side-walk's grainy concrete—they were finally good for something—and shoved with all my strength.

"Come on, Les, you can do better than that," he said, laughing as he stood his ground.

"I am stron ..." I said with gritted teeth as he let up on his weight, and I fell toward him. The street came up to meet me fast, but Johnny caught me mid-fall. He pulled me toward him, our faces mere inches apart. The world stopped. I dared not move.

In all the books I'd ever read, this is when the boy would lower his lips to hers for a kiss and declare undying love. I could feel my eyes flutter closed as I lifted my face even closer to his, but he released me from his hold.

I stepped back, and my heart thumped back into working—in fact, it raced so fast I was afraid my chest would be physi-cally throbbing and bouncing about.

"Come on." He grabbed my hand and pulled me with him as he turned down a side street. His voice sounded gruff, and I followed without question. A car drove by as Johnny pulled me into a nook behind the red brick building's false front. From the side street, it appeared the building continued for another five feet around the corner, but in reality, it was a brick wall built to frame in the side. The result was a private nook five feet deep and three feet wide.

Johnny pushed me into the deepest corner against the wall and kissed me hard on the lips. A stench of stale urine filled the space along with dog poop. I didn't know what to do. It didn't feel romantic. His lips slammed into mine, and the pressure smushed my lips tight against my teeth. His tongue pried them apart and darted into my mouth. Every nerve in my entire body lit up and stood at attention. The initial shock of his tongue gave way to a burning desire to devour him. Shocked, my eyes flew open, but the lids quickly melted closed to savor and devour his taste. Heat radiated from my belly and throbbed through my entire body with each pump of my heart. A feverish heat overwhelmed my neck and chest as Johnny ground his body against mine. Mother called them private parts, but they sang and twitched in a dance of yearning and desire. In unison, we rocked and convulsed, trying to get ever closer.

"I love you," he mumbled as he pulled his face back, spittle creating a bridge between us. "You make me so horny." He brushed the hair from my face and kissed me again.

"You make me so happy, too." I sighed. The second kiss was different, hungry, and demanding. He kneaded my breasts through my thick sweater, which ignited another fire throughout my body. My back arched against him and fed his desire. With each move, an inferno engulfed my world. Nothing else mattered—only the hunger I felt for his touch against my ever-ready body.

The alcove became our secret place. The next time we went, we found a discarded piece of cardboard and swept the area clean of cigarette butts, broken glass, and piles of dog turds. It was a perfect spot affording us privacy as the side block was a no-parking zone, and if we pressed ourselves into the corner deep enough, no one could see us unless they came right up to us.

I already knew I loved him. It was the first time in my life I sensed that another person actually saw me, loved me. School was torture as he laughed with his buddies and ignored me, but I knew. The secret was ours, and, though he pretended not to know me, sometimes I'd catch him studying me from across the room. It made my heart awaken from its sluggish slumber to signal my body to ready itself for his touch.

In study hall, he stared at me, and I thought of the day before when we had spread out damp newspaper to protect us from the ground as we cuddled in our spot. It felt like forever ago. Later that same day, I saw him in the hallway grinning and slapping his friend on the back as he whistled and gestured at a tall, leggy girl walking down the hallway.

Sometimes it's better not to watch if you don't want to see.

Chapter Eleven

NOW

LESLIE

Tall, imposing doors to the courthouse loomed before me as I approached the entrance. The deposition meeting to determine ongoing alimony and support had finally arrived. The only thing between me and the meeting was the expansive lobby and hordes of mingling people.

Max said to dress professionally and prepare for battle. All I wanted to do was tuck back into my overstuffed chair with my snacks and binoculars. This was the first time in five years I'd worn heels. When you work in your pajamas all day, there's no need for fancy shoes or suits. This whole court thing was a play on real life. Phillip knows how uncomfortable and ill such public displays make me feel, and yet there we were. The muscles in my gut—such as they were—scrunched and churned over and over. It would be a miracle if I made it through this without having to run to the bathroom every two minutes. *I'd much rather be at home with the cat and a bottle of wine. Shit, I want to tuck deep into a hole, pull a blanket over it, and not come out again. Why should I have to defend myself against him when he was the one out screwing around making babies with someone else?*

Damn. With each step, sweat pooled at the band of my skirt and trickled lower. The tingle of a speedy sweat rivulet inched down onto my butt cheek, making me even more uncomfortable.

Just as I thought I might bolt for freedom, I saw Max. The building's enormous windows reflected the area's well-appointed landscaping and framed him perfectly in his form-fitting navy suit as he scrolled through his phone. He waved and came toward me.

"Hello, Leslie." He hugged me. "You look very nice today. Do you remember what we talked about?"

"Yes, I'm fine." I took a deep breath and reiterated what Max had told me before. "Answer yes, no, or I don't recall. Don't elaborate. Don't explain."

"Good. And there's no need to look at Phillip either. This meeting is all preliminary, but it is on the record." Max placed his hand ever so slightly on the small of my back to guide me in. "Come on, we're due on the second floor in a couple of minutes."

When we entered the building, I slipped off my shoes, belt, and watch before being allowed to walk through the metal detector. A security guard took my leather purse and, with hands the size of oven mitts, pawed through the compartments of it. A tea bag and lint-covered mint fell as he yanked out my cell phone and examined it. Without so much as a glance in my direction, he shoved everything at me and went to the next person in line.

I put it all back in my purse as the building's chilly air conditioning found my damp, sweaty skin. An involuntary shiver ran the length of my body, and I rubbed my hands over my exposed arms.

"This way." Max cocked his head as he strode toward the elevators.

The doors are right there. I could easily slip right back out— back home to snuggle into my chair and watch the park. This is such crap. Seeing him that night at the store was enough. I don't want to see him. Why should I have to do this?

I fell in step behind Max as he pushed through a heavy wooden door to a boardroom. Phillip sat at the table. I could tell from the tan lines on his neck that his full, thick blond hair had recently been cut. Our eyes locked for the briefest moment, and I remembered how I couldn't wait to rip off his clothes and be with him. The heat of the memory coursed through my body. He was a generous lover. Slow and thorough. I cleared my throat.

"Hi, Les. You know Barbara ..." He half stood out of his chair and nodded toward the woman sitting next to him—the one I'd failed to see because Phillip's presence alone filled the room.

My brain ceased operational status. *Why is she here? What do I do? She stole my husband. Where the fuck am I supposed to look? Shit. Every time I glanced over, she stared at me. Is this a strategic tactic to get to me? What did Phillip tell her? Oh, I bet there were lots of secrets spilled.*

"Max?" Where was he? "Max..."

I clasped the nearby chair to steady myself, but it didn't help. The air in the room came in rippling waves. It was like being under water with my eyes open. The pressure squeezed my chest in a tight, vice-like grip. Breathing was difficult, and nothing was where it should have been. The woman beside Phillip held a baby in her arms.

I stumbled back as though slammed in the gut. My heart hung motionless within me. My throat folded in upon itself, as if it was full of wadded-up tissue. The noise of underwater turbulence bounced off the walls in slow motion swells and mixed with the undulating air. A baby? *The baby should be mine.*

Max? Where did he go? I tried to scream, but nothing came out. *Why is that woman holding my baby?*

My body jerked forward and slammed into the heavy wooden table—an obstacle in my quest to exit the room and find air.

Gulping, I pulled the door open and scurried out on what little oxygen existed within me. This was all wrong. Why was I all alone in there? No one was on my side. They came to slaughter me—to teach me a lesson like Mother always told me they would.

An aura of white light surrounded me, but still, I couldn't breathe. I gulped, but my throat was closed, and I couldn't swallow. It was a tease.

The air ...

The baby ...

Everything ...

Why are they so cruel? My baby ... Where is my baby? Why did Phillip take my baby away?

My legs drove me forward. Nothing was familiar except the clicking of my heels against the marble floor. Strangers gawked at me like I was crazy.

Why are they staring at me? Did they take my baby?

Heavy footsteps sounded behind me. A man was chasing me—Johnny?

No. I shook my head as the air became more difficult to find.

Falling ...

I reached out, but darkness claimed me first.

Cold water dripped down the front of my neck. I was on my back, and the trickle was uncomfortable as water pooled around my ears. I tried to reach up, but someone held my wrist.

"Relax, ma'am. I'm taking your pulse."

Hushed whispers from strangers floated through the air and clung to me.

"Yeah, she fell right there," one said.

"I think she's mentally ill," another said.

"Oh, for sure. She was screaming about a baby." A man's voice boomed across to me.

"She's a wacko-doodle if I ever saw one."

I kept my eyes closed. I didn't want to put faces and voices together. I knew from experience they didn't care about me, but simply wanted to see a horror unfold before them. This would probably be their social media chat for the week. *Shit, there'd be pictures.* In the distance, there was a faint cry of a baby. I couldn't help it. The baby? I turned and bore witness to the entire fiasco before me. I had single-handedly made a complete and utter ass of myself in front of everyone.

"Leslie? It's Max. Are you all right?" His hand was on mine. "Did you hit your head when you fell? Do you know where you are?"

I wanted to scream, but I pushed myself to a sitting position. Nausea overtook me, and I laid back down. I took the towel off my head and wiped it on my neck to stop the dripping.

"I'm fine. Please. Everyone stop." I held my hand up to the

first responder, and all those gathered around me. "I need some air. Can I go outside? Max?"

"Les, the paramedic thinks you may have hit your head."

"Max, I assure you, I'm fine." I tried to stand up. "The paramedic can come outside with us if he wants."

"Okay?" The paramedic nodded, and Max slipped his arm under mine to guide me from the floor. "Lean on me. We'll go slow." The paramedic followed with an oxygen tank and his chest of medical tools.

"I'm completely mortified." I tucked in under his arm and kept my head down. "I don't know what came over me."

"The show's over, folks." Max cleared the way as he led me toward the elevator. "Go back to whatever you were doing. She's fine. Not to worry."

When we finally stepped outside, I breathed in the fresh air, and the fog lifted from my brain. I crumpled onto the step beside Max.

"I saw the baby, and I lost it." I stared at the ground, hoping the burning behind my eyes would stop, but the tears poured unchecked down my cheeks to splash on the smooth step below. The tears overwhelmed me to the point of new understanding.

Max sat beside me and held me as I recognized this surge of reality hitting me. The paramedic stayed close by and monitored my heart rate and oxygen levels.

"You know Max, when Phillip left me I didn't fight him. I was so numb and hey, let's face it, there's nothing a bottle of wine and a good juicy burger won't fix, right?" I studied the clouds that held the promise of rain. "My heart is still in shreds and is so fuckin' raw it feels like it happened yesterday."

"I know. I know." Max said as he patted my arm.

"Ma'am, I think you're in good hands right now," the paramedic said. He loosened the cuff around my arm. "I'd like you to follow up with your family doctor tomorrow, and please watch for signs of concussion—headache, blurred vision— anything like that please go to the Emergency."

He left me to sit dazed with Max as life buzzed on around us. I knew better. Nothing stops because you're hurting. It was a life lesson I'd learned and forgotten a long time ago.

"All the work,"—I took a ragged breath—"... the drugs, the surgeries, the emotional rollercoaster, oh, Max." A sob exploded from me. "I tried everything to have a baby, and he goes out, and boom."

"I'm sorry, Les." Max rubbed my shoulder. "I don't know what to say. I didn't know he was bringing her to the meeting."

"You know, Max, I don't think it matters much anymore." And I meant it. "When Phillip and I went through all the fertility treatments, it was a hormonal rollercoaster. Terrible ..." I focused my gaze out into the world—somewhere far away—as I talked. "What should've been a positive time in our life was a fucking nightmare. I dove into my work. Hell, I wrote a best-seller, but I also put on over fifty pounds and became a crazy lady. Once he left, I never got back on track, and I've been floundering for too long."

"Les, you don't need to tell me all this."

"I have to, Max, because I'm stuck. You've always been my person. You know that." I wanted him to understand. "We took out a second mortgage for fertility treatments. We always said we'd save, but we didn't, and I'm drowning in debt. As it stands, if I don't have Phillip's financial support, I could lose the house. I've already lost so much. And why? Because I couldn't have a baby? He gets his perfect little family and leaves me high and dry? I feel so abandoned and broken right now, it's not even funny. Seeing his younger, more perfect wife holding a baby today reminded me how unworthy I am."

"Les." He cleared his throat. "You need to see a therapist."

"Max, you're the closest thing I have to a friend and therapist. You've seen the down and dirty. You know my finances and my history." I squeezed his hand. "Seriously, I don't need a therapist. All those long talks are still with me. Remember the detective?"

"Yeah, I sure do." He studied the face of his phone, then turned it off. "You're going to open that envelope soon. The results of that investigation have been waiting way too long." Max shoved himself to a standing position and held out his hand. "Come on. We have to go back and finish this meeting. I'm going to sue his sweet little ass, so he doesn't know whether he's coming or going."

I allowed him to pull me to a standing position, and we returned to the same room for the meeting. A hush fell over the room when we walked in, and everyone stared.

"We apologize for the delay in getting started," Max said to the room as he shuffled some papers in front of him. "My client was not expecting such a, let's say, she wasn't expecting such a full room. She now suffers from panic attacks because, in the middle of fertility treatments, she was abandoned by her husband, who strayed from the marital bed and got another female pregnant. Through no fault of her own, my client's ability to produce quality work for her employer has suffered a tremendous blow, as has her income. We are therefore countering the request for decreased spousal support with a motion to increase said support and also to have the courts consider the pain and suffering of my client. She deserves an increase in support income so she can maintain her standard of living, which was, shall we say, rudely interrupted and changed by her ex-husband's infidelities. And, as we all witnessed today, there is a need for ongoing medical and psychological support, which we see as being the plaintiff's responsibility as he abandoned his wife when she was going through every treatment known to medical science to fulfill his dream of becoming a father."

"This is bullshit. She was nuts before I married her." Phillip stood so hastily his chair nearly toppled over.

I did what Max told me to do. I lowered my eyes and stared at my hands. Papers were shuffled, and Phillip continued to rant and shake his finger at Max as the baby cried and someone asked for quiet.

Hmm, I wonder what cans I should put in the trash for Prince tonight.

After the deposition at the courthouse, I returned home and went to bed. The incident had drained me both physically and emotionally. I napped the afternoon away, only to wake to the telephone vibrating on the bedside table. Max's name filled the screen. The time was 3:04 p.m. I let it go to voicemail.

I stared at the ceiling, searching for the motivation to move forward. What difference did any of this make? No matter what, I couldn't have a baby and was defective in so many ways no one would ever want me. I knew it would take a long time to get the memory of Phillip and his new family out of my mind.

Bastard.

I forced myself from the bed. It was clear I wasn't only tossed aside but also long forgotten. It was the story of my life. A tease with happiness, then a violent yank to make sure I fell flat on my fat, ugly face. The bottle of chardonnay I bought on the way home today whispered my name. *Lessssslie,* it mumbled, *come on. Have a glass, and you'll feel better.*

Who was I to ignore the inner voice? I padded down the carpeted stairs, poured a glass of wine, and went to stand before the large floor-to-ceiling window. Within minutes, the school bus pulled up to return the students to where they'd started the day. They piled off and scattered in different directions. There she was. She was hard to miss. I should've paid better attention, then I could've followed her. Hell, I wasn't even dressed yet.

With the binoculars, I watched Selena walk up the pebble path. She kept her head bowed and her shoulders slouched with the burden of her school backpack. Even from this distance, I could tell the girl didn't walk with an ego or air of superiority, but with a shy confidence.

"What's your story, little one?" I dropped the binoculars back on the chair. All the students had left, and the unkempt park suddenly pissed me off. Why was it so neglected? The patchy grass needed fertilizing, weeds needed to be sprayed, and even the faded bench where Prince sat every morning needed a fresh coat of paint. There was a plaque on the bench, so someone dedicated it in the name of a loved one. Now, look at it.

I searched for the number of City Hall.

"Yes, my name is Leslie Richter, and I live in the Oakville Place townhouses on 21st and Oak Street. I'd like to know why the little triangle park across the street is in such rough shape. It's a hub for the buses and a lot of people, but it's looking shabby. I pay huge taxes to make sure the neighborhood doesn't fall into disrepair." The lady on the other end assured me someone would attend to it. My Prince shouldn't have to sit on a crumbling bench—no sirree—I'd make sure my people were taken care of.

Chapter Twelve

SELENA

It was Thursday. Thanks to Leslie, who dropped me at school, I actually arrived before the bus. It was nice not to start the morning squished into the bus with a bunch of idiots who think they're better than me. I had Spanish for the first block, but I needed to go to the office.

"Can I help you with something?" one of the secretaries asked.

"Yes. My name is Selena Henderson, and I'd like to see the school nurse, please."

"Okay. I need you to fill out this form for our records, then I'll see if she's available."

I took the clipboard with the dangling pen on a string tied through the small hole in the shiny silver metal clip. I perched on the side of one of the fabric covered chairs in the waiting room and filled out the sheet.

"Hi Selena," came the friendly voice of the nurse. "It's so

good to see you again. Come on in." She stood holding open the heavy door to the staff sanctuary.

"Thanks for seeing me this morning, Mrs. Bonder."

"Come in here, and we can talk privately." I followed her down the long hallway and into her office. "What can I do for you today?"

"I'd like to ask your advice on something if it's all right. I'm not sure who to talk to."

"Ask away." Her face scrunched up as she blinked. "That's why I'm here."

"Well, it's sort of ... bad."

"Bad? Has something happened to you?" Blink. Scrunch. "You know, anything you tell me here is confidential."

"My sister, she's only eleven ... she told me something." As soon as I opened my mouth, it was like the whole thing was real. Tears cascaded down my cheeks, and I couldn't wipe them away quickly enough. Nothing I did stopped them, and truthfully, I didn't want them to. A weight lifted from me as the story tumbled out. I never would've forgiven myself if anything happened to Victoria or Sofia.

"Oh, Selena." The nurse handed me a box of tissue as she listened, then spoke in a hushed tone. "Let's be thankful your little sister spoke up. I'm going to have to report this. I know I told you everything would be confidential, but with things involving child welfare, I have an obligation to report."

"I want you to report it. I need you to report it. I didn't know where to go or who to tell. My mom's going to be so pissed off."

"Don't worry about your mother. I'll take the blame. I'm going to call the girls' school first and make sure they're safe, then I'm going to call the child protection services and have them take over." Mrs. Bonder paused and placed a hand on my arm. Squeeze. Blink. "Selena, are you in danger in any way? Has he touched you?"

"No. I'm fine. Seriously. I'll talk to Mom, but I'm fine. Thank you." A stream of air escaped from me like a pressure valve had finally opened, but a lump of overwhelming anxiety still stabbed me in the center of my chest. "They'll be safe, right? Like there won't be any teenage boys or old men living in the next room?"

Did I just make a huge mistake? Shit, kids were killed and hurt in foster care all the time. I'm such an idiot. At least at home, I could watch them. Why didn't I just take them myself? I just sent my sisters to their new users and abusers. Fuck. People only foster for the money. I want to throw up. I wanted to throw myself across the desk and make Mrs. Bonder tell me where they were going. I was possibly the worst sister in America.

"Thank you for trusting me with this, Selena. We'll chat later. In the meantime, here are some pads for when you need them." She went to the cabinet, filled a plastic bag, and handed them across the desk. "You come talk to me anytime. In fact, I'm going to leave your name at the front desk, so you don't have to do all the paperwork and wait each time." She walked beside me to the door and touched my hand. "One more thing, Selena. Check the lost and found to find some trousers. If you can't find anything, let me know."

She squeezed my shoulder, and I nodded as I tucked the bag into my backpack. Part of me wanted to curl into her warmth and stay protected by her quiet kindness, but the girls would need me.

"I'm sorry all this is happening to you," she said.

"Me too," I whispered.

Mrs. Bonder was already on the phone to the girls' school

as I went back down the inner hallway, then out the locked door to the rest of the school. I didn't look back.

The lost and found at a rich kids' school is like going to the mall. We'd only been in school for a few weeks, but I found yoga pants, a pair of high-waisted jeans, and two tops. I shoved them into my backpack. *Was it shoplifting if I wasn't in a store?* My mind wandered to the girls, and I worried all day. Did someone go to the girls' school and ask questions? I hoped they would throw Gilbert into a cell with a bunch of violent psycho killers. The day's first two classes were over, and I'd heard nothing. Checking my phone again, I realized it was nearly noon, and Mom would've been home two hours ago from the first part of her split shift. Thursdays, Mom worked five-thirty a.m. to ten a.m., then went back for the noon lunch rush until two, sometimes three, if it was busy. The not knowing what was happening was freaking me out.

As I trudged down the hall, peals of laughter and sounds of fun filled the air. The noise bounced off every wall and crept around every corner. It left me with a sense of missing out. The struggle for the girls' welfare weighed heavily, and no one really got it. I felt like those soldiers laden down with a shit ton of gear but still putting one foot in front of the other. The kids around here were just clutter in my life. I slipped into the bathroom for a break from all the turbulence.

I tied my hair up, then checked the stalls to make sure no one was in the room before I pulled out an empty plastic water bottle and filled it with the liquid soap from the dispenser. When it was full, I screwed the lid on tight and shoved it to the bottom of my bag. I was now set for showers and hair washing for at least a couple of weeks.

I yanked the bathroom door open and immediately spotted Chad across the hallway. He leaned against the brick wall with one foot on the floor and the other casually propped on the wall. He stood straight and came toward me. My heart pounded, and a trickle of sweat formed at the base of my neck as the heat crept into my face. It was an instant physical response that took my breath away.

"Hey, Selena." He reached out and pushed a few errant hairs from my face. "I hope you don't think I'm annoying." He raised one eyebrow and smiled. "I wanted to let you know I'm officially your assigned stalker. They used to give out private bodyguards, but all they had left were stalkers."

"I'm too late, huh?"

"Yup." He winked. "You're way too late. But you'll be happy to know this current model of stalker before you is special in its own way."

"How?"

"Ah, I like it when you smile." He looked straight into my eyes.

The heat rose in my cheeks and I brought my hand up to cool it.

"Yeah, as I was saying," he said, clearing his throat, "with this model of stalker, you never have to say 'follow me,' 'cause he will anyway and ..." he glanced at his shoes and put his hands deep in his pockets, "and, I'm here for you any time you need me. You're my target." He stared down at the floor and shuffled his feet, then added, "I want to like really get to know you better."

"You're so sweet." I stepped so close to him that his warm breath swirled around my ear. He closed his eyes, and I let my hand brush against the front of his jeans. He quivered as he took a sharp intake of air, then let a soft moan escape. "It's nice to know someone's looking out for me. I have to work until nine tonight, but if you'd like to meet after, we could talk—you know, stalker to target."

"Deal."

"Sealed with a kiss," I said as my lips brushed his. "Come on." I clasped his hand in mine, and together we walked to history class.

The school day dragged beyond an eternity. I had to work at four, so I slipped out of school early in order to race home and check on the girls and Mom, which wasn't easy when the city bus was my primary source of transportation. When I arrived, no one was home. There had been no text or phone call, so the whole Gilbert thing must've been dealt with. I hoped Gilbert would rot in jail for an eternity.

I rushed back to the bus stop in time to arrive ten minutes before my shift. I flew into the back, washed up, and put on my apron. The day had turned out better than expected.

"Welcome to Java Jenny's. What can I get for you?"

"Large non-fat chai latte, extra foam, extra hot."

I listened carefully and shouted the order over my shoulder to the barista.

"Okay, that'll be $4.75. What's your name?" I stood poised with my sharpie.

The customer tossed the change in the tip jar and moved to the side counter to collect the order. I loved my job.

The night flew by quickly, and as my shift wound down, I saw Chad sitting on the concrete planter outside the store. My heart pumped blood into every nether region of my body. Any place there could be a pulse throbbed in anticipation of a touch, a kiss, a stroke. I didn't hear my boss come up behind me.

"Why don't you go wipe the tables and chairs? Then you can call it a night."

For the first time since starting, I couldn't wait to walk out the front door.

"Let's walk." Chad took my hand.

There was no hesitation, and it felt natural to fall into step beside him.

"Where're we going?"

"Does it matter so long as it's you and me?"

I didn't answer because he was right. So long as he was beside me, I didn't care. We'd been together for two months, and I was falling hard. It wasn't just sex anymore, but my last boyfriend had said he loved me, then slept with my best friend. It would've been comical if it hadn't hurt so much. Mom tried to warn me—said he was a smooth operator—but I didn't listen. And now, with Chad, I could feel the longing again.

I snuck a peek at him as we walked side by side. We were close to the same height. I wanted to grab him. Couldn't he feel the magnetic force I emitted to bring him closer?

"What're you smiling about? You look like you have a secret."

"I was thinking about magnets." I laughed and gently hip checked him.

Red blotches crept up his neck as he pulled me close. His bleach-blond, curly hair gave him more height and made his green eyes stand out in his long face. I let my finger trail down his long straight nose, trace his full lips, then slip right into his waiting mouth. When my finger entered the wetness of his mouth, my entire body shuddered as bursts of pent-up energy exploded. I was more than ready for him.

He swooped in, brought me close to him, and pushed himself against me. Finally, those full lips were on mine, and I melted into him, so our bodies became one. For that moment, nothing else except the roaring fire within me mattered. The horrible lurking shadows of my world disappeared, and I wasn't alone.

"Come on. Let's go to my place." He dug in his back pocket to produce a key fob. He pushed a button, and as light flooded the darkness, he pulled me with him.

The car smelled like leather polish and greasy french fries.

My tummy grumbled, and my mouth watered at the thought of fries, but right now, it didn't matter because what I wanted sat right beside me. He pushed the start button and put the car in gear. Every inch of me rippled in anticipation of his touch as I studied his profile. I wanted to taste every single piece of him. His beauty was feral and masculine, and his kindness edgy and daring. He pulled the car into a driveway and parked close to the fence—away from the automatic garage doors.

With my hand in his, I fell into step behind him. He pulled me through a side door and into the garage. It was full of cardboard boxes, luggage, tools, and exercise equipment. A funky stench wafted over from the far corner, and I saw the trash can with the lid lying on the ground beside it. There was room left for one vehicle to park inside. Chad punched a code into the door pad, which beeped three times and blinked green. He opened the door, and took off his shoes, adding them to an already neat lineup of sneakers, boots, and sandals. I slipped out of my shoes and added them to the line. We went down a short hallway. Framed family pictures—so many faces, old, young, and everything in between smiling back— filled the walls. The idea of a real family made me warm on the inside.

He stopped before a door. It had a Do Not Disturb sign dangling from the knob.

"Welcome back," he growled as he pulled me close and grabbed my butt.

I felt welcomed by the familiar room. It felt like a home, a place of emotional safety and love. Is that possible after only five times in someone's home? And I wasn't in the house, just his bedroom. Throughout our time together, we had used his room if his parents were away; otherwise, we made do with the back seat, the park, and sometimes his friend's place. He grabbed the handle, and we stepped through the door. The room, littered with empty pizza boxes and piles of clothes, smelled like stale sweat, damp dog, and dried marinara.

A framed picture of him and some girl at the beach stared back at me from the top of the cluttered dresser. His arm dangled over her taut, sun-kissed shoulder to hover over her near-naked breast. He told me they went out for a while, but I didn't ask why the picture was still there. After all, we didn't come here to talk. I placed the picture face down, then turned to Chad as he put on some music.

The rhythmic beat reverberated off the walls as the smell of weed filled the air. I took a deep, long toke, ran my hands through my hair, and swayed to the music. I kept my eye on him as he watched me from where he lay on the bed. I took another drag on the pipe as I lightly slid my hands over my breasts and stomach. He didn't move.

I pulled my T-shirt over my head and flung it at him. He caught it and held it to his face as he breathed in deeply.

"Oh my god, you are fucking amazing," he said, scrambling out of his clothes.

I slowly lowered the waistband of my new-to-me Lulu's and inched my fingertips along the length of my body to remove them. Naked, my eyes never left his. I crawled on all fours across the bed. Everything within me was ready. Dripping. Waiting. Alert for his touch. His hands on my skin were like wildfire, raging through dry tinder. The flames jumped and danced from one nerve to the next, drinking up the eager and willing fuel of desire. Ready, he reached for me as I straddled him and let him fill me. He didn't move, but I could feel him palpitate inside of me. I arched my back to take all of him. A cry of full surrender flew from my lips as I allowed him to flip me on my back and move with me. We were one. Nothing between us. No cares in the world.

"It's late." I stretched out beside him. "I have to get home.

Mom's going to kill me as it is. I don't think I can avoid it any longer."

"No worries. I'll drive you home, but I have to see what's on your neck first."

"What? Is it a spider or something?" I sat up and felt my neck. The tickle of spidery legs trickled down my chest as I flailed my hand at the imaginary intruder.

"No," Chad said, drawing me close. "It's my lips, silly." He rolled over, taking me with him.

As the night went on, Chad turned off the music, and we cuddled under the thin blanket, then made love a third time.

"You've completely drained me, I swear. I need to close my eyes for a minute," he said. Within seconds, he was softly snoring.

The next thing I knew, I woke to see the sun streaming through the window. Beside me, Chad, spread eagle, was still fast asleep.

"Chad?" I shook his shoulder. "Chad, it's morning."

"What?" His gaze was confused and glassy—like he didn't recognize me.

I slipped his shirt over my head and tiptoed across the hall and down to the bathroom. A woman's voice came from somewhere in the house, but I couldn't make out what she was saying. I locked the door behind me and peed as quietly as possible. Staring back at me in the mirror was a young woman with rumpled hair and flushed skin who looked like she'd just had sex. There were three hickeys on my neck and beard burns all over my face and body.

I splashed my face with cold water and opened the bathroom door to get Chad.

"Good morning." A woman stood before me. "I'm going to assume you're a friend of Chad's, so I don't have to call the police to have you thrown out of the house."

"Um ... yeah. Hi, I'm Selena. Um, Chad and I ..." Heat crept up to my face. "We're friends."

"Hmm ... yes." She appeared to consider the situation. "I'm sure you are."

"It's nice to meet you. If you'll excuse me ..." And with that, I slunk back to Chad's room and closed the door.

"I think I met your mother."

"What? Shit." He threw the cover off himself. "They weren't supposed to be home until later today. We better go, but I can't move with this hard-on. We need to fix it."

"You are insatiable." I giggled as I threw the shirt back off and climbed in beside him.

We pulled the blanket over us and fought not to laugh. His fingers pinched and stroked me until I had to bite my lip to stop from crying out. He traced the inside of my thighs with a feather touch, then, with my help, he traced small circles over and over again until he almost drove me mad.

"I need you to fuck me." I wrapped my legs around him. "Now."

He didn't argue, and we quickly found our release. What a perfect way to start the day. Together, we dressed and retraced our steps back to the car.

"We'll talk about this later, Chadwick," a voice called out.

I'm not stupid. I know. Later, like when the slut is gone. Christ, why not just tell me I'm a skanky bitch and get it over with? I've never felt so fucking nullified in my entire life.

Chad pulled into the dirt driveway. Mom's orange pinto with the missing back window covered with plastic and duct tape was backed in close to the house. The clear plastic flapped with the slight breeze.

Gilbert's motorcycle wasn't there. Maybe things would finally get back to normal.

"Is this where you live?"

"Yeah, this is it." I didn't blame him for his judgment. It was a shitty pit of a neighborhood, and believe me, if I had a choice, I wouldn't be there either. "I guess I better go. I have a feeling there's going to be some fireworks."

"Why? Is it because you didn't come home last night?" Chad reached for my hand. "Do you want me to explain it to them?"

"You're sweet, but it's a long story, and it's totally separate from you and me. I'm sure it'll be fine."

"Okay, good." He sighed like he'd been holding his breath. "Cause last night was fucking fantastic, if you know what I mean."

I nodded. The specialness wasn't lost on me. I knew I loved him, and I wanted to tell him. He was the best thing in my life. He gave me hope. But now was not the time for a talk or declaration of love. I noticed the thin curtain covering fluttering behind the front door window. Someone was watching us.

"I should go." I grabbed my school bag and reached for the handle.

"Yeah, me too. My mom sounded pretty pissed. Is it," he checked his mirrors, "is it safe around here? Like for me?"

"Yeah, nobody'll touch you."

"Good. Listen, can I see you tonight?"

"I don't know what's going on. I may have to stay with my little sisters. Can I text you later?"

"Sure. Whatever."

"Chad," I couldn't look right at him. "I had a great time last night. I ah ..."

"Yeah, I know, and believe me, you were amazing. You blew my mind, not to mention a few other things."

"Oh, my God." I punched him on the arm. "I can't believe you said that."

"It was the best. Later, okay?"

He cradled my head in his hands and gave me a small kiss on the lips. Before he could pull away, I drew him back to meet his heated tongue and promised passion.

"Fuuuuck, you don't make it easy, do you?" I pried myself away from him and forced myself from the car. Part of me didn't care about anything except our bodies enmeshing as one, but the reality in the shape of a shitty, dilapidated shack and the secrets within needed to be dealt with first. "Thanks. I lo ..." I paused and stepped back. "Talk tomorrow, okay?" I closed the car door and waved.

He drove away, and I climbed the three worn steps to the front door. On the second step, the tip of my shoe caught a rusty nail that had worked its way out, and I stumbled onto the front landing. The six-panel door was decrepit, tired, and filthy.

I turned the knob and shoved it with my shoulder at the same time. The house, dark except for the glowing ember of Mom's cigarette, was freezing. A draft flowed through the room as a shiver raced down my spine—I was afraid I'd walked in on an execution, namely my own.

"Mom?"

"Well, you finally showed up, huh? You best turn yourself right around and get out of here. Don't come back."

"Mom, you know I can't leave. I need to stay here with you. We're a team, remember?"

"The team died when you called in the social workers. How could you?"

"Oh my God, what happened? I didn't call any social workers. I swear. Mom, you have to believe me. Please, Mom." I fell at her feet. The couch was a dark chocolate brown corduroy material, worn through the arms and seat cushions. Mom sat with her feet tucked under herself while an ashtray perched nearby, overflowed and threatening to tip its contents. I stared at a hair-thin thread from the couch cushion wound through Mom's toes.

"They took the girls." Her eyes brimmed with tears as she glared at me. "The state worker said the girls aren't safe with me because I'm not looking after them properly."

"Oh, Mom, you have to believe me. I didn't know they took the girls. I came home after school, and no one was home. You know I'd never let anyone take the girls."

"They told me you reported Gilbert—said he was doing unspeakable things."

"I didn't report Gilbert." I fought to stay calm and hide my racing heart. Technically, I was telling the truth, but I also know Mom wasn't stupid.

"They told me you said he had plans to molest the girls."

"Shit, Mom. He was eyeing Vic this morning. He told her she could stay home from school, and they'd do stuff together. Mom, I came home from school the other day to find Sofia topless and Vic adjusting her clothes."

"What are you talking about? I've asked Gilbert, and he says he's not interested in little girls. I don't have any reason not to believe him." Mom leaned forward and stubbed out her cigarette. Ashes from the already full tray spilled onto the table and puffed softly into the air to fall to the floor like volcanic snow. A cough erupted from deep in her rattling chest. It shook her entire body as she spat into the tissue in her hand. Spittle of blood and saliva fell to her chin, and she wiped at it with the back of her hand. She picked up her package of cigarettes, shook one loose, and took another between her teeth to light it. "Gilbert wouldn't touch any of you. He's got me."

"Mom," I whispered as I kneeled on the floor in front of her. "Mom, he's no good." There was no easy way to do this, and I knew Mom would be heartbroken for both the girls and Gilbert.

"What're you saying? Gilbert loves you girls like you're his own. He promised he'd never touch any of you."

"I walked the girls to school this morning." Mom pulled her hand away as soon as I began. I needed her to hear me. "Vic told me about a secret pact she made with Gilbert about being his special model." My voice broke, and tears fell. I glanced up. Mom's eyes were closed, and, except for her clenched fists, you'd never know she was upset. "Gilbert told her she'd make lots of money, and together they'd get rich." I clasped her hands and held them tight. "Mom, Vic told me flat out that Gilbert wanted to see her without her clothes on so he could take pictures."

I put all my weight onto one knee and stared at the floor. The last part was a lie, but I desperately needed Mom to believe me. It wasn't far from the truth anyway, and I didn't mean for any of this mess to actually happen.

She pushed me away, and a gut-wrenching scream erupted from her seemingly frail frame. She hit herself in the face, not once, but twice.

"Mom, stop!" I scrambled along the wooden floor to get closer. In my haste, my foot kicked the coffee table, sending empty beer cans and newspapers flying. "Mom, Victoria told me nothing had happened yet. He hadn't touched her."

"Oh Selena, I failed you," she wailed. She tried to hit herself again as coughs erupted and she hawked a wad of bloody spit onto the floor. "I'm a terrible mother and don't deserve to live."

What's going on here? This isn't the way I pictured this going down. Right now, I want to be back in Chad's warm bed and pretend none of this exists. It's all my fault. How could I be so stupid? I should've known they'd take the girls before they even touched Gilbert. Assholes. I pushed myself up off the floor and, in the process, knocked the ashtray from the rickety side table. Clouds of near-disintegrated ash filled the air with a poof while the larger particulates drifted farther afield to land all over everything.

"Shit. Sorry." I swatted to clear the surrounding air. "It's going to be okay. You're a great mom. I'll tell them. We can move—the girls and us. A place where Gilbert won't find us. We'll be fine. We always are."

"Selena, you've been taking care of me for too long. It needs to stop now."

"Don't say that. I'm not going anywhere." I searched her face. She was so thin. The skin around her neck and chest was filled with huge brown blotches resembling bruises. And blood? Why did she spit blood?

"There's no use." She wiped her face with her raw, swollen hand. "I'm so tired. I can't fight anymore."

"I'll do the fighting, Mom. I'm strong. You don't have to worry about Gilbert. It'll be the four of us again." I leaned in to hold her hand. "Remember how much fun we used to have?"

The entire situation was like an old black and white movie set to fast music. I wanted to hold and comfort her, but Mom slumped back away from me and pulled out a bottle of gin she had tucked in tight beside her.

"Oh, Mom ..." I stepped back, but with a quick snap, she removed the cap and took a long pull on the bottle. "Why, Mom? It's been over five years. You promised."

"I've lost everything. Two baby girls taken away by the state, and you—you've got one foot out the door already, don't you?" She didn't look at me as she coughed and wiped her face. "All I have is ..." She took another drink from the bottle. The clear liquid dribbled down her chin and fell to her chest, where ashes had settled. The droplets slinked down between her sunken breasts, leaving a blackened trail. "All I have is Gilbert."

"No!" My voice ricocheted off the thin walls, and I knew I

needed to calm down. "Mom, you have me. I'm here. He's poison." I took her hand again. "Mom, he did secret things with the girls. We don't know half of it."

"He loves me. He told me it was all a lie, and Victoria made it up because he gave her heck for messing up the kitchen."

"Mom, listen," I said. "Please. Vic and Sofia will be home soon. Mom, I'm here for you. Please."

"Selena, you've always been a good girl, but it's time you move on. I told Gilbert I believe him," Mom whispered with her lips near the bottle. She took another swig and wiped her mouth with the back of her hand.

"Mom? Are you choosing him over me? Over the girls?"

"You don't understand. You're so young. You have your whole life ahead of you. He takes good care of me."

"I'll take care of you." I stood before her as she gulped from the bottle. My heart skittered out of control, but it wasn't from the feel-good excitement like I'd experienced the previous night. This was different. A sheen of sweat draped itself over me as I braced for a fight. "Mom, you're being ridiculous. Don't do this. We'll find Victoria and Sofia, and we'll be a family."

"Selena, it's already done." Tears rolled unchecked down her tired, puckered face. "Someday, you'll understand."

"Why're you doing this? Mom, you know as well as I do that the girls will get sucked further into the system, then God knows what'll happen. Mom, please ..." I pleaded before her. "Please."

Though all my senses were heightened, I didn't hear him enter the house. My knees turned to mush when I heard his voice.

"You want it all, don'tcha, Selena. You wanna whore around all night when yer mama here is worried sick, then you want yer baby sisters to run amok and not hafta listen to anyone but you."

"Oh, Gilbert, I'm glad you're home," Mom slurred from her chair.

I turned and glared at him. I wanted to punch him so hard and knock him on his pompous ass. His eyes roamed slowly from my feet to my head. He made me feel filthy with a mere glance.

"You can't let this happen," I begged. "Look at her." I turned to see Mom nod off. The dark red spots where she'd hit herself glowed with white ash. "She shouldn't be drinking. It'll kill her. She can't even think straight. You have to leave."

"Why, you lil' bitch," he sneered at me and stepped closer, "don't tell me what I should 'n shouldn't do. I'm the one who pays the rent in this here house, not yer ma. This is my house, 'n yer no longer welcome. Yer nothing but a visitor here, so if anyone's gonna leave, it ain't gonna be me. Yer nothin' but a lil' slut. I can smell it on you jus' like I put it there myself."

"Mom! Did you hear that?" I spun on my heel to where Mom slouched in her chair with an unlit cigarette in her hand, resting by her leg.

"Me and yer ma already had us a lil' talk 'n yer the one who hasta go. Like I said, you and yer lies 'n bullshit ain't welcome here no more." He raised his hand, and I leaped back. "Well, lookie there—someone done branded ya all over yer neck. Yer a lying lil' slut who'll spread her legs at the drop of nickel, ain'tcha? You go stay with yer man. Maybe he'll teach you a lesson or two 'bout being a proper woman."

"Selena, you go now," Mom slurred. "The girls aren't coming back, and it's no use fighting anymore. I haven't got no fight left in me."

I couldn't believe it. Something must've happened because normally she wouldn't let anything tear her away from us. She worked her fingers to the bone, doing split shifts to keep us together. Five years ago, she swore off booze with a vengeance filled with courage and tenacity. Everything was fine until he wormed himself into our family and poisoned everything.

"Mom? Come with me." I kneeled before her so she could see me. "It's not too late. We don't need him. You're working, and so am I—we can do it together. We can find our own place, Mom. Please, for Vic and Sof. Don't let him ruin our family." I yanked her hand as I begged, but her eyes were empty. I knew then I'd lost her.

"You hafta understand the world's not all 'bout you," his voice boomed. "Me and yer ma are a family. It'd be best if'n you'd take those love bites 'n git movin' on outta my house."

I checked Mom, who'd somehow lit a cigarette which was ready to drop to the floor as she fell further into a drunken sleep. I took the cigarette and snuffed it out. Mom slouched down on the couch. The self-inflicted blows were now welts and needed ice, but Gilbert stood between us with arms crossed. I knew I needed to go. The alcohol dulled Mom's common sense, and the power passed silently to Gilbert.

"You got ten minutes to get yer stuff 'n git da fuck outta my house. Is that clear?" He scratched himself, removed his coat, and tossed it over top of Mom's head onto the far end of the couch. "If'n y'all stay longer, I'm gonna assume ya wanna give a real man a try. Yer choice."

Bile burned in my throat. I swallowed hard and sidestepped around him to go to the room I shared with the girls. Drawers were open, and things strewn everywhere. Someone, a social worker probably, had come in and done a quick grab of stuff for the girls. I picked up one of Sofia's favorite books—Mr. Grumpy Cat—which she'd got from the Christmas hamper last year and carried everywhere. Damn it. It wasn't supposed to be this way. Talking to Mrs. Bonder was supposed to get rid of Gilbert, not tear my family apart.

"Five minutes!" he yelled from the other room. "Should I get myself ready fer ya?"

I went to the kitchen and took one black garbage bag Mom pocketed at work. I jammed it full of whatever I could grab. Victoria's ratty old stuffed lamb sat propped on her pillow.

"Oh Vic, I'm so sorry," I whispered as I shoved the lamb into the bag. "Please be together and be safe."

I didn't have a lot of clothes, but between the three of us, there was enough stuff to fill the bag halfway. Before I tied it up, I went to the bathroom, took all the toilet paper and soap I'd collected over the last couple of weeks, and shoved them in my school bag. I certainly wouldn't leave it for him.

"Ya gots 'bout three minutes," he chuckled through the doorway.

How long had he been standing there? He turned, and the roar of rushing adrenaline deafened me but made me move faster than I ever had in my life. I couldn't see straight. I searched for another garbage bag, but all I could find was a plastic grocery bag. Like a madwoman, I tore things off the walls. Special pictures made by the girls and one of my own treasures. It was a picture of me, around age ten, with the only father I ever knew. He and Mom married when I was six. In the picture, Victoria was a baby. Less than three years later, when Sofia was a newborn, he died from an aneurism, and Mom started drinking again. It's like we'd come back full circle to a terrible place and time. Tears blurred my vision, but I checked to make sure he wasn't behind me. I ran into Mom's room, grabbed her jewelry box, and tossed it in the bag. I double looped the handles and tied a knot. With the two bags, I went to the front door and stopped. Mom had fallen sideways on the couch and snored with her near toothless mouth wide open.

The room was still hazy from cigarette smoke and strewn ashes, and though I didn't want to leave, there was no choice.

"Okay, little one, come jump on. I'm all ready fer ya," he yelled from the kitchen.

I threw my school backpack over my shoulder, grabbed the two bags, and raced out the door and down the steps to the alley. Mom chose him over the girls and me. She'd live with a bottle tucked under her arm and embrace a man she thought she deserved.

"Love you, Mom." A lone tear snuck down my cheek. I wiped it away and kept walking.

I had no idea where to go.

Chapter Thirteen

NOW

LESLIE

I saluted Prince with my coffee as he rooted through the trash. Every night this past week, I'd stuffed the trashcan full of empties. Such a simple thing to do, and my heart sang when I saw him grin.

As fall approached, days grew shorter, and the morning light was shallow and dull. It was as if nature was tired of all the sunshine energy and needed a break. The rains and constant cool dampness of the Pacific Northwest took over, and umbrellas became the norm. The commuter traffic, along with the hustle and bustle of the work week, appeared slower, too.

All last week, I picked Selena up after she missed the bus. It was a new routine borne out of necessity. Yesterday she told me about her Thursday morning dilemma of having to walk the girls to school and I offered to be the solution. Selena wouldn't stick out her thumb anymore if I had anything to say about it. She should be coming any minute now.

My phone showed 7:59, and Selena still hadn't shown. The bus always arrived at 8:01. Hmm ... it was Monday. Where was she? After the first hitchhiking incident, I made sure I was dressed and ready to go at a minute's notice. The phone said 8:00. *Okay, Selena should sprint past here and get in line for the bus any minute. Come on. Come on. Where are you?*

I zoomed in with the binoculars as far as I could. Limpy-Mommy wore a multi-colored poncho today, and the baby had his/her hand sticking out the side. Up, down, up, down—the young woman's labored movement mesmerized me—it was like watching a well-oiled piston in motion.

Selena was nowhere to be seen. I lowered the binoculars as the bus pulled up with a hiss, and all the students moved forward.

"Come on, girl. Where are you?" My breath stuck in my throat as I waited.

I scanned the area again through the binoculars, but my stomach was knotted with worry. *Maybe she's sick? Maybe she's moved?* Something wasn't right. My heart beat like drums at a rock concert. My hollow breath failed to fill me. I wiped my sweaty palms against my legs, which left them pasty and doughy. *Shit. It's like I'm back at the courthouse.* I shook my hands and bounced my legs to wake up my brain. *Come on, I'm not going down that humiliating path again. Stop being so stupid ... damn, I'm acting like some kind of fervent idiot. She's nothing but a familiar stranger.* There was something I couldn't figure out about Selena, though. It was how she moved and spoke—I'd seen it all before. The false bravado and tenacious survival instinct had me both enamored and intrigued. I was the same way at her age, and no one looked out for me. *She needs me whether she realizes it or not.*

Car. I need to get to the car. I grabbed the keys, charged down the stairs, and went out to the garage. The precious seconds when Selena could come running over the knoll couldn't be sacrificed. The last thing I wanted to do was miss her all together. My blood pumped so fast I could probably pound out a marathon and not break a sweat. *Invincible, that's what I am!* I wanted Selena to be invincible, too. I'd picked her up several times now. She was always polite, grateful, and recognizable in her mannerisms. I needed to figure this out. She was a soul akin to my own, and I wanted to show her not all people, like some of those other students, were jerks.

With practiced efficiency, I closed the garage door and drove the narrow lane to the end, where the small triangular park was visible. With my driver's window open, I caught a whiff of billowing diesel exhaust as the school bus pulled away.

Selena was still nowhere in sight. She'd crest the hill any second, out of breath and needing a ride to school. Then I could sweep in to pick her up—what a great way to start the day. I checked my phone for the time. Selena was never this late.

"I live nearby, and I'm on my way to work," I told her. "Dropping you at the school is no problem."

"Thanks. Some days it's hard to take the bus on time." She always held her bag on her lap.

We chatted about school and her job at Java Jenny's. It was lovely to be so near her. To get the opportunity to study her up close. She had long slim fingers, like those of a pianist. Her fingernails were short and clean; she smelled of cigarette smoke and detergent. Her manners and decorum were impeccable. It was obvious she'd learned to behave properly, but there was also a mysterious aura surrounding the girl—one of solitude and melancholy.

My adrenaline slowed to a crawl as I panted and gripped the steering wheel so tightly my knuckles turned white, and I could no longer feel the flesh of my palms. *Please, Selena. Where are you?* Sitting at the stop sign near the driveway entrance, my vision was murky as pressure beat at my temples. All I could do was wait.

I steered into the bus stop, put on the four-way flashers, and waited to see if Selena would show up. The traffic whipped by me and the empty park.

My temples throbbed. *This is insane. I don't know where the girl is. Hell, she's a stranger. What the fuck am I doing? I need to, though. She told me about her mom's nasty boyfriend. Why didn't I give her my cell number? She could've called me for help, but no, I'm too dumb to consider the obvious. All I can do is hope she's not hurt.*

I slid into traffic and headed toward the school. What if something happened to her? What if she was in the hospital? Or worse? And if she was, what could I do about it?

I pulled into the high school parking lot and watched as a massive sea of students meandered about the grounds. I craned my neck to cover as much area as possible. She had to be here somewhere.

I stayed until the bell rang and all the students went into the school.

The sudden absence of the hubbub and buzz of students left an eerie stillness that gripped my gut and didn't want to let go. *Do I wait here or go home? Okay. Breathe, Leslie.* The skunky stench of weed and the sweetness of nearby lilacs clung to the thick air. I couldn't draw any air deep enough to make a difference. Gone was the resolve of strength, as a helplessness of weakness and uncertainty crept in. I didn't know whether to wait or leave. Was there actually a choice?

An hour later, I was still sitting in my car in the parking lot. I tried everything to make her appear—to will it to happen. I made deals with the universe and promises to God—if only Selena would step out the front door.

With classes in session, there was little to see. I'd been in the same spot for an extended period, and yet no security—or anyone—asked me why. I could have been a shooter or someone with ill intent or a grudge—what kind of school was this? After I found Selena, I fully intended to speak to the principal.

I had to pee, so I gave up and drove home. *Where could she be?* I perched myself atop the nesting chair and checked out the triangle park. It was full of strangers now. A woman dressed in a long, torn coat dug through the trash can. I wanted to shoo her away. Tell her this trashcan belonged to Prince. Strangers waited for the city bus in the same spot where Selena should've been this morning. I wrung my hands and drew my legs under me to rock back and forth as I continued to search each face. Something bad had happened—I could feel it.

Far off in the distance, a phone rang. The melodic tune was familiar. I realized it was the ring tone I assigned to Phillip.

At one time, I would've done anything for him. I'd loved him so much, but now he was a mere annoyance pushing into my life when my mind was on other things. A chill ran down the length of my exposed skin and I realized I'd fallen asleep in my chair with my phone beside me. I pulled the nearby throw-blanket over myself, and let my mind drift.

Phillip and I were supposed to conquer the world together. I believed every word out of his mouth. Even now, I fantasized about being back in his arms, snuggled warmly against him. Familiar. Safe. Oblivious to the world. I was smart enough now, though, to recognize that what I really wanted was the feeling, not him.

Mother's voice echoed through my head. *Don't you forget—you're damaged, soiled goods, so the fact any man wants you is a blessing.*

Was I damaged? I never told him all of what happened to me because of my shame. I knew Phillip wouldn't understand. He'd hate me. Hell, I hate me.

It was all my fault. Over the years, Mother reminded me at every opportunity. Even now, the echo of her voice pecked away at the same raw spot every chance it got. The pregnancy, the humiliation, the loss... All my fault.

I couldn't help but wonder, though, what our life would've been like without the secrets and insecurities. Would I've been freer to love him better? Perhaps he wouldn't have cheated. Was it my fault he sought out another woman? He deserved better. I pinched and twisted the soft flesh under my upper arm. The phone vibrated against my leg and I fumbled to answer it.

"Hi Max," I said. "What can I do for you?"

"I wanted to congratulate you. The judge threw Phillip's lawsuit out and accepted your countersuit for ongoing spousal support."

"Great." I tried to muster up some enthusiasm, but what I wanted was Phillip—not his money. Even through the far reaches of my romance writer's imagination, I couldn't think of a scenario where we'd reunite. And Selena. Where was she?

"Les, are you all right? I know how stressful this whole thing has been on you."

"I don't know, Max. I really don't. I ... I feel so alone." *Oh my God, I can't believe I blurted out my truth.* "Sorry. Seriously, I'm fine. I guess I'm feeling down, is all."

"Do you want me to come over? I can bring dinner or some-thing. What do you think?"

"No, Max, please don't. Seriously, that's very kind, but I seriously need to learn how to cope with this whole thing by myself. I'll be fine. Really..." I took a deep breath and tucked the blanket around my feet. "You've done enough. I need to be more thankful, and I am. Thankful, I mean."

"Leslie, I'm worried about you."

"Please don't worry. We'll do dinner soon, I promise—I'm fine."

"Well, if you're sure. I'll send you an email about the docu-ments. You need to sign and return them by week's end."

"Thanks, Max. You're the absolute best." I dug deep to force some energy into my voice and fought to sound cheerful. To my ears, it sounded ridiculous and put on, but I knew it was what Max needed.

"And you, my friend, are very welcome. Glad to be of service. We'll talk soon."

"Yeah, soon." I hung up and curled back into my chair. It was nearly three o'clock in the afternoon, and I hoped Selena would be on the school bus.

I scanned the area with the binoculars and waited, but Selena didn't show.

The floor-to-ceiling windows which opened the room to the world felt like a barrier, revealing nothing. I paced back and forth for what felt like hours, and still nothing. *What if she's hurt? Should I go to the police and tell them? Tell them what? The young girl I've been watching didn't turn up today? Shit, they'd toss me into the psych ward for sure.* I took a deep breath and tried to block the endless loop of things that could've happened to her. *She's in a ditch somewhere—calling weakly for help. Or perhaps she has a high fever and is comatose in the hospital. What if she was kidnapped? Or murdered?*

I nearly foamed at the mouth with all the possibilities. I had to do something, though what, I didn't know. Grabbing the car keys, I bolted down the steps to the front entrance foyer, put on my coat, hat, and gloves, then swung open the oversized front door.

I seldom used this door because I always parked in the back garage, but lately, I'd taken cans out this way for Prince. I locked the door with the push of a button and made my way down the wide sidewalk with its intricate brick inlay and old-fashioned wrought iron lamp posts. Glancing both ways before I crossed the four-lane highway, I went to the bench where Prince sat every morning.

"Dedicated to my loving husband, Edgar. You'll be missed," the engraved bench plaque said.

I nodded at Edgar and made my way to the pebbled path on the horizon. From my window perch, it always appeared so far away, but it was the incline that gave the impression that it was much larger than expected. The path had a deep, quick-sand effect that would slow anyone to a near standstill. *Wow, hat's off, and full respect to Limpy-Mommy.*

I trudged farther and recognized how rundown, and in need of repair, everything was. It was definitely worse than I realized. Just past the path, the cracked sidewalks heaved every couple of feet and spewed tenacious weeds through the worn porous surface. *Poor Limpy-Mommy must have a heck of a time with all these tripping hazards.*

At the end of the short path was a broken gate in a chain-link fence. The overgrown grass was home to fast-food wrappers, drink cups, and cigarette butts. It was a stark contrast to my own street and its perfectly coifed lawns and pruned trees.

The gaping hole in the fence was ominous, but a compulsion beyond my control pushed me forward into a path bordered by tall weeds and strewn trash. If I said I was shocked, it would be an understatement because I had no idea this area even existed, especially so close to home.

I could picture myself dodging along this dangerous path as though I was in a horror film where the idiot woman always goes through the door that's half open. In the back of my mind, watchers screamed for me to stop—*don't keep going, you stupid fool, you're walking into a trap... you're going to get yourself killed...* But I blindly inched forward and didn't care. Selena came from this direction every morning, so it was worth checking out, even if my spidey senses told me to turn back.

The path narrowed, and to the left was a patchy grass field and school with a jungle gym and swings. Wow, I had no clue there was a school so close, though I probably paid taxes for it every year. To the right was a pockmarked alley with shacks lining both sides. *How will I know which one is Selena's?* The house on the corner had a trampled-down path worn through the wild grasses and weeds to what appeared to be a flimsy front door. A board was nailed to the side, and the faded and worn wooden porch barely clung to the front of the shack. Dead, colorless flowers flanked the door in cracked clay pots adorned by a grinning garden gnome with half its head missing. At the property edge, a Beware of Dog sign dangled on a flimsy rusted chain, and even though a dog was not readily visible, huge piles of dog poop punctuated the yard. There was no way I was going to hang around to meet the obviously large pooch.

Farther down the lane, the next yard was strewn with trash, as though the dog from next door had visited and obliterated everything in sight. In the middle of the yard, an overstuffed chair with a missing cushion and worn green fabric on the arms oozed cotton stuffing as it sat right next to a car up on blocks. A frayed half of an American flag flapped in the steady wind.

The next house had a clothesline full of men's clothes.

Boxes and crates were everywhere, but right near the back door, there was a broom and a covered sandbox with a mesh bin of neatly stacked toys beside it. It looked like an oasis in the middle of a bomb field. I thought of Limpy-Mommy and wondered.

The entire area was something out of one of those cop shows where they chased gangsters into the seediest part of town. *Why didn't I know this when it's practically my front yard?* I checked over my shoulder and sped up my pace. *This can't be where Selena lives. Maybe there's a different neighborhood on the other side. Something fresher. Newer.*

The alleyway went on forever, though. The farther I got away from the break in the fence, the more squalid it got. I glanced up to see a man sitting on a back step smoking a cigarette. He didn't have a shirt on, even in the cool fall weather. His all-over tattooed belly fell low over his pants. He cocked his head at me. He knew I didn't belong here. Behind him, the windows were covered in tinfoil with randomly shaped pieces of plywood nailed over. On the side, someone had spray-painted, "I exercise my 2nd Amendment rights—Keep Out."

Holy shit. Sweat broke along my hairline as a fear of what could've happened to Selena grabbed and shook me to the core. Was she being held against her will? Was she captive in one of these shacks? Most of these places should have been condemned and, who knows, maybe already were.

My breath came in short gulps as my legs weakened in my quest to get back to the broken gate. There was no other way out. This was Selena's escape from this part of her world.

I realized I needed to pay more attention. I'd never watched to see where any of the other kids at the bus stop came from. They just appeared. As far as I could remember, Selena was the only student who came over the hill every morning. It was even more clear to me now that Selena needed my protection. All I had to do was find her.

Chapter Fourteen

SELENA

I carried the two plastic bags down the alley toward the city bus. The heavy bags cut into my fingers and every few feet I had to stop to readjust the weight, so it wasn't all on one side. It made for a slow walk, but all I could do at this point was put one foot in front of the other to get distance between me and that monster. How did this happen?

At the bus, I set the bags on the ground and straddled them so they wouldn't topple over. I took my student bus pass out of my backpack, and, within a couple of minutes, the bus pulled up to the stop with a forcefully expelled hiss as the door slapped open. Even though the stuff in the black garbage bag had settled to fill half the bag, it was bulky and cumbersome. The plastic knot stretched away from the bag, threatening to separate all together. I was still standing as the bus door slammed shut and we rolled away from the curb. The seats designated for handicapped or elderly were empty, and right then, I felt disabled and broken, so I plopped down. I leaned against the seat and rocked with the swaying motion of the bus. I wanted to close my eyes and make everything disappear. Chad. My mind drifted back to the night before.

The bus lurched, startling me out of my daze. I tucked my leg around the black bag on the floor and held tight to the small one I'd placed beside me on the long blue bench seat. We neared my stop when I turned to pull the cord to signal the driver I wanted the next stop. As I reached up, the small bag tumbled to the floor. I scrambled to catch it, but it shot into the air and launched itself across the aisle. It was like a kick in the head. I grabbed the knot on the black bag and dove to retrieve the other bag, only to have the plastic stretch until there was a gaping hole in the side. My underwear and T-shirts spilled out. Everything happened so fast my brain couldn't keep up. The clothes unfurled, and a small water bottle half-filled with hand soap rolled toward the driver's feet, then a hairbrush slid along the grooved floor. It was like an avalanche gathering speed and power, and I had no way to stop it.

"Stop," I whispered as tears burned at the backs of my eyes. I fought them off. There'd be time for that later. Right now, I needed to get my stuff back in the bags and get off this crazy ride.

On my hands and knees, I braced myself against the careening motion of the bus. I swept all the clothing within arm's reach and pulled them into a pile before me. My hands were covered in dirt and a pebble embedded itself into my knee. The bus driver bounced in his seat with each slight bump and turn. He didn't realize a bottle of soap was headed for his feet, and I was helpless to stop it as it skipped and rolled in motion with the bus. I plopped down on my butt and put everything between my legs to stop it from sliding. My eyes watered again, then I spotted a discarded condom stuck to the bottom of a nearby seat. I gagged, forced myself to take a deep breath, and started re-stuffing the bag.

"Here, dear, let me help you," a white-haired elderly woman said as she handed me a cloth bag. "I have another one here in my purse, too. My husband, Edgar, always insisted I keep them in my purse because you never know when you're going to need them, and it appears this is a situation in which they're needed."

"Thank you," I whispered. Those tears threatened again. I could barely speak, and I knew if I looked her in the eye, I'd lose it. I took the cloth grocery bag and stuffed it full of clothes.

"It's not a problem. Let's get all this scooped up and back in order, shall we?"

The old lady got down on her knees and re-bagged my treasures while a young boy rushed to pick up stuff that had rolled and slid beyond my reach.

"Here you go." He handed things back to me, glancing over his shoulder at his mom, who smiled and nodded.

"Thank you." I smiled as best I could at the boy, who quickly turned and scampered back to his seat.

The older lady's efficiency surprised me. She scooped things up, handing them to me to stuff into the cloth bag, which I then shoved into the larger plastic bag. Her hands were steady, and though she was tiny in stature, I had a feeling she was strong and capable.

"I think I've seen you before—maybe around the school bus stop," she said. "Sometimes I'm getting off one bus and you're getting on the school bus. It's a small world, isn't it? But it appears as though you're moving."

"Yah, I guess you could say that."

"Do you have a plan, dear? A place to go?"

I met the older woman's eyes and recognized the concern. Tears welled up in my eyes as there was more care and concern from this stranger than I'd seen from my mother in the last few hours. I clutched my things close to me as the tears blurred my vision, and I nodded.

"I wouldn't want you to be on the streets. You hear such horrible stories on the news."

"I'll... I'll be all right," I said as I sniffed and wiped my nose with the end of my sleeve. I scanned the aisle—there were so many kinds and sizes of shoes, and I knew it echoed the world's largeness and mishmash. "I have a ... a friend."

"Well, that's such a relief, isn't it? You have no idea how happy that makes me." The woman smiled and handed me another bag. "You don't need to return the bags, but if you ever see someone who needs them, you can pass them along." The older woman pulled herself back up to the seat and smiled. "That's the most exercise I've had in a long time."

The bus pulled to a stop, and the door slapped open. There were no words. I nodded at the lady, gathered my things—even the bottle of soap from under the bus driver's feet, which he kicked out for me to grab—and I stepped off the bus.

The chill in the air hit me immediately and reminded me of how insignificant I am. I hooked one bag over my wrist and carried the other with both hands to ensure it wouldn't spill or rip. My backpack, still in place, pulled against my shoulders. I jumped up to adjust it, but the weight increased with each movement. I scanned the area to see if I could spot an abandoned shopping cart. *Then, I'd look the part of a homeless waif.* With a deep breath and a sigh, I walked.

I ended up tucked around the side corner of Java Jenny's. The plastic bags kept me warm and sorta dry, but didn't conceal my presence. People could still see me, but I'd actually never felt more invisible in my life. I know it sounds crazy, but I needed to be alone. The idea of someone gawking at me with pity in their eyes blocked the flow of common sense. During the day, I saw some kids from school. I turned my head and pulled my hoodie down over my face as far as I could, but I didn't know whether they recognized me. It had been a long day. I'd arrived at the store sometime around eight-thirty a.m. Mindy opened at seven-thirty and would finish up around five p.m.

All day, I leaned against the brick and tried to ignore the cold seeping into my bones. The rain almost drove me into the shop's warmth. If a smooth-talking guy had approached me and promised a nice warm bed and some food, I couldn't say I wouldn't have gone. Is that what had happened to Mom? This whole thing weighed on me. *How could a jerk like Gilbert get so much power over her?* My brain felt like sludge, thick and slow.

Every time the door opened, I smelled the coffee's warm, rich aroma. My stomach growled, and my mouth watered at the thought of the enticing fare inside. I should have gone in and waited in the back, but every time I went to move, I was paralyzed with dread. I wasn't ready to share the truth, or face it.

I nodded off, only to wake to see Leslie frantically run into the coffee shop. Her face was ultra-pale, and she had one big crease across her forehead. She dashed through the door, then raced out a few seconds later without a coffee, jumped in her Jeep, and tore out of the parking lot like a crazy lady.

Finally, there was no one in the store, so I gathered up my stuff and staggered in to stand in front of Mindy.

"Selena? Oh my God, Selena? What're you doing here?" The shock was obvious on Mindy's face as she froze in place and raised her brows.

"Sorry..." I studied the floor. "I didn't know where else to go."

"You must be freezing. Oh, my God. Come on, I have a blanket in the back. I was worried when you said you couldn't work today." Mindy wrapped me in a musty-smelling blanket and rubbed my arms. "I've been so worried about you."

"I'm sorry. I didn't mean to make you worry. I didn't want to see anyone. I have all my stuff. My step-dad kicked me out." *Did I make a mistake by coming here? This was my workplace. I should've gone to Chad's, but I knew his mom would freak out. I could hear it now—'what is she doing here, Chadwick?'*

"I didn't know what else to do, so I waited outside." My voice cracked, and I took a deep breath to stop myself from totally losing it. "I need a place to stay for a couple of days until I can get a plan together."

"Well, you're coming home with me. I won't take no for an answer. God, you could catch pneumonia out here. Do you have any dry clothes to put on?"

It surprised me how Mindy administered to my needs, so gentle and caring. But it was the home situation that weighed on me. The separation from my sisters had caused the flames of a primal rage within my gut. Nothing else, especially my comfort, really mattered right now.

"Okay, let's get you back to my place so you can clean up properly and get some sleep."

Mindy wrapped her arms around my largest bag and carried it for me. I followed her. She didn't ask me what happened or judge me, she just smiled. I knew I'd be safe.

We got on the same bus I'd have taken if I headed home. We got close to my regular stop, and my heart pounded furiously. A cold sweat broke out across my brow as we neared my stop by the small park. Mindy's warm leg pressed against mine as we sat side by side and swayed with the motion of the bus. I wanted to leap off and rush home to take care of Mom and tell Gilbert to go fuck himself. He'd ruined everything, and now my life was in shambles. But I didn't jump out. I sat quietly as the bus continued past the stop.

"Here we are," Mindy said a few minutes later. "This is our stop. Hope you don't mind sleeping on the couch. You're going to have to excuse the mess. I haven't been home much lately, and I don't entertain a lot."

We got off one stop past where I normally got off to go home. I followed her down a narrow concrete sidewalk leading to a strip mall's rear loading lot. Tree roots reached through the cracked and bumpy path and would easily trip up anyone. At this point, I didn't care. My toes and fingers were numb to the point of nonexistence. As we trudged behind the strip mall, the all-consuming intoxicating smell of fried chicken and french fries made my stomach grumble and mouth water. I hadn't eaten since lunch the day before.

"We don't have far to go now." I followed as Mindy stepped onto a makeshift bridge consisting of loose planks placed over a ditch. As we stepped on them, they bowed into the dampness, then bounced back up for the next person. "This shortcut makes the walk so much faster. If you take the streets, it adds another ten minutes, and I don't know about you, but I want to get home."

Mindy stopped at the front door of a flat gray stucco apartment building. It was like an enormous cube, with eyes in every corner. Mindy jiggled the key into the lock and pulled the glass door open. The smell of boiled cabbage and fried bacon immediately assaulted my senses. My mouth watered as my tummy growled.

I wanted to put my backpack and bag down and have the world stop spinning for a minute or two. We walked up three flights of stairs because the elevator was out of service. We reached the apartment door, and Mindy opened it. A powerful sour stench smacked me right between the eyes, forcing me to take a step back.

"Whoa, that's nasty, isn't it? Sorry. I guess I forgot to put the trash out. I had tuna a few nights ago. When I get home from work, I'm so tired, I eat and go to bed. I'll warn you now, taking out the trash and scrubbing toilets are definitely not my forte."

"Don't worry about me. Can I use the bathroom? I need to get out of these clothes. Do you mind if I have a shower?"

"Sure. No problem. It's right through there."

"Thanks."

I dug out some fresh underwear, lost-and-found tights, a T-shirt, and my bottle of liquid soap. I turned on the water and stripped off my clothes, leaving them in a damp heap in front of the toilet. The water rushed over me, and I'd never been so thankful for warmth in my entire life. My body and brain returned and melted back to normal as the warmth soaked through my skin and into my bones.

The liquid soap stripped all the dirt from my hair, leaving it feeling coarse but clean. I borrowed some of Mindy's conditioner and smoothed it through my long hair. After an active night with Chad then all day outside waiting, it was a relief to feel fresh again.

The bathroom door opened, and I froze.

"I just brought you a towel," she said.

I stood unmoving as the water ran down the curtain and bounced off the outer side into a puddle on the mustard-colored linoleum. I yanked on the stray curtain and pulled it back into the tub.

"I'll finish my shower and be right out if that's okay."

"No worries. Take your time. Didn't mean to intrude."

The door clicked closed, and I released my breath.

I finished my shower and found the crumpled but clean towel beside the sink. I dressed quickly and draped the towel over the tub's edge to dry.

Even with the conditioner, there was no way I'd be able to

get my fingers through to untangle my long hair. The mindless activity of working on the tangles, though, let my mind wander. *Chad. Did he miss me?* I touched my neck where he'd branded me, and I closed my eyes. It had been a perfect night, and I had no regrets. It was the one shining positive in the last twenty-four hours.

"Are you gonna stay in there all night?" Mindy asked.

"No. I'm just brushing my hair. I'll be out in a minute."

When I returned to the living room, the window was open, and it didn't smell as bad anymore. "Here, come sit." Mindy slapped the ratty orange and red plaid fabric couch, sending a poof of dust into the air. "I thought you might be hungry, so I made you a snack. Do you want a beer or soda? Tell me what happened."

"Well, long story short." I sipped the beer Mindy offered, and ate some salty chips. The taste explosion in my mouth was orgasmic, and I'm sure my eyes rolled to the back of my head. I sunk into the couch. "Yesterday morning, social services took my two little sisters. Mom started drinking again after being dry for nearly five years, and my asshole step-dad told me to put out or get out."

"Holy shit. That's intense. Is he the one who gave you all those hickeys?"

"Oh, fuck no! The guy's a supreme dickhead. These came from—" I could feel the heat in my cheeks. "His name is Chad." I raised my hand to my face at the memory of being with him. It already felt like it was a million years ago.

"Is he your boyfriend?"

"Yeah, we've been going out a couple of months. We get along very well."

"Awesome. To be honest, every time he's been in the shop, I found him to be really nice." She smiled.

"Yeah, I think he's pretty special for sure."

"I'm glad you were comfortable enough to come to me."
She pulled her legs up under her and laid her arm along the top
of the couch. "I've seen some girls really lose their shit, you
know, and I don't want that for you. You really seem like a
together person, and, well, I'm here to help."

"Mindy, thank you so much. It means a lot, like, seriously.
I'll make it up to you somehow. I don't want to be a burden. I'll
find another place as soon as I can."

"Don't be silly. We can be besties."

I smiled and suspected she was serious.

My mind wouldn't stop twirling in an endless circle.
Mindy knocked me off balance, and I wasn't sure about her, so I
accepted the blanket and pillow and laid down fully dressed. I
found it difficult to fall asleep as I tossed and turned for what
seemed like hours. Dogs barked and sirens wailed all night. My
head ached—probably from not eating much — and I'd developed a painful kink in my neck.

I was trying to stretch my neck to one side to release the
tension when I heard the toilet flushed, and I scrambled to find
the blanket to cover myself. I closed my eyes, breathed deeply,
and pretended to sleep. The soft barefoot steps padded to the
couch and paused at the end for a few seconds before continuing on. I opened my eyes in time to see the flutter of her long
nightgown reenter her bedroom and shut the door. The whole
thing was weird, but sleep eventually overtook me, and I
zonked right out.

I woke up to the sound of the shower.

Mindy ambled toward her bedroom a few minutes later.
"Good morning. Did you sleep all right? There's bread in the
freezer if you want toast or something."

"Oh, thanks." I hadn't heard her leave the bathroom and
enter the room. "I had a great sleep. Just trying to find my apron
for work. It's Saturday, right?"

"Yeah, you're on the schedule for the entire weekend. You have a city bus pass, right?" She yawned.

"Yeah, I have a pass. Is it okay to come back here tonight?"

"No problem." She pulled the tie on her robe tight. "If you're still here Monday, all you need to do is take the bus back one stop, and you'll connect with your district school bus. I never really know when I'll be home, but I'll see you at the shop all weekend and then Monday after school, right?"

"Absolutely." I stared down at my bag. "Thank you again. Is it okay to leave my stuff here?"

"Sure, no problem. Don't worry about it." She turned and returned to her room. "I'm going back to bed. If I'm not home, the key will be under the mat outside. See you later."

I made toast and ate it dry. It was the best-damned toast I'd ever had. I shook my head and pushed all the weird stuff to the side of my mind so I could get ready for work. Deep in the bag, I found another pair of yoga pants and an oversized T-shirt. This was much better than the ripped jeans that showed so much skin they were barely there. The hoodie was still damp from last night, so it would be a jacket-free day. I slung my backpack over my shoulder and opened the door. The hallways now smelled like heavy lilac air freshener that would cling to anything, given the chance.

I bolted down the three flights of stairs and straight over to the water-filled ditch. The plank appeared narrower than before, and it held a sheen of slippery slime that wanted to toss me right into the water. I adjusted my backpack and sucked in my stomach to stabilize myself as I walked heel-to-toe over the ditch. With a leap at the end, I ran down the bumpy path behind the strip mall, then let my breath go. My stomach growled, so I knew my first stop would be to check the trash where we threw out all the expired bakery items. The bus pulled up as I arrived. It was the same bus driver from the day before when I'd dropped my bags. He sat there in his chair with no flicker of recognition on his face as he waited for me to board so he could close the door.

I got off in front of the coffee shop, walked into work, and checked the trash can. I pulled out two expired croissants, a fudge brownie, and a lemon loaf. I opened the expired loaf and took a huge bite. The sweet, moist glaze melted in my mouth as the lemon flavors percolated on my palate. I don't think I'd ever tasted anything quite so delectable. I ate the entire piece in two more bites and shoved the other stuff into my bag. It was time for work. From somewhere deep inside me, I pulled out the veil I donned to make it through the day. People smiled and threw money in the tip jar as I numbly went through the day with a smile plastered across my face.

Not wanting to return to Mindy's until I had to, I sat in the back room until closing time. I tried and tried to formulate some sort of plan to find the girls and get Mom back on track so we could move forward with a normal life. Gilbert needed to go, but how do I make that happen?

My head and back ached as I prepared to return to Mindy's. I rang up her unit, but there was no answer. The key was right where she said it would be, so I let myself in. I snuggled on the couch and pulled the blanket around me as my eyes drooped with fatigue. Darkness overtook me quickly. It was the best sleep I'd had in a long time.

Time passed in a fog. Work kept me busy, but my brain never stopped considering the girls and what I needed to do. On Sunday night, as I lay on the couch for my third night in a row, I knew what I needed to do.

Monday morning, I got off the city bus at the little park where students gathered to wait for the school bus. A wave of relief calmed my step as I took my place at the back. The cool fall breeze gave an edge of rawness to the air as it blew it through my thin shirt, reminding me of my still damp hoodie that I'd left behind. I crossed my arms and tried to ignore my shivering—just as everyone ignored me. It was like I didn't exist, so why would it matter if I was uncomfortable in the cold?

I didn't matter.

It was all a blur.

As everyone loaded onto the school bus I picked up a vibe that there was a secret I wasn't in on. It wasn't anything specific. The routine was the same as always, but something felt off... it was weird. The hairs on the back of my neck stood up with a tingly sense that something wasn't quite right.

We arrived at school and shuffled off the bus. In an effort to get warm, I hugged myself as I sprinted for the front door.

Chad.

There was a flutter in my chest when I saw him standing halfway down the hall with his back to me. I couldn't stop the excited frenzy in my belly as sparkles of warmth spread through me. I headed toward him but stopped as some girl cozied up against him. She pulled him closer and ran her hand along his back. I couldn't hear what she said, but it looked playful and familiar. Then it hit me—she was the girl in the picture in Chad's room—the one I always turned over. My gut fizzled and seized in a knot as the redhead leaned into Chad and kissed him. *What the fuck? This has to be a fucking joke, right?* I couldn't turn away. I tried, but it was like a train wreck —one that shattered hearts and left people stranded.

The fight wasn't in me right now. Another fucking kick to the gut. I squeezed my eyes together, tucked my chin into my chest, and forced myself to turn away as I headed to the office in search of Mrs. Bonder.

The entire weekend had been a nightmare. I didn't know which way to turn, but I needed to figure it out, and quickly.

"Oh my goodness, Selena," Mrs. Bonder waved me into her

office. "You're having a terrible time, aren't you? Here, put this sweater on before you catch a cold."

"You need to find my sisters." I put the thin red sweater on over my T-shirt. It made my arms itchy and smelled of lavender, but I was thankful to have it. "They must be terrified. Everything happened so fast, and the girls did not know social workers would take them away from home."

"I don't know any details, but let me make a few phone calls and see what I can find out. In the meantime, I'm more worried about you. You're looking, how shall I say, somewhat— bruised and tired."

"I'm so stupid." I hung my head and brought my hand to my neck. I knew she was talking about the hickeys. The sharp sting of shame burned in the back of my eyes. Any energy I had to fight vanished. "I think I might be in trouble."

"Oh, my goodness." The nurse passed a box of tissues across the desk. "Whatever it is, we'll figure it out. What's his name?"

"Chad Spenser, and I thought ..." I shook my head as I grabbed a tissue. "I don't know what I thought, but it doesn't matter because I saw him kissing someone else in the hallway."

My hands shook, tears rolled down my face, and I sank to the floor. *Fuck, I nearly told him I loved him the other night. So stupid. He's just another pretty smile with fast hands. How gullible am I?*

"I feel so stupid." I blew into the tissue and wiped the tears with the back of my hand. "So, so stupid."

"We've all had days like that, dear. Let's focus on your sisters, shall we? I'm going to find out where they are, and hopefully, this Chad situation will blow over sooner rather than later."

I nodded at her words. I was thankful she'd help me find

the girls, but Chad—how could I be so blind? Why was everything so complicated?

"Selena, when was the last time you ate?"

"I don't know. I had some toast."

"Okay, here, take these." She opened her drawer and pulled out a Ziploc baggie filled with crackers. "You go to class and come back and see me at lunchtime. Hopefully, by then, I'll have some more information about your sisters for you."

I walked outside the office and shoved two crackers into my mouth.

I kept my shoulders hunched and my head down when I walked into my first class. I slumped into a seat and held my breath as Chad slowed his walk by my desk, only to be pushed along by Scottie.

I'd been played, and everyone knew it. I wanted to go back and smack him across the face, but a tight lump of scorching agony filled my chest and rendered me helpless. I wanted to cry —to scream—to punch and kick, but instead, I chewed on the hangnail on my thumb. The salt from the crackers seeped into my mouth and mixed with the raw skin to remind me I could still feel.

Later that day, I sat in Mrs. Bonder's office and waited. As soon as she saw me, she led me to the back, sat me down, then left the room.

"Here you go." She burst back into the room, panting like she'd been running. "Sorry, I meant to scoot down to the cafeteria before the lunch rush, but I got caught up with phone calls. I figured you probably didn't have any lunch, so I got this for you." She passed me a bag with a sandwich, cookie, and a bottle of water. She didn't even allow me to respond before continuing. "So, this is what I know so far. The Child Protection Services wouldn't release any specific information, only that the girls are healthy and safe."

"Do you know whether they're together?" I took a huge bite. Ham and cheese, my favorite. The tangy mustard played on my tongue, and I forgot everything else. My stomach lurched at the food as though grabbing it quickly before it disappeared again.

"I'm sorry, Selena. As I said, I don't have specifics, but I'm sure they're with a nice family."

The bread's soft white pastiness turned to glue in my mouth. Were the girls really with a nice family? I tried to chew through what was in my mouth, but my appetite disappeared, and a chill raced down my spine.

"I also have it on good authority your mother signed over her parental rights."

"No, that's not true." I dropped the sandwich on the desk, tipping over the open water bottle. "My mom is all about family and wouldn't give her kids away. She wouldn't. I know her."

"Selena," Mrs. Bonder said, sopping up the water on the desk. "Desperate people sometimes do desperate things."

"You don't know what you're talking about. My mom wasn't desperate. She loves us."

"Of course, she loves you." Mrs. Bonder reached for more paper towels. "I know this is all upsetting, but you need to keep your voice down. I don't want the principal to think something's wrong."

"But ... but ... something is wrong." I couldn't catch my breath. It wasn't true. It couldn't be. "My mom ... loves us ..." I hiccuped.

"I'm so sorry, Selena. Perhaps there's more to the story we don't know."

"Did ... did the police charge Gilbert?"

"The social worker told me the girls were interviewed, and neither spoke of any touching or abuse."

I couldn't hold it anymore. A guttural cry of pure relief escaped—unchallenged and unheeded. I had been gripped by terror, not knowing, and the energy seeped from me as bits of bread fell from my mouth onto the floor like sticky globs of gunk.

"Listen to me." Mrs. Bonder kneeled beside me and took my hands in her warm, soft grasp. She smelled like cinnamon and vanilla—I couldn't help but think of cookies and wondered if she baked in her spare time. "Both girls are safe. I shouldn't tell you this, but I think they're still at their same school for now, though it's likely temporary because of logistics. Your sisters are being strictly monitored and aren't allowed to leave with anyone except a foster parent."

"Can I visit? Can I see them?"

"I'm working on it. Right now, they want the girls to settle into their new home with as little disruption as possible."

"So, I'm a disruption? Seriously?"

"No, Selena, that's not what I said." She shook my hands and made me look at her. "This situation is not about you right now. We need to let things settle for the safety of your sisters."

I nodded. I knew she was right, but I also knew I had caused this whole situation. I needed to see the girls. I needed to explain.

"Selena, we need to get you set up, too." She stood and grabbed some papers from her desk. "Some foster families will take in older children. I have some names here."

"Can I go stay with my sisters? Please. I could take care of them and help."

"I don't think so, but I'll ask, okay? When do you turn eighteen?"

"February."

"Foster kids age out at eighteen, for the most part. There

are teen group homes available where you could go short-term until your birthday. You'd be warm and provided with meals."

"I'm staying with a friend." I pushed the chair away from the desk. The tightness in my chest like hard molten rock returned, but this time the sense of pain stabbed deep like a honed dagger trying to dig out my heart. "I'll be fine," I breathed. "You don't need to worry about me."

"Oh Selena, I wouldn't be human if I weren't worried about you." Mrs. Bonder squeezed her eyes closed, then, a moment later, they burst open. "I'll need an address where you're staying for the school records—whenever you get a chance."

I didn't answer her. I couldn't. I didn't know Mindy's address, and besides, I didn't know how long I'd be there. The girls were fine, so I had to hang onto that for now. They have each other. *If anyone dares lay a hand on them, I'll kill them.*

"Selena? Did you hear me?"

"What?" I didn't want to hear anymore. I wanted to curl up and go to sleep forever. I simply wanted this nightmare to end.

"Selena? Did you talk to Chad?"

"Um, Chad's not even an issue, so long as my sisters are with strangers and are probably scared out of their minds."

"You're right. Boy troubles can wait." She nodded. "You certainly have enough on your plate, don't you?" The older woman stood beside me.

"Well, you don't need to worry about me. I'm a survivor. Always have been. There was nothing impulsive about being with Chad. Hell, we've been together for over two months, and I'm not stupid. I'm really not."

"Selena—"

"Seriously, don't worry about me." I smiled the biggest and widest smile I could. "My priority is my sisters, so if you could arrange a visit, I'd be grateful. Other than that, I'm good." It was like all the air was sucked from the room, and I couldn't draw in a deep breath. The longer I stood there, the less in control I felt. A sourness rose in my throat, threatening to explode all over the desktop. I had to force the words from me. "I know it was all my fault—everything—I just didn't realize I had loser plastered across my forehead."

"Selena, please don't go. Stay, and we'll make a plan—"

"I don't need a plan." I turned to leave. "I need a fucking new life, is what I need."

"Please come see me tomorrow. Are you sure you've got a place to stay?"

"Thanks, Mrs. Bonder. I'll be fine."

Every time I walked down the hallway, I held my head high and proud. The entire school probably knew what had happened by now, but I didn't care. They were all a bunch of two-faced assholes, and no matter what I did or didn't do, made no difference. I was here to finish school, not make friends.

"Selena. Wait..."

I heard his voice, and every muscle in my body stiffened. I forced myself to keep walking while maintaining my aloofness and not panicking. If I looked him in the eye now, I'd probably cave and babble incoherent nonsense. His footsteps echoed against the hallway's polished floor, but as he got closer, the bell rang, and students flooded the space from every direction. I turned to see him stop his pursuit as I quickened my step.

"Watch it, bitch."

"Who're you calling bitch?" I didn't want to fight. In fact, I didn't have the energy to even defend myself, but the shock of her words struck me. I glanced down at the young girl—she couldn't have been any more than thirteen years old and eighty pounds, but her attitude far outweighed any fragile persona.

"I heard you slept with my sister's boyfriend. In my book,

that makes you a bitch." A numbness overcame me. I couldn't respond and was alone like never before.

While school was a bastion of hell and abuse, work was a haven. The pace was quick and constant, which helped me keep my mind occupied.

"Hey, Selena, how was school? You look great this afternoon." Mindy smiled. "You must've had a good sleep."

"Hi, Mindy." I tried my best to smile back. "I'll wash up and grab my apron. What would you like me to do this afternoon?"

"I'd like you to get more comfortable prepping some coffee orders, so I'll have you spend some time with Emily. Shadow her and do what she says. She's, like, totally amazing."

"Okay, I'll be right back."

The pace at the barista station was fast and furious. There were a lot of things to remember—the foam, the whip, the milks, and non-milks. It totally took my mind off the rest of my day, and the hours passed quickly as the cashier shouted coffee orders.

The lineup never let up as I helped Emily. I grabbed my latest creation and shouted out to the customers, "Leslie, large non-fat soy latte, no foam with a shot of espresso, all ready for you."

"Thanks, Selena," Leslie said. "How are you?"

"Oh, hey." I smiled. "Yeah, thanks. I'm okay. Busy. Enjoy your coffee." I wiped the counter and tucked the cloth back into my apron as the door buzzer signaled more customers.

"Selena, you're a natural," Emily said. "Don't forget to put the empty bottles in the bin. It's important to keep your station clean."

"Thanks for letting me do this. It's been the best part of my day." I took a second to read off the next order. "Large full fat chai with whip and two-shot vanilla for Ch—" the name caught in my throat. I took a deep breath. "For Chad." I slid the drink across the counter and turned away before he got too close.

"Selena," he called after me. "You have to talk to me some time."

"Who's the hottie? I know he's not here for me." Emily elbowed me in the side. "Why don't you take your break and talk to him? He looks like a puppy who's lost his ball, poor baby. Look at that face."

"He's a douche, and I don't want to talk to him."

"Hmm, really? Too bad. He hasn't taken his eyes off you. Is he your boyfriend?"

"No. I don't have a boyfriend."

"Well, I think you may need to go talk to your nonexistent boyfriend. I don't think he's going anywhere, anytime soon."

Chad glanced in my direction from outside the front door.

"Okay, I'll go settle this once and for all. I'm telling you, the guy's an asshole."

"Go." Emily waved me out from behind the counter.

My head spun in every direction. The store was nearly empty as we neared closing time. I nodded and smiled at Leslie as I pulled open the front door and stepped outside.

"I wanted to talk to you all day," Chad said.

"Why? So you could join the masses and call me names, too?"

"No. I need to explain. I adore you. It's complicated, you and me. We're so good together, well, you know..."

"Chad, you're a fucking prick. I don't even know why I'm standing here talking to you. I've been replaced by some redhead who practically dry-humped you at your locker, and some punk-ass kid called me a bitch today."

"Yeah, sorry." He kicked a rock with the toe of his sneaker.

"I guess I should've told you a while ago I'm kinda seeing someone."

"You played me, you asshole. How could I be so fucking stupid?" I crossed my arms and moved closer to the door. "Like what the fuck? We've been together for almost two months. Where do you get off seeing another girl?"

"Wait a sec," he said as he moved closer. "Hear me out. Her whole family moved to New York. I didn't think I'd ever see her again, so we never broke it off officially... but then it seems like New York didn't work out."

"Oh my fucking God, and you think that makes it all better?" I wanted to slap those lips right off his face. "Don't worry about it. Be with your snooty little girlfriend—I don't care. It was nice knowing you. Now get the fuck out of my life."

"No, Selena, listen," he stammered. "You need to understand. We've been together since kindergarten. I owe her—"

"Hey, no problem. It's been nice knowing you, but I don't have time for bullshit games." I squared my shoulders, turned toward the door, and prayed over and over to myself that he'd follow me, take me in his arms and kiss me like I knew I deserved to be kissed. He never moved. "She can have you," I called over my shoulder.

I stomped back into the store and went to the cramped storage room that also doubled as a staff room. I sat on a box and forced myself to breathe. My hands trembled, and my knee bounced nervously. The buzzer above the door dinged over and over. The thought of him out there waiting for me made my heart race. I wondered if he came back in. *Maybe he's waiting for me right now?*

I washed my hands and went back to the barista. The sounds of the store were amplified. The milk steamer pushed its air and hissed. New customer voices echoed and bounced around the room repeatedly as the required soft rock played through the speakers. I finally spotted him, and my gut sank to my knees. He stood in the same place outside, but his arm was around Scottie, whose hand was placed on the center of Chad's chest. She laughed as Chad pouted.

No one needed to tell me she was laughing at me.

Chapter Fifteen

NOW

LESLIE

I sat in my chair in front of the window for the entire weekend. I scribbled in my notebook as I studied the street and its diametric contradictions of living conditions and opportunity. A story idea bubbled and took steam in my head. I named the protagonist Selena, a princess switched at birth and raised in poverty. My mind worked overtime as I studied the view.

"There! There she is!" Adrenaline coursed through me as I jumped atop the chair and bounced in jubilation. Nothing else in my life compared to this. It was like Selena had come back from the dead. A huge cry erupted from me as my body folded in on itself. The relief left me breathless. "Where have you been, my girl? I've been worried sick about you." I grabbed the binoculars and brought Selena closer into view. "Thank God you're safe. You look as rough as I feel, though, and hey, what the hell are those things on your neck?"

The hickeys threw me for a loop as Selena didn't seem the type to get into such situations. What was the type? I remembered the writhing passion I experienced with my first boyfriend. The way time stood still as flashes popped throughout my young and eager flesh. With a sudden heat in my cheeks, I lowered the binoculars and thought about it for a minute.

I paused and thought of my perception of Selena and the fact she ended up with all those hickeys on her neck. I closed my eyes and pictured Selena laying down and a boy on top of her—his lips touched hers, and his teeth nibbled at her neck—a sensuous and highly sensitive spot on the body. Jesus, stop it. What the hell am I doing? I pinched myself under my arm and opened my eyes. The pit of my gut twisted into a tight knot. I wanted to pull the boy off and hit him with a stick.

Little bastard.

I raised the binoculars again. "He better be treating you with love and respect."

I stepped back and considered this disturbing thought. What was Selena to me? Who was she, really?

The romance writer in me wouldn't let it go because something didn't ring true. Through the binoculars, I saw Selena at the back with her backpack hanging from one shoulder. She wasn't wearing a jacket, and it was near freezing. Damn. I desperately wanted to run across the street with a heavy sweater and drape it around her shoulders like a protective shroud. She always appeared so lost and alone.

The yellow bus pulled into the stop just then. Otherwise, I'd have thrown on some clothes and gone to offer Selena a ride. She was too good for such riffraff.

I glanced over as Prince put the last of his treasures into his cart to push it toward the sidewalk.

They all went their separate ways, and I snuggled back into my chair with my notebook and laptop. The day flew by with refreshed enthusiasm and inspiration. I set the alarm and brought a half-eaten bag of chips closer as I let my fingers rip over the keyboard.

At two o'clock, the priority was to be at the school to see Selena come out the front doors. I took some snacks and my water bottle, knowing there'd be a bit of a wait, but when I arrived, parking was at a premium. Vehicles, all occupied, lined the street. Many scrolled or talked with an earpiece dangling out of their ear. One driver glowed with blue-light casting off her laptop. These were obviously parents picking up their kids after school, even though there was at least another half hour before they were out. No one even noticed me. As far as they knew, I was another parent.

I pulled in behind another car, turned off the engine, and waited. At exactly three o'clock, the bell rang, and, within seconds, the front doors opened, and kids spilled out like confetti. They were everywhere. Some moved fast, while others sauntered around. Where was Selena? All the girls with long dark hair looked alike. They all wore jeans and sneakers. How was I going to find her in this sea of sameness? My heart beat faster, my eyes darted everywhere, trying to see her, and my chest tightened. *How could I be so stupid? Did I think she'd simply waltz out and stand in the middle of the road for me to see her? Shit, I'm so stupid.*

I twisted and turned to see above the crowd until I finally spotted her. Someone had given her a sweater, an ugly one, but it served the purpose. Alone, Selena walked directly toward me. I froze. *Does she recognize me? Or the vehicle? Is she going to get in? Oh, my God. Oh, my God.*

I sucked in my breath and didn't dare move, but without so much as a flicker of recognition, she marched right past and continued down the block.

I fanned my face and tried to calm my pulse. *What the hell am I doing?* Selena could've recognized the car. So stupid. I needed to park farther down the block to avoid detection. I shook my head like my brain needed waking. *Selena has been in the Jeep several times, but I think I dodged a bullet.*

Within fifteen minutes, the crowds, along with all the cars, wove their way back into traffic, which left only me parked there. I put on my turn signal, pulled out, and drove two blocks to Java Jenny's.

It only made sense since Selena didn't head for the bus, she went to work. I parked as far from the front door as possible, turned off the engine, and slumped down in the seat. I knew Selena wouldn't start work until three-thirty or four, so I waited and watched as the stream of non-stop customers emerged from the shop with steaming cups. Everyone moved quickly and with purpose—like they had to be somewhere and were already late. The opposite was true for me, as a calmness reclaimed me after finding Selena again.

When the time was right, I went into the store, ordered a coffee, then watched Selena prepare it with the other girl. The hickeys stood out like beacons by the sea. It gave me a heavy feeling for her, as the marks sent a message of sensuality and took away some professionalism. I didn't like the idea of anyone judging her.

Selena called my name.

"Thanks, Selena." I took the coffee and smiled. "How are you?"

"Oh, hi, Leslie." Selena smiled. "Yeah, thanks. I'm okay. Busy. Enjoy your coffee."

Buoyed by her presence. That's the only way to describe

my mood as I grabbed a newspaper and took the table over by the restrooms. From my vantage point, I could see the entire store. The staff enjoyed themselves, and it showed.

I pulled the newspaper open to use as a shield. Staring was so passe. This was the most fun I'd had in forever. I overheard the orders, which turned into a dance of preparation, presentation, and delivery. I loved it.

I half-listened to the girls' voices as I sipped my coffee and scanned the paper.

"Ch—Chad?" Selena called out. There was a hint of surprise and hesitation in her voice. My curiosity piqued, I tipped the newspaper down and saw a young man approach the counter. He wore torn jeans, a close-fit button-up shirt, red sneakers, and had a head full of bleach-blond curls over dark roots hanging down to his shoulders. So, that must be Chad. Hmm ... I wonder if this is hickey boy.

The two young people talked briefly when he picked up his coffee, but no matter how hard I tried to hear, the grinder and other noises drowned out their low voices. Chad went outside, and Selena visibly deflated as her shoulders slumped and her actions slowed. The barista leaned over and talked to her.

I picked up my phone and pretended to be reading something as Selena glanced in my direction. Without even thinking, I snapped a picture. I held my phone in front of me and shifted to see Selena with mysterious Chad outside the front door. It was only a few minutes before the front door opened, letting in an icy breeze.

Selena's eyes were flat, her shoulders square, and her face stark white. I didn't know what had transpired between them, but I swear I heard the actual break of her heart.

Without thinking, I stepped out the front door and stood to the side, pretending to talk on the phone. A thin, red-haired, Barbie-doll type joined the boy and laughed.

"Stupid bitch," the girl said. "She's lucky I'm so under-standing. You're going to have to make it up to me, Chad. You've been a very naughty boy."

"Yeah, whatever. Fuck it ..." he said.

"Now, now, there's no need to get all upset," the girl said. "Remember, she's a poor girl in search of the American dream."

"Yeah, well, I seriously fucked everything up. I didn't know you were coming back. What was I supposed to do? Shit."

I overheard some choice words and knew they were talking about Selena. These two little assholes had hurt her. Damn it. I should've grabbed a nice hot coffee before I came outside; I would've happily dumped it right into their laps.

Instead, I strode toward them and deliberately turned my ankle as I neared them. I fell right into Chad. He didn't see me coming, and with all my weight, I shoved him backward into the concrete planter. His back bowed, and his feet went out from under him. He landed hard on his tailbone with a whooshing thud. I let myself fall with him and smacked my head against his face. *Oopsy, sorry. Jerk.*

"Hhhrrumph ..."

"Hey lady, what the hell," the skinny girl said. "Chad? Are you all right?"

"I'm so sorry." I pushed myself to my knees and gazed into his face. There were tears, and a trickle of blood seeped from his nose and split lip.

"I'm okay. I'm okay," he said through clenched teeth as he pushed himself off the ground. He touched his nose, and his eyes grew large when he saw the blood. "Look." He held out his hand. "I'm bleeding—I'm fucking bleeding."

"I don't know what happened. I'm so embarrassed. My ankle ... I tripped. I feel so stupid. Is there anything I can do? Here, I think I have a tissue." I dug deep into my pocket and brought out a crumpled wad of tissue. "We should go into Java

Jenny's. The girls who work here are so nice. They'll have a first-aid kit, I'm sure."

"No. Seriously, I'm fine." He wiped the blood with the back of his hand. "I don't need any help."

"You stupid old bitch," the rude Barbie doll spat. "Watch where you're walking. Jesus, you're going to kill someone, for Christ's sake. Why don't you leave?"

"Scottie, shut up. Listen, lady, I'm fine." Chad stared at me. "The damage is done, so you should probably move along?"

"Are you sure you don't want to go into the coffee shop with me? Perhaps I can buy you a cup of tea."

"Lady! For fuck's sake, he asked you to leave him alone. Come on, Chad." The girl clutched his arm. "Lean on me. I'll take you home."

He limped and groaned with every step toward the parking lot. I couldn't help but smile. *That snippy little red-haired bimbo needs to watch her mouth, but the two obviously deserve each other.* It made me sad Selena had to deal with such idiots, and I hoped she was okay.

The two drove away, and I headed to the Jeep. I planned to wait until Selena's shift was over before leaving. I flipped open the center console between the front seats and pulled out a package of sanitized wipes to erase any Chad germs before I reached for the cookies.

I slouched in the Jeep for about an hour before Selena emerged from the store with her two co-workers. The manager locked the door, then yanked on the handle before putting her keys in her bag. Selena stayed with the manager as the other young girl walked in the opposite direction.

I opened the window, hoping to hear the plan.

"See you tomorrow, Em. Thanks for a great shift," the manager said. "Okay, Selena, we better get going, or we'll miss the bus."

Selena and the manager rushed toward Main Street. I started the Jeep and circled around the block. They got on the bus, and I followed as best I could. Following a bus is difficult. They pull off, and the rest of the traffic keeps moving. The frustration and threat of an accident weren't worth it, so I pulled into the parking lot of a chicken place. I was about to turn around and go home when I saw the bus in the mirror, and both girls got off. They walked right toward the vehicle. It was like déjà vu from after school. I couldn't drive right past them. Selena would recognize me for sure. I turned my back and crouched down as far as I could. Their voices carried into the car as they passed.

"I'm glad you finally got some sleep last night."

"Yeah, it makes a big difference..." Selena said.

"Well, you'd probably be ..."

I couldn't hear any more as they turned the corner around the strip mall. *Why is Selena staying with the manager?* It certainly explains why she turned up on the city bus today and didn't come over the knoll like normal. *I need to be ready for tomorrow morning. I hereby appoint myself as the official daily Selena driver.* There was no way she needed to ride on the same bus as those awful, foul-mouthed creatures. Something was going on, and I suspected Selena needed my help.

Chapter Sixteen

SELENA

The bus ride back to the apartment wasn't long, but any downtime meant having to relive the day, and it was one I'd rather forget. The whole day had been a Selena bash-fest. Like, what the hell was wrong with people? My universe was like a brain-twisting labyrinth where I always took the wrong turn. No matter how fast I ran or how smart or cautious I thought I was, I ended up at a dead end. *Shit, right now, if I accept the reality, I'm a homeless teen with my family scattered to the winds.*

The bus jerked to a stop, and Mindy's leg bounced against mine as we both reached to brace ourselves. I didn't want to admit it, but outside the store, she was weird. Hey, it was probably me. I was terrible at reading people and wouldn't normally notice if it held me down and shoved it in my face. What choice did I have? Foster care? Group home? I knew what went on in those places. If you weren't being groped or raped by the person in charge, then your bunk mate was sniffing around.

My world had fallen apart, and I needed to stay strong and focused. Maybe it was time to give up on graduating high school to concentrate on a full-time job and make a home for my sisters. But who was I trying to fool? My best chance at getting them back was to graduate high school and get a job where I could actually pay the rent. Mom was always so proud of my school work, and she wanted me to succeed, not drop out. 'Education is the way out,' she always said.

The bus pulled up to our stop, and we got off.

"Do you want to stop and get something to eat?" I asked.

"Naw, I got tuna at home. But if you wanna stop, it's all good."

"I'm fine. I'm so beat I just want to sleep."

"I hear ya. It's been a long day. Sorry about the boyfriend thing."

"Wasn't your fault, but yeah, it sucks."

"Let's hurry up and get out of this cold," Mindy said.

Chapter Seventeen

NOW

LESLIE

Prince prepared his cart, and this was my cue to leave.

My morning routine now included picking up Selena and dropping her at school. The girl never questioned my presence and always readily got into the Jeep. For me, it brought out a maternal protectiveness toward her. I wanted to know her, honestly. Her dreams and desires. Her secrets and problems. She obviously needed someone in her life, and why shouldn't it be me? I hoped today would be a day of connection.

I laced up my shoes and placed the car keys on top of my purse. Ready. I went back to the window and scanned the park to find Selena.

"There you are." I smiled as Selena arrived before the other students. "Hmm, what's the matter this morning, young lady? You look like you've got something on your mind." I watched through the binoculars. Selena appeared distracted and fidgety as she paused by Queenie, who walked by every morning. For a second, I thought Selena was going to talk to her, but the old lady kept walking.

Selena appeared more lost than usual. The girl obviously lived on the outside of life and had little to no support. She was a prettier, more with-it version of my younger self.

She needed understanding and security. Heck, people said the same about me, too, but this was different. Mother kept me on such a tight rein that my insecurities, social ignorance, and inane fears held me back. Selena bears the weight of too much seriousness atop her as obvious signs of worry and stress warped her youthful glow, with tensed jaw muscles and a roundness in the back and shoulders.

I wanted to know her story. Hear her dreams and be her friend. With my purse and keys in hand, I zipped down the stairs and out the back door leading to the garage. I swung my keys on my fingers and hummed on my way to the Jeep. The traffic was busy, which meant making a left turn proved difficult this morning, so the bus had already pulled out.

Okay. Plan B. If nothing else, I'd make sure Selena got to school safely. I shook off the sudden negativity and drove toward the school.

As I slowed on the tree-lined street I searched for a parking spot. I didn't want to have to loop around the block—I could miss Selena that way. Just then a student exited a vehicle, and the driver put on the car's blinker to leave. I slipped right into the spot. Perfect. See, the day was all falling back into place. I reclined the seat and waited. The bus showed up three minutes later.

60

It pulled into the alcove, slammed open its door, and students spilled out everywhere. The boy Selena spoke to the night before—the boy I, ah, inadvertently knocked over—limped to the front, draped his arm around the first girl off the bus, and disappeared around the corner. I wished I had my binoculars in the Jeep. The kids were too far away, so I couldn't detect any details of their faces.

There were other buses coming and going in loops. They'd drop and go. A wave of relief swept through me. Selena would be next. But the bus driver closed the door and rolled away. What? Something wasn't right.

I leaned forward in the seat and strained to see around the bus. Cars and students obstructed my line of sight, but then the bus pulled forward to go wherever buses go when not in use. A girl with long dark hair caught my eye, and a jolt of exhilaration shot through me, but it faded quickly when I saw it wasn't Selena.

Something was very wrong. All my muscles tightened, ready to lash out and strike. Blood flooded my head and whirled the thoughts around like dry leaves caught in a fall breeze. Selena was at the stop. I saw her. Now she was gone. *How does one disappear between here and there? Oh, my God. She's in trouble. I can feel it in my chest. What happened? Where is she?*

A sour bile rose in my throat as I tried to make sense of this fiasco. Mother always said I was a failure at planning anything. This was no different. Loser. I tapped the steering wheel with my forehead—the forehead with a big L written across the center. *Why am I here? What the hell am I doing trying to connect with this girl? It's all so useless, and I'm grasping at straws. She's a teenager, and I'm a grown woman. Why? Maybe Phillip was right when he told me I'd be alone for the rest of my life.*

I fought to find some focus. My eyes, my brain, and even my heart bounced around in confusion. I had lost her—there was nothing I could do.

Chapter Eighteen

SELENA

The next morning, I hurried to the bus in order to make my connections. As I got off the city bus, I spotted the old lady who'd helped me gather all my things on the bus the other night. She had her coat buttoned right up under her chin and a sassy red hat with a dainty swinging tassel perched on top of her snow-white hair. I smiled, but she walked by me with a determined focus to get to wherever she was going—she didn't even see me.

Other students arrived, including Scottie. The thought of being near them or facing Chad and his group made my stomach churn. The rocky path back home and to the girls' school beckoned. There was no time to sprint there and get back on time—I knew that. Even though it had only been a couple of days, I missed Mom so much. I wanted to hug her, to ask her what had happened with the social workers. I had a feeling Gilbert had more to do with what happened than anyone else.

I caught the up-down motion of a lady pushing a baby stroller. The line formed for the bus as the homeless man stood and pushed his cart. Everyone around me was on the move—going somewhere—doing something. I turned and bolted up the rocky path, past the baby carriage and away from the bus.

Everything was the same. The worn curtain hung sadly in the window, giving nothing away. I'm not sure what I had expected in a few days. In my fantasy, Mom, sick with worry, searched for the girls and me. She trudged through wilderness and urban sprawl to find and reclaim her babies. But fantasies didn't cut it. I learned a long time ago to remain a realist because I spun fantasies, which turned quickly to delusions, and fucked with my head. I drew in a deep breath and heeded the complete stillness engulfing the tiny shack. Before I did anything, I checked to make sure Gilbert's motorcycle wasn't on the other side. Often, he drove into the long scraggly grass—he said it was his way of maintaining the yard. Relief washed over me as I saw he wasn't home. Jittery energy shot through me as I sprinted to the front door and twisted the knob. It was unlocked.

"Mom?" I leaned in through the opening. "Mom? Are you here? It's me—Selena."

I met silence and stillness. I checked over my shoulder and spied the neighbor across the dirt lane. He sat in a green plastic lawn chair, his undershirt barely covering his huge hairy chest and belly. He took a long pull from a can and stared straight ahead. Beside him, a dog that was all muscle and teeth strained against the chain that held him to the rotting lattice fence at the base of their porch. Shivers raced down my spine as I quickly stepped into the house. The click of the latch echoed behind me and made me stop in my tracks as the sound filled the small

space. There goes any element of surprise. I let my eyes adjust
to the dim light and was quickly reminded that this place had
always been disgusting, but now it made my skin crawl.

"Mom? It's me. Are you here?"

The room reeked of stale cigarette smoke. Dampness
hugged the walls, offering a bouquet of mold and mildew. I was
used to ignoring the smells, whether it was tuna, booze, or cigarettes. My nose probably didn't even work anymore. I followed
the worn red and black checkerboard linoleum down the
hallway into the kitchen. I half expected to see Mom passed out
across the table, but Chinese food cartons, four empty whiskey
bottles, and an overflowing ashtray filled the small space.
Someone had propped the window above the kitchen sink open
with a stick which looked like it could snap at any second. I
rubbed my arms to keep the chill away as I pushed a chair
under the table.

I tiptoed down the narrow hallway. I swear the walls moved
closer together as I inched my way down toward the bedrooms.
I hurried for fear the all-knowing walls would reach out and
stroke my arm. When we'd moved in, Gilbert had removed the
door to the girls' and my room, as he didn't want us slamming
doors. I'd tacked a sheet up for some privacy, but knew he
could enter any time. The thin sheet now hung from a lone tack
in the corner. The room was as I'd left it—a frenzied mess of
spare socks, stained mattresses, and the girls' doodling papers
splattered with smiling faces and flowers.

The bathroom next to our bedroom was fully closed. I
cupped the loose rattling doorknob in my icy hand, then
paused. The possibility of finding Mom passed out on the floor
niggled in my self-consciousness. I turned the knob and pushed
my shoulder against the bowed door. With a protesting pop, the
door let go but quivered from the force. The room was empty.

"Phew!" I laughed as I kicked the door, which rippled like a giant suspended jellyfish on a hinge. "No dead bodies—that's a good sign."

I went to the last room—Mom's. A thin line of light surrounded the door like a halo of radiant grandeur that belied the truth of what lay behind. I pushed the flimsy door with my fingertip—it protested as it creaked open an inch at a time. I poked my head in first. The brightness from the open curtains assaulted my eyes, and I blinked a few times before I could see things clearly.

"What the hell?" I stood in the doorway, scanning the room. It was impeccable—no junk or errant clothes tossed on the floor. The bed, covered in its dull, butter-yellow comforter with frayed edges and plumped pillows, freaked the shit out of me. Mom's room was always a mess of dirty clothes, Gilbert's chaps, and full ashtrays, but now the room smelled of vanilla with hints of a rose or jasmine—I couldn't tell. The sickly sweet scent clung to the air and got ingested with each breath, to the point where I could taste it. Why was everything so neat and in its place? An eerie shutter ran the length of my body.

A glass-framed photograph caught my eye. I picked it up to examine. It was something from another planet. There, sitting on Gilbert's lap, was my mom like I'd never seen her. Her head tossed back in laughter, she appeared free of worry—full of life as he grinned at the camera with bright eyes, his hand on her thigh. They looked so happy. I'd never seen this picture before. Mom was about twenty pounds heavier in the photo, so it had to be at least a year old. I glanced around the room Mom shared with Gilbert—it was a private sanctum where I didn't belong. Everything was so orderly, unlike their lives—or at least the side I knew. Mom said she was happy with him. Did I read too much into this whole thing?

"I don't get it." I placed the photo back on the side table and scanned the room again. The emptiness turned to a deafening silence that raced up my legs like hundreds of baby spiders let out to play for the first time.

I sensed the sound of the door before I heard it. Little hairs stood on the back of my neck and my muscles clenched. I felt another person nearby. I held my breath and turned slowly toward the door. A long black gun barrel poised midway through the door pointed straight at my chest.

My heart zoomed blood through me so fast that my legs wobbled, and my head floated from my body. A prepared room? A gun? I wondered if I'd ever see my sisters again.

Chapter Nineteen

NOW

LESLIE

Not knowing what to do, I remained parked at the school, willing Selena to show up. In times of such intense stress like this, I wished I smoked dope. Wine, I could drink wine, but people who smoked marijuana always appeared calm and functioning. The idea of being numb to the world was so seductive right now that it was all-consuming. Anything —hell, even sex —sounded better than what I was going through. Maybe I should go downtown, pick out some guy and fuck his brains out all day.

Shit, even my mother called me a goodie-goodie-two-shoes. The idea of doing something illegal or dangerous to let off steam warmed my blood but also turned my stomach. It wasn't a guy, or drugs, or booze I wanted. It was Selena—or her safety, at least. My failure rebounded within me and sucked and carried me to a place beyond the school's tree-lined street, down to a place where core logic and understanding were targets of past demons and degradations.

At the thought of Selena, my insides ached. Knowing she was out there alone somewhere was torture. I tucked my head down to my chest as a shallow wail escaped from somewhere deep within me. Hazy likenesses of Phillip, the baby, Selena, and even Mother filled my consciousness, my soul. The pain was sharp and filled me with a feverish pitch that convulsed with each breath.

Selena's disappearance totally disarmed and immobilized my ability to act. The Jeep was a safe place for me to sit and think. But a quick flash of a shadow caught my eye, followed by a sharp tap on the window. Every nerve ending fired adrenalin directly into my heart as I jumped and slammed my knee into the door. Jarred back to reality, I abruptly emerged from the depths of my misery to face this new threat.

There, by my car, stood a man bent at the waist with his face inches from the window, staring at me. I jerked back in shock and panic at the sudden intrusion and lost all sense of self. Warmth flooded my lap—powerless to stop the flow, a puddle formed beneath me on the leather seat.

I pushed myself as far from the door as possible. The man gazed right at me. His suit jacket hung open, and his tie flopped forward as he continued to stare. Time froze, along with any ability to think past this stranger. He rapped on the window again with his knuckle. I pushed the start button on the car and rolled down the window a couple of inches so I could hear him.

"Hello, sorry, I didn't mean to frighten you. My name is Will Freeman. I'm the principal here at the school. I noticed you were in distress and wondered if you needed any help."

I studied the geometric pattern in his tie. The triangles melded into the circles, then back again.

"Ma'am?"

"Yes, sorry..." I gulped for air and shook my head. "Thank you. I'm fine."

"Do you want to come into the school for a glass of water? I could call someone for you."

"No. Thank you, though. You're very kind, but I ... I got a call ..." The lie caught in my throat. "My mother ... she just ... died," I yelped, racing to catch my breath.

"I'm so sorry." He leaned even closer to the car. "What's your name? Do you have a child attending the school?"

"No, I don't." My voice sounded high-pitched and screechy as I pressed firmly on the brake and put the car into drive. "I dropped off my neighbor's daughter. Thank you for your concern, but I have to go." I pushed the button to close the window and signaled to turn onto the road. As I drove away, I kept my eye on the rearview mirror and watched as the principal stepped onto the sidewalk and tucked his tie back in place before returning to the school.

Numb, I drove five miles back to the townhouse. On autopilot, I flicked my finger to signal a right turn into the alley, where I glanced over my shoulder to see Selena standing on the sidewalk with her thumb out.

I vomited all over the shiny dash.

Chapter Twenty

SELENA

All I could see was the dull metal of the gun barrel fixed right on me, quivering in the air. I didn't so much as twitch as I held my breath. The faded panel door swung inch by inch into the room. My heart exploded every time the hinges squeaked.

"Mom? Is that you?" The sun-filtered dust filled the room. "It's me, Selena."

"Selena? I thought you were a burglar. I hid behind Gilbert's chair when you came in." She lowered the gun and held it, dangling from the tips of her fingers. "What're you doing here? I thought you left for good."

"I came to see you. I needed to know you were okay."

"Don't need to worry about me. I'm fine." She tossed the gun on the bed, where it bounced and came to rest in the center of a pale, tired, stenciled daisy.

"Mom," I rushed forward and took her hand. "Come with

me." Her fingers were cool to the touch and so delicate. The contrast of the blue of her veins against the paper-thin skin was more pronounced. I ran my thumb gently back and forth over the top of her hand. "We'll get the girls back and start again— without him. We've done it before. Come on, Mom, what do you say?" I shook her hand to get her full attention. "Let's do it."

"It's different this time, Selena. I gave up my rights to the welfare people. The girls are fine, and you, well, I'm not worried about you."

What was going on? Mom wasn't the same. A smell of defeat and surrender enveloped her. It was briny and pungent, like gunk left to fester and rot at the bottom of the heap of slimy fish carcasses.

"Mom, we can fight to stay together. I've got a good job now, and I can help you. Mom, you can't stay here with him. He's a monster."

"You hush that trash talk. Gilbert loves me, and we're good together. Selena, you don't understand." Mom shuffled to the bed. She wouldn't look at me. "You're off with your boyfriends, so your sisters were on their own, anyway."

"Mom ... " The prick of tears stung the back of my eyes. "Mom, please come with me. I'll take care of you, and I'll figure out how to get the girls back. I promise."

"Gilbert's right," she said, as though she didn't even hear me. She rearranged the pillow on the bed and spoke without looking up. "I had such high hopes for you, Selena, but you like the boys, don't you?" Her voice dripped with bitterness and accusation as she finally turned and glared at me. "You remember we moved here because you were whoring around and got all them girls after you."

"Mom, you know that's not why we moved here." I shook my head and bit back the tears. "It was Gilbert who wanted to leave. Remember those biker guys who came to the house? Mom, what's going on? Why are you so mean?"

I wanted to snuggle up on her lap and let her stroke my hair. I wanted to tell her about Chad and how badly my heart hurt. Oh, how I wanted to tell her how much I missed her and how Gilbert was pulling her down the wrong path.

"Selena, things have changed." She let out a breath of air and coughed a deep, wet, chesty cough that rattled the entire length of her frail body. She spat blood and phlegm into a crumpled tissue she took from her pocket. "They say I've got cancer or something," she whispered. "It's best you get out of my house. You're not welcome here anymore. Me and Gilbert have our life, and we're better off alone."

I studied her face. She'd changed so much since the move, but I'd been so busy with my stuff and the girls I hadn't noticed how worn out and haggard she looked. Her eyes sunk deep into her face, and her once rosy cheeks were the color of dull cement. Her thin lips, once so ready with a smile, appeared as a tight line across her nearly toothless mouth. The sallowness of her skin highlighted the dark circles encapsulating her eyes. Her skin hung, and her bones jutted out everywhere. She resembled pictures in my history books of prisoners of war.

"Mom? Cancer? I can take care of you. You're not yourself. We can see a doctor. You know that, right, Mom?"

"Selena, it's better this way. It's just me and Gilbert. He doesn't like you much."

It was like a knife plunged into my heart over and over. Mom wouldn't, or couldn't, look at me. I took a deep, shaky breath and pulled back my shoulders. I stood tall and strong in front of her.

"Don't worry, I'll find the girls. Mom, I can take of you, too. You don't need Gilbert. Please, Mom. He's evil."

"Someday you'll understand ... someday. And, believe me, I

know what Gilbert is." She took the gun from the bed, placed it on the bedside table, then opened her arms.

I crossed the room in two steps and eased into her hug. There was nothing left of her. She was a skeleton, and I was afraid if I squeezed too tight, her ribs would snap.

"I understand, Mom. I do."

"Your daddy would've been so proud." She hugged me back tight. Her tiny body was stronger than I imagined. "I know you're a good girl," she whispered. "You make your sisters know how much I love all of you. They need to know. I plan to die on a bed of daisies."

"What are you talking about? You're not making any sense. I promise I'll find the girls and bring them to see you. Somehow. I will."

She didn't answer my questions as we stood and clung to each other. I was that little girl again as Mom stroked my hair and pulled me closer. The magic shattered when a familiar voice invaded the space.

"Susie, you home?" Gilbert called from the kitchen.

Mom stiffened. She jumped back and grabbed my shoulders.

"You need to get out of here, now." She pushed me toward the grime-caked window. "Go quickly. I love you." Mom picked up the gun from the table and turned from the room. "Gilbert, I'll be right there," she called. "Selena, remember what I told you," she said as she grabbed my hand. "Now, get out of here."

I nodded as Mom wiped tears from her face, then strode toward the door. I tossed my backpack through the small window and shimmied head-first through the narrow opening. My heart raced as I tried to hurry, but my yoga pants snagged on the lock latch on the windowsill. I pulled so hard they ripped, and I whacked my knee on the edge of the weather-beaten wood as the stretchy material gave way. I reached my hands out and hoped I wouldn't break my neck in the five-foot fall to the uneven ground.

As my hips passed the threshold of the window, an explosion—then another, and another, and still another—filled the air behind me. A scream pierced the air like a frantic mother dragon swooping down to protect her young. I knew it was Mom. It echoed around me as I caught a whiff of a peppery acrid smell like fireworks.

A nameless resolve reverberated through my chest, leaving me breathless as I hit the ground hard against my hands and knees, landing on top of my backpack. I crouched in the overgrown grass under the open window. Flakes of sunbaked chipped paint floated down around me. The explosions came again and again—so loud and close; I knew they were gunshots. I suspected Gilbert probably found out I was there and was shooting at me. My insides trembled with each pop as I sidled against the outer wall beneath the bedroom window and tried to make myself as small as possible.

There was one more bang right above me, then stillness. I waited in a tight fetal position with my hands over my ears. I don't know how long I stayed like that—it may have been three minutes; it could've been thirty. My entire body shook like a lone leaf on a tree, and an unfamiliar emptiness surrounded my heart. *Mom?*

A long piece of dry grass moved with the slight breeze. It tickled my arm and woke me from the shock. I crawled along the damp unkempt side yard to the front. The man and dog from across the lane, now perched on their back step, watching keenly as a stillness engulfed the area. I listened for the far-off howl of sirens. Nothing. I inched around the corner on my knees and came face to face with Gilbert's bike. A loathing so deep-seated bubbled up in me I could taste the acrid brackishness of hatred.

"Hey girl, what ya doin' there?" a stranger's voice called from a distance. "You best move along a'fore I reports ya to the poe-leese."

I couldn't be there when the police showed up. They wouldn't understand. Before I realized what I was doing, I pushed through the long grass and leaped over the spindly line of bushes dividing the yard from the back alley. I needed to put as much distance between me and the house as possible. I raced as fast as my feet would move. My arms pumped in time with my heart as I checked over my shoulder to make sure no one followed. My backpack bounced as I sped down the back alley toward the elementary school the girls attended. I hurried like I had a rabid dog at my heels. In one way, I wanted to stop and let it rip me apart, but the deep-borne need to survive pushed me forward. I don't know how I continued as I fought to draw in air. Tears leaked from me as the cold air bashed against the sensitivity of my eyes.

In one way, I wanted to escape completely—let the world swallow me up and end my misery. But nothing ever went as planned. I reached the path leading to the bus stop, but my legs had a mind of their own and turned the opposite direction to the side street.

I jogged until I reached the playground. Children were everywhere. I blindly searched for Victoria and Sofia. If only I knew what they were wearing. I turned one girl around, thinking it was Victoria with her long blond hair, but when I looked into the startled face, I didn't recognize the child.

There! Across the field, I spotted a friend of Sofia's. They played in the park before school started. I dropped my backpack at my feet and raced across the playground. A teacher, or maybe it was a parent, watched me and walked in my direction. I changed course and circled around the swing to where the child played in the sandbox near the monkey bars.

"Hey ..." I kneeled in front of the little girl. My chest heaved as I fought to catch my breath. The girl looked up at me with big, startled eyes as she pushed herself across the sand on her bottom. "It's okay. I won't hurt you. Do you remember me from the park? My name is Selena. Do you remember? Sofia—she's my baby sister. Do you know where she is?"

The little girl looked at me as though an alien was speaking to her.

"You! You there in the blue hoodie—stay where you are," a woman called as she ran toward me. "I need to talk to you."

The lady, whose girth was substantial, panted and bounced as she headed straight for me.

"My name is Selena." I stood and backed away from the little girl. "I'm looking for my sisters, Victoria and Sofia Henderson. I need to find my sisters."

"Your sisters aren't here." The lady walked the last few yards toward me. Short of breath, she swung her arms as she came closer. "You need to leave, or I'll call the police."

I searched her face for an answer, but I could see she spoke the truth. She had no reason to lie.

"You need to go now." The lady stopped. "I'm sure they're fine, but they're not here. That's all I know."

It was like a giant club came down from the sky and slammed me across the back. I stumbled to the fence. My feet were like concrete weights being sucked down by the deep dampness of grass surrounding the playground. I picked up my backpack, pushed the hair from my face, and squared my shoulders as I walked back to the alley. I turned down the path toward the bus stop—sinking into the tiny pebbles—the only path left open to me.

Chapter Twenty-One

NOW

LESLIE

Oh my God... Oh my God! Selena was at the bus stop! Right there—right now! I used the remote to open the parking garage, parked the Jeep, and rushed to open the door that led into the house. I needed to get to her before she got on a bus or some creep picked her up.

"Come. On." The faster I pushed the buttons to the keypad lock, the more my hands shook. I dropped my hand and forced a deep breath. With a gentle touch, the code blinked green, and the door burst open. I flew through the short hallway to enter the foyer by the front door. As I neared, my wet feet slipped on the polished tiles, and my knee bashed into the doorjamb.

"Shit ..." It was the same knee I'd whacked in the car. It didn't hurt, but it slowed me to the point of panic. My fingers didn't work right as they fumbled and slipped against the cold metal deadbolt on the front door—it was like trying to escape quicksand, with each step full of suction against forward momentum. In my haste, I smacked my knuckle on the lock, and blood spewed out as the door popped open, then I raced outside to the sidewalk.

"Selena!" I yelled as loud as I could while I waved both arms. "Selena!" I dashed onto the sidewalk and waved my arms over my head. I wiped my mouth with the back of my sleeve and immediately regretted it. I spat onto the pavement, and the smell of vomit wafted up and made me gag. I drew the chill air as deep into my lungs as I could. I wanted—no, needed—to have Selena respond and answer. I needed her. We needed each other—I was sure of it.

I stumbled between fast cars to the center island that divided the highway.

"Hey, you crazy old hag," a voice called from a car as it screeched to a halt next to me. "Get the fuck off the road."

The air exploded with a cacophony of horns and voices as I froze in the middle of the street. Were they yelling at me? Everything was suspended and dusty in my brain, as though in a bad dream. Not quite real, but jagged and hazy around the edges. My knees buckled while a hand swooped in, grabbed me, and yanked hard to move me to the side. I laid down on my back.

"Are you all right?"

"Sel ... ena?" I reached to touch her cheek. A stunning rainbow aura radiated from her as she bent over me. "I'm ..." No words came. *My God, how can I make a bigger ass of myself?* A shiver snaked up the length of my body as a breeze shifted to catch all the dampness. I wanted to be swallowed by the ground and disappear. *How did I get to this point of crazy? I'd talked myself into the ridiculousness of this Selena fantasy.*

How sick is that? Me, a grown woman stalking a young girl. I squeezed my eyes tight. All I heard was my mother's laugh as she gazed down and shook her head.

"Come sit down." Selena nodded toward Prince's bench.

"Thanks." I stumbled over and slumped onto the bench. As I shifted position, a bouquet of body odor laced with vomit wafted through the air. I shuddered with revulsion as I adjusted my jacket. I lightened my voice and smiled. "I guess I look a bit rough, huh?"

Selena didn't answer. She appeared to be a million miles away, cloaked in a shield of distant thought. Her torn yoga pants, covered in grass stains, and embedded dirt at the knees, revealed apparent recent happenings that consumed her.

"Could you help me get home?" I broke the silence. "I live right across the street." I pointed to the door that gaped open.

"Yeah, sure," Selena shook her head as though bringing herself back to the moment at hand. She slung her backpack over her shoulder and helped me to my feet.

"I appreciate your help. I'm not having the best day." I allowed Selena to lead me to the crosswalk.

We arrived at the house. The front door begged us to enter, but Selena stopped. She stood between the two large potted trees that framed the oversized door. I wished I had my phone to capture the moment forever.

"You're welcome to come in. You're safe here." I stood back from the door, waved my arm in welcome, and waited.

Selena hesitated, then shrugged and entered.

"Be careful, the floor is slippery," I said.

Chapter Twenty-Two

THEN

LESLIE

"Mother, I can't do this." I searched her face for any softness. Any forgiveness. "Please don't make me. Please, Mother." I begged as I lay on a plastic sheet atop the slatted wooden floor in the living room. My hand was outstretched to her. She didn't even so much as glance down at me. The contractions had been sporadic at first, but there was little relief from the overpowering agony encompassing my entire being. "Ohhh, it hurts. I don't think I can do this."

"Don't be silly." Mother yanked on my nightgown, jerking me forward. "Women have been having babies since the beginning of time. Believe me, you're not special. This is God's retribution for all your sins."

Sweat ran in rivulets down my face. It dampened my hair

and made my ear itchy. I tossed my head back and forth to shake the pain from my mind. The skin across my belly stretched beyond my imagination and continued to jump with the baby's movements. Nothing else existed at that moment.

Mother faded into a ghostly figure. She came and went without a word. Time ceased, and the air thickened with my own murky thoughts. The baby—oh, how I already loved him. I didn't know the intricacies of childbirth, but I knew enough.

Before Mother found out, I talked to the school nurse, and she gave me pamphlets to read. Shocked by what I read, I realized how sheltered I'd been from the realities of life. Mother had told me my period was a monthly reminder from God because he spilled his blood for our sins, so I was to remain humble and indebted. She never uttered the words uterus, eggs, or baby. Nor did she ever mention sperm, sex, or childbirth... The school nurse was aghast at how little I knew, but when I told her I'd been homeschooled, she'd pursed her lips and nodded.

"Leslie-Anne? Can you hear me?" Someone shook my shoulders. "It's time. You need to push now."

"No, please don't make me." I tried to look at her, but my eyes wouldn't focus. "I can't do it." I could barely lift my arm anymore, let alone push a baby out of me. My belly turned rock-solid, and pain radiated like lightning bolts in all directions —even behind my eyes and toes. No part was exempt from the sharp jolts. "Is this labor, Mother? Make it stop."

"God is reminding you a baby doesn't belong inside of you." Mother stood above me. "And this baby isn't yours. It's His. Don't you ever forget that."

"Mother, he's coming." I searched for her as a roaring, rumbling agony consumed me.

"Get up here." Mother grabbed me under the arm and rolled me forward. "Now push."

I sucked in my breath and focused it on the baby with all my might. I stopped, leaned my head back, and pushed again and again. Mother stooped between my legs, but I couldn't feel anything. Even the baby seemed done with the whole thing. An intense heaviness of fatigue and apathy swaddled me in its warmth to secure refuge. All I wanted to do was give over to sleep, but Mother slapped the inside of my thigh.

"Come on, you lazy cow of a girl." She smacked me again. "You need to push again."

"I can't ... I can't."

"Yes, you can! And you will!" This time, mother pinched and twisted the soft flesh of my inner thigh. The sharp jab got my attention.

A contraction ripped through me like an intense, aggravated bull ready for battle. I propped myself up onto my elbows and bore down with all I had in me. A blistering scream tore from a chasm deep within me as a whoosh rushed over my body and left me devoid of not only the agony of the flesh, but of that which had filled me for so long.

Mother stood over me, holding the baby covered in white goop and blood. A long, thin, curly cord hung from its tiny body. Mother pinched two clothes pins onto the cord, then cut between them. There was a mewl like the sound of a kitten. My baby. Where was he? A robust cry filled the surrounding air, then silence. He needed me. Where did Mother take my baby?

My heart raced as the still room echoed loudly around me. The ticking clock filled the abyss mockingly with an admonition of secrecy and solitude.

A pressure from my belly urged me to push again, but I ignored it, hoping it would pass. Was there another baby? Oh, my insides felt all twisted, and I didn't know what to do.

"Mother? Where are you? I need you."

Without thought or intent, my head curled toward my

chest, and I pushed. Something fell from me as I cried. Was it another baby?

"The afterbirth." Mother said as she stood at the end of the table. "You can clean that up later. Right now, you can go to bed."

"The baby? I want to see my baby. Why isn't he crying?"

"Put these on." Mother handed me an adult diaper. "You'll bleed for a while."

"Mother, the baby?"

"The birth was too much for him. He's dead."

It was like someone took a sledgehammer and swung it hard against my head. Everything careened out of control as I recoiled in all-encompassing pain. The words shot through me like rampant bullets tearing apart my insides inch by inch. No part of me was exempt from the anguish.

My eyes shot open as another sharp prick on my hip broke through my consciousness. Mother stood beside me with something in her hand. It was orange and shiny. A needle? My eyes became heavy, and my head fell to the side as though no longer attached. Mother had a look on her face—a slight upward turn in her pursed lips and her brows lifted—not quite a smile but a, ugh, I couldn't think of the word. Everything swam before me. I fought to focus on her face—to put a word to her look—when I heard low, muffled crying.

My baby. He's crying.

Mother's head snapped toward the sound as darkness overtook me.

Chapter Twenty-Three

SELENA

It was the way she waved her arm that made me follow her inside. It was the most genuine thing I'd seen all day.

"You're welcome to come in. You're safe here." Leslie spread her arms in welcome.

I caught a whiff of the stench covering her and stepped back.

"Oh my God, I'm so sorry. I know I stink. Tell you what, come on upstairs and make yourself at home. I'll go have a quick shower." Leslie turned and started up the steps.

It was like being swept gently into the house. I didn't know why, but I followed. A murkiness filled my head. But this house —Leslie—felt safe. She was goofy and helpful, like a friend's mom wanting to help but waiting to be asked. I believed she genuinely cared about me.

"I live alone. It's just you and me. No one's lurking around the corner." She said with a smile. "I'll be right back. Help yourself to anything you can find in the fridge."

I watched Leslie gingerly tiptoe up the stairs. The living room and kitchen were one large open space. Everything was so beautiful—shiny and new. On the far wall, a huge painting hung off-center over the fireplace. I didn't know how long I stared at it, but the colors and shapes calmed my rattled nerves. I heard the shower upstairs as my eyes gently traced a path down the mantle, coming to rest in front of three ornate silver frames—all empty. Weird.

Nothing was real. I felt like I was floating through the air, watching myself from above. I knew that if I thought too much, my skull would crack, and my brains would splatter everywhere. *I don't belong here.* I turned to leave and found myself beside a huge, round, charcoal gray chair strewn with pillows of various sizes, shapes, and colors. The chair, with its soft, worn fabric, had to be six feet across. It faced the floor-to-ceiling windows looking across to the park and bus stop. It was like a private nook where you could watch the world go by. There were empty potato chip bags stuffed between some pillows and fast-food containers wadded up by the side. On the table between the window and the chair, there must've been fifty cans of empty diet coke. I plopped down on the edge of the chair and stroked its softness. As I pulled my phone from my pocket, a pair of binoculars fell to the floor and landed right by my foot.

I leaped up and stared at the black, half-folded spyware. *Why does Leslie have binoculars? Is she a bird nerd? Why did I come here? Will the police even come if I call? Who's dead? Did Gilbert kill her?*

"I see you found my favorite spot in the house."

"Ah, yeah." I turned to Leslie, who wore a long, thick robe cinched at the waist. "Uhh, I need to go. My mom ... I shouldn't

be here. I need to leave." My feet bounced on the floor in opposite directions as my eye tried to find the door. "I need to go."

"It's all right. I can drive you anywhere you need." She
shook her wet hair out and studied me as if seeing me for the
first time. "Selena, are you okay? Your hands are shaking."

"I need to go to school." I turned in a big circle, trying to get
my bearings. I couldn't remember where I'd dropped my backpack. Every time I moved, the room spun. The motion made
me dizzy and off-kilter.

"Selena?" Leslie said as she caught me mid-fall.

"My mom ..." I crouched low and squeezed my eyes tight as
I covered my ears to block out the sounds. The gunfire. The
fear. Cancer. Right before me, the window framed the triangular park across the street. Now empty, I stared at the spot
where the bus stopped every morning. My head hurt, and my
heart raced. I could hear the repeated gun shots in my head.
Pop, pop, pop, pop ... pause ... pop. I leaped up and sprinted
across the room. "I'm late. I need to go. I ... I ... it's been."

"Selena? What happened? Are you okay?"

"I have to go." I found my backpack on the floor by the fireplace and made a beeline for the stairs. "I'll see you around.
Gotta go."

"Selena! Wait! Please." Leslie followed me down the stairs
to the front door. Her voice was louder now. Spilling with fear
which mixed with her own. "Are you okay? I'm worried about
you."

I grabbed the doorknob and froze. Worried? She was
worried? Nothing in the world was right. My entire world was
jolted, dumped upside down, and strewn about. I had nowhere
to go except Mindy's. And I didn't know if Mom was dead or
alive. All control was gone. I couldn't stop shaking as the
teeniest voice formed in the dry recesses of my throat and
scratched its way to the surface.

"It's my fault. All of it. My sisters are gone." I gasped as though trying to grab my family back. "My mother ... gunshots ... my fault. You're worried for me? Oh my fucking God, it's my fault." A dam opened, and my fears gushed from me like a passion-filled flash flood. The release barged through all my walls as nothing held me up anymore. My legs—exhausted and weak—crumbled below me as the reality of life smothered me. "It's all my fault."

"Oh, Selena." Leslie caught me before I hit the floor. "Poor baby." She stoked my hair, and I leaned into her to rock me. "Shh, it's going to be okay. I saw the fight you had with your boyfriend the other night, but with all this family stuff, too ... it's overwhelming."

"Oh, yeah." I groaned at the absurdity of everything. "He's not my boyfriend, but I'll add him to the list."

"Why don't you come back to the kitchen and let me make you a sandwich or something? It sounds to me like you really need to talk about this."

I couldn't move. Now that I'd said everything out loud, my energy and bravado vanished. It was all real, and it belonged to me.

"I don't know what to do." I cried as I pulled my knees into my chest. I could smell the sweet floral scent of her soap as she rubbed my back. Leslie was down on the floor with me, holding me from behind as my body shook with sobs.

She never left my side or asked me questions, and for the first time in a long time, I felt safe.

Chapter Twenty-Four

THEN

LESLIE

I woke to silence. I held my breath and waited. My head cushioned by a pillow, I turned and saw the familiar room. Someone had moved me. My patchwork quilt lay folded at the foot of my dark brown, wrought iron bed, and the curtains were closed against the day. Or was it night? I had no idea. I raised myself to a half-sitting position. It felt like my insides had been ripped from me. Where was my baby?

I know I heard him cry. He needs me.

"Mother," I called toward the closed door. My voice merely squeaked in the air. I winced as I forced myself to stand. Blood trickled down the inside of my leg and dripped onto the bare slat-wood floor. My head floated as I fought to keep my balance.

I grabbed a chair, but it skidded and fell backward under my weight, taking me with it.

The door led to my baby. I needed to get to the door. Slapping my damp palms against the floor, I pulled with all my might. It was useless.

"Mother ..." But the stillness remained.

Chapter Twenty-Five

SELENA

"I need to go."

I'd never cried so long or so hard in my entire life. Leslie held and soothed me as my tears poured out. My head was an upset jumble of questions and uncertainty. I needed to check on things. I needed to go.

"My car's a mess. Can I get you a taxi?"

"Don't worry, I have my bus pass." I shook my head. "I don't know what—"

"Shh, you don't need to explain anything to me." Leslie held up her hand. "I wish you'd stay and let me get you some lunch, but I understand you need to do what you need to do."

It was difficult, but I left and caught the next city bus going in the school's direction.

"I'm sorry, Selena, but there's no further news about your sisters," Mrs. Bonder said as she squeezed her eyes shut and pushed her glasses farther into her face, only to have them slide down again as her eyes burst open. "I know they're safe. They won't tell me where they are, and apparently, because of the proximity to the family home and threat of interference, they moved the girls to a different school."

"So, now I'm interference? I'm their sister, for Christ's sake. They need me."

"They know you're eager to make contact, and I'll keep working on getting more information."

With each minute that passed, everything slipped further away—always out of my reach. The girls could be anywhere and dealing with God knows what or who. I shut my brain down before I went to those dark places. And what if they liked where they were and preferred their new family? My gut clenched at the thought.

"Tell me how you are." Mrs. Bonder leaned in my direction.

"Me? I'm fine. I want my sisters."

"Selena, I'm worried about you. I've heard some talk around the school about you and Chad Spenser."

It was like my bones went soft. I might as well have been a pile of shit on the floor for people to walk all over. *How could I have been so stupid? You'd think I'd know better by now, but it certainly didn't appear that way.*

"How is he portraying me? Wait." I held up my hand to stop her from answering. "Don't tell me. I don't want to know. I made a fucking mistake." A surge of angry energy pulsed through me, ready to erupt everywhere. I pushed the chair back with my legs as I jumped up and studied Mrs. Bonder. "I guess it only takes one mistake to ruin your whole life, huh? Well, it seems like I've made my fair share in the last few months, and I can live with that. Chad and his asshole friends can go pound it because this girl is going to get back on track and take control."

"I like your fire, Selena." Mrs. Bonder also stood. "Concentrate on your studies and move forward."

"Thank you." I slung my backpack over my shoulder and left without a glance. I marched straight to the nearest bathroom. With the stall door closed, I leaned my forehead against the cool metal and forced myself to breathe. I stepped back as the door creaked, and announced other people.

I waited in the stall until they left. It was close to noon, and I hadn't been to class yet, so why go now? I splashed some cold water on my face, left the bathroom, and walked straight past the office and out the front door.

The fresh air hit me immediately. The coolness against my damp skin refreshed my thinking. I needed to take my power back—like I told Mrs. Bonder. No one controlled me before. Why would I let it start now? With my shoulders back, I strolled toward work. There was no other place to go, and I didn't know what else to do.

"Hey Selena," Mindy called when I entered the store. "What're you doing here? You're not on the schedule."

"I couldn't stay at school today." I kept my voice light. "Too many morons and idiots in my way, if you know what I mean."

"Oh, I know exactly what you mean. We're gearing up for the lunch rush, but I've got a full crew. You can hang in the back if you like."

"Thanks. It'll give me a chance to do some homework."

My clammy hands shook as I grabbed a coffee and returned to the staff/storage area. The warm, rich, intoxicating smell of coffee was everywhere. Instead of sitting on the hard-backed chair at the table, I sandwiched myself between two stacked rows of supply boxes. I relaxed against the wall, letting the boxes hug and support me from the sides. This was the worst day of my life. It still made no sense. My heart raced, and each breath was thick and clogging in my chest—the air unsatisfying as it failed to penetrate my lungs. Unable to hold my eyes open any longer, I rested my head against the sturdy cardboard and willed myself to relax. My exhausted mind wandered as sweat poured from me. I tried to calm my breathing.

"Selena, it's all better now."

"Mom? Is that you? Oh, thank God, I thought you were dead."

"Yes, it's me, and I've never felt better in my whole life."

"Mom? You don't look very good. You've got blood all over your dress. The hole in your head—it's leaking."

"Oh, don't you worry about this old thing." She swished her skirt and grinned. "You've always been so serious, Selena. You need to relax now."

"Mommy! Mommy!" I watched as Victoria and Sofia clambered onto Mom's lap. They smiled and waved, but they too had huge gaping holes in the sides of their heads. Blood and brains poured from them unchecked and spilled down their fronts onto Mom's legs.

"You need help!" I tried to scream as I reached forward, but the girls laughed and pulled farther away. "Let me help you."

"Selena, come get me," Sofia laughed. Blood gurgled from her mouth. Her teeth were stained red.

"Selena?"

I couldn't move. Something had my foot. I tugged and pulled, but a force larger than me yanked my leg as I slammed into a towering wall. It jerked me hard.

"You bastard, get away from me!" I screamed with all my strength. Sweat dripped down my brow and into my eyes. I flailed my arms as I fought to see ...

"Selena, wake up." Mindy shook my leg. "Selena, it's me, Mindy. You're having a nightmare. Selena, can you hear me?"

"I hear you." I shook my head to clear the cobwebs. "My

sisters. My mom ... it was so real." I yanked away from Mindy and pulled my knees up to my chest.

"Sounds pretty fierce. You okay?"

"Yeah, yeah ..." I struggled out from between the boxes. "I'm fine. Sorry about the fuss—bad dreams." I forced a laugh as I brushed the floor dirt off my butt.

"No fuss. Really, I'm here for you," Mindy said. "Listen, I need to tell you I have some company coming over tonight. Pretty casual. A few beers, maybe play some cards. You're welcome to join us. I just wanted to give you a heads up."

"Thanks. You need your space. I have a friend I can stay with. She's cool."

"Are you sure? I don't want to push you out or anything. Seriously."

"Nah, I'll be fine." Shivers raced up my body. "Hey, you work hard for your space and should be able to enjoy it. I'll stay at my friend's tonight and pick up my stuff tomorrow. Does that work?"

"You don't need to leave. It's just for tonight." Mindy side-hugged me.

"I'd rather move on. I don't want to ruin our friendship. You know? Is it okay if I hang here for a while longer, though?"

"Oh yeah, for sure." Mindy waved her arm. "The whole staff room is yours until you're ready to leave."

"Thanks. I'm going to finish my homework, then I'll get going."

"No rush," she called over her shoulder as she returned to work.

I sat on the straight-backed chair and tried to figure out what I was going to do, but I already knew.

I needed to go home.

Chapter Twenty-Six

NOW

LESLIE

I turned and walked up the stairs after she left. Selena ...

What a shocking turn of events. Heck, there I sat all that time in my Jeep being questioned by the Principal and she was here the whole time. At first, I thought my mind was playing tricks. Damn, to run out there covered in pee and vomit, I must've looked like an escapee from the psych ward.

Selena didn't say a word about it, though. She appeared to be in shock. Her hands shook and her knees were all grubby. Something wasn't right. The poor girl had more going on than I ever suspected. Two sisters? And a mom? I hadn't even considered her family. She always seemed so aloof that I assumed she was alone in the world.

It was good to connect outside the car—even though I

resembled a lunatic—and maybe once her life settled, we'd reconnect. I was sure we would. The day's happenings banged around in my head as I bounced up the stairs to my office.

The office was actually the third bedroom. My computer and desk filled the lower length of one wall, while the upper part had framed book sleeves with all my books. There was the first, The Seductive Glance, followed by The Seductive Smile, then, of course, The Seductive Whisper. There were twelve in all, with another set to release next year. Writing romance allowed me to mingle my imagination with hope—the stuff of fantasy. It was my job to convince readers that someone full of stature, desire, and improbable truths could fall madly in love and truly devote themselves even to the most unlikely of people —which, of course, was me.

I lowered myself into my chair in front of my desk. There, to the left, was the secret picture I'd taken of Selena at Java Jenny's. When I got home, I had printed it out and studied it. She possessed such a sweet innocence in her face, yet so much awareness in her eyes. The half-smile showed off Selena's full lips and high cheekbones—a true and natural beauty. I remembered my own senior year and saw myself in her eyes. I shook myself back to the task at hand and picked up the phone.

I wheeled the chair closer to the computer. My Selena Princess story was progressing well, and the first draft was near completion.

When Selena first left, I returned to the car to find the door still open after I'd sprinted into the house. No one had touched it—the smell alone was enough to knock a grown man through a wall. I called an auto detailer and hired them to take care of the Jeep, which my non-existent grandmother had vomited in and peed all over. This was such a relief, and for the first time in a long time, a buoyancy embraced my spirit. I walked from the office to the bathroom and stepped on the bathroom scale. I knew better. This lapse in thinking wiped away any zeal and smashed my mood to shreds.

"Oh my God, I'm so fucking fat. Up nearly ten pounds in the last month. Tomorrow. I'll start tomorrow."

As a young girl, Mother called me lazy and fat daily. She said I sucked every calorie from everywhere, whether it was mine or not. Even as a baby, I'd become so pudgy, normal baby clothes wouldn't fit.

The repeated words echoed through my mind, countered by flashes of Selena in the house. I wasn't stupid, though my actions rarely showed that. I knew I didn't deserve any better. Life proved it to me time and time again. All day long, I'd say I don't care what people think, but I knew what a pile of crap that was.

I grabbed the phone and scrolled through to the Grubhub home page. On the menu, I entered two cheeseburgers with extra cheese and pickles, two large fries, and two large diet cokes. I was ordering from a stranger, but I needed them to think it was for two people. I was about to hit send, but opted to add two chocolate fudge sundaes with extra topping and sprinkles. A confirmation text and a tracking number arrived immediately, with an estimated delivery time of thirty minutes.

I next scrolled to the Best Grocery app and ordered two bottles of red wine, two pints of choco-mint ice cream, three bags of chips, one head of broccoli, and four Granny Smith apples. Heaven forbid the grocery people judge my purchase as completely unhealthy. The estimated time for delivery was one hour.

I went to my favorite chair, curled up, and waited.

The aftermath of my impulsive binge ordering made me realize how alone and empty my life had become. The food solved nothing, but fixed everything in that moment. Mother's voice still seeped through everything.

It scratched at me—the denial and shunned reality—the blame and humiliation, the birth of my baby. There were no pictures, no paperwork, and most importantly, no baby. Mother wiped an entire year away with her smug stance and self-appointed God's blessings.

I knew my baby was real. I still had the stretch marks and scars to prove it. I only ever told four people about the baby. Phillip was one of them. When we realized getting pregnant wouldn't be as easy as planned, we went to a fertility specialist.

The doctor called it secondary infertility because I'd carried to term before. After tests, I learned that uterine scarring because of a past infection was stopping the egg from implanting in the uterus. In plain language, it was my fault we couldn't get pregnant. Everything changed, though it had always been the same for me, as my brain went right back to lying on the plastic sheet on the floor. In my marriage, I'd always been a supportive wife. I would've been his biggest cheerleader had the issue been with him, but his sperm count was normal, and it was all on me.

Oh, my God. How could I expect Phillip to accept such damaged goods? With the news, a part of me shut off completely—maybe it was hope that died, or it maybe it was the belief I didn't deserve to be a mother. A baby had already been ripped from my life—God, how I hated Mother and her glib attitude. I deserved better. I would've loved and cherished the gift of a child like no other. Never again would I experience the secret bond of an unborn baby rolling and stretching within my belly. Phillip deserved better. I couldn't blame anyone but me, as it seemed anything I touched or loved hurt me. I'm more broken than the billion grains of rice that fill the fields to be harvested individually. So many itty-bitty pieces.

I cringed as the bright light from a nearby streetlight shone through the window as I ate both burgers, washed them down with wine, then continued on to the fries and ice cream. I couldn't stop until it was gone. My mouth was dry, and my head pounded with every breath. I heaved myself to a sitting position and covered my face with clammy hands.

"Why?" I groaned. "Why do I do that to myself?"

Dammit, will I ever grow up? My stomach rolled, and for a second, I thought I was going to puke. That would be the icing on the cake after the car. Stupid fat cow. I seriously need to tap into some self-control. So stupid. I pulled my bruised knees closer and fought off another wave of nausea.

The doorbell rang, and I froze as the sound reverberated off every wall, then still echoed for a follow-up.

Everything ceased for a split second, and I fell into a fantasy state of overindulgent suspended animation where I floated over myself and surveyed the scene. Pathetic. The clock ticked, the fridge hummed, and I breathed.

The doorbell rang again.

There's no one in my life to ring the bell. I'm fucking trash. Why would anyone want to come here? I held a cushion over my ears. Mother's words echoed around me. No one wants to be your friend. You're selfish. No one will love you. I squeezed the cushion harder, but I could still hear.

Biiiingggg Boooooonnnggg. It echoed up the hall.

I waited for the nausea to calm, then pushed myself to stand. I rubbed my eyes and scanned the coffee table for the security camera remote. With all the empty cans and fast-food wrappers, I couldn't find it, but the ringing finally stopped.

I peeked out the window and saw a police officer getting back in the front seat of a police car.

"What the ..." Did the school principal figure out who I was? I grabbed the binoculars to get a closer look. "Shit!" In my haste, I slammed my baby toe against the coffee table leg. Empty bags, cans, and wrappers crashed and flitted through the air to land on the floor. The empties echoed with a tinniness that would have been funny if it hadn't been so damn painful and messy.

I hobbled back to the window. The police car was about to reenter traffic when I held the binoculars up to my face. There, in the back seat of the police car, was Selena.

Chapter Twenty-Seven

THEN

LESLIE

I dared not move for fear of waking the pain. Someone had come in and picked me up from the floor. I had no memory of it, but it had been a long night, and every time I moved, I couldn't help but cry out, which made it even worse. Blood pooled beneath me, and I knew in my heart I was going to die.

It was my punishment for going back for more.

Johnny and I met at the building alcove as often as we could for weeks. When she asked, I told Mother I was studying at the library or researching an essay.

No one knew. No one suspected.

We ignored each other at school and met in our secret place. Things went sideways on a Thursday. Mother worked late, and I snuck out to meet him at the park at the river bank.

The night, lit only by the half-moon, allowed for privacy and anonymity. Johnny always brought a blanket, and we'd lie together until forced by the clock to separate.

That Thursday was different, though. Johnny's friends followed him.

"So, I see you got fat Leslie in a nice isolated spot," they teased as they circled the blanket.

"Hey, we're just talking here. It has nothing to do with you guys," Johnny said.

"It has everything to do with me, Johnny," one boy growled. "She made me look like an idiot in gym class. She fucking tripped me, and I fell on my face. The whole class laughed—including her."

"You tripped over your own two feet. I never tripped you," I said.

"You have a fucking big mouth, don'tcha?" He shook his fist at me. "I suggest you keep it closed unless you want my dick in it so you can suck me off."

They all laughed and slapped the boy on the back. They were like a pack of wild dogs, salivating and nipping at the vulnerable prey before them—the posturing and puffed chests grew larger. I sensed trouble as I studied the path that led back to the parking lot and onto the road.

"Johnny, I think I better go."

"Why're you even here with her? Are you two screwing?"

"Get lost, you guys, and leave her alone. She's helping me with some homework." Johnny shrugged. "The teacher paired us up, and I had no choice."

Heat rose in my face. I realized then I was on my own.

"Where ya goin', sweetheart?" One boy blocked the path.

One pawed at me and touched my breast, while another pulled at my skirt. Another covered my mouth while I fought wildly against him as he tore my clothes, and grinded against me. My legs kicked and flailed as the boys pulled my hair and grabbed my private places.

"Jesus, you're fuckin' brave to take her on. Look at the fight she has in her."

"Hey guys, lay off!" Johnny screamed as he scrambled to his feet. "You're hurting her."

"Go fuck yourself, Johnny. She's a fat, easy fuck. You just wanna keep her all to yourself."

"I said, leave her alone." Johnny pulled my arm and freed me from the clutches of another boy. "All o' you get the fuck outta here. Now!"

"Whoa, Johnny. We're having a bit of fun. No one's gonna hurt anyone. Jesus Christ, do you love her or something?"

I stood behind Johnny, my eyes averted. Johnny was red in the face and wild-eyed. I knew he'd fight, and it took a minute, but the unwelcome boys recognized it, too.

"There's no need to foam at the mouth, Johnny. It's fat Leslie, but we'll go, won't we guys?" They all mumbled as a group and ambled away as though nothing had happened.

"You okay?" Johnny asked as he stared at the grass. "Sorry, I didn't know they were going to do anything. I shouldn't have told them we were meeting here."

I'd loved him the first time I saw him and knew it was divine intervention that brought us together. Mother had always told me that if God wanted you to have something, he'd put it in front of you as a glorious gift.

Johnny was a gift.

"Can I get you anything? Are you hurt?"

"I think I'll be okay. I need to clean up, you know. I can still smell them." I adjusted my clothes and wiped the tears that started again. "I'd like to get out of here, though."

"Come on. I know where we can go."

I followed blindly. During the melee, I had twisted my

ankle, but I was otherwise no worse for wear if you didn't count the bites and bruises, and violation of my body, mind, and soul.

"Those fucking bastards, I should report them." He shoved his hands deep into his pockets. "They're no better than a bunch of criminals. I'm sorry I wasn't able to stop them. You understand, right?" He looked me straight in the eye. "You don't think I had anything to do with the guys, do you?"

I crossed my arms to keep my breasts from jiggling with every step, and I put my torn bra in my pocket. I needed to sew it without Mother seeing it.

"I know it wasn't your fault."

"I don't blame you if you want to go home."

"No," I stared at the ground. "I'll stay."

"Okay, great." He took his hands from his pockets and cracked his knuckles. "Oh, and by the way, I thought it was hilarious when Dean tripped over his own feet and did that face-plant in gym class. Too bad it didn't knock some sense into his fucking empty head." His hands shook, and I thought I saw tears in his eyes. "I have a sister, and if any guy treated her like that, I'd be ... I'd be ... I'd want to kill them."

I knew this was a gift sitting before me. A gift full of love, honor, and integrity. I loved that he defended me in the park.

He was my destiny.

I massaged my aching breasts. They were rock hard and shot burning spurs down through my armpits. I wept for the death of my baby, for the misery, and because things should have been different.

I lied in my bed wearing nothing but a diaper and a short red silky nightgown I didn't recognize. The stiff lace pulled across my breasts and itched.

"Mother, please help me. Mother?" I felt the torn flesh of my body and didn't know what to do. "Mother, are you there?"

"You're awake." The door opened, and light flooded the room.

"Mother." I stretched my hand toward the looming figure above me. "Oh, Mother, I hurt so bad."

"Well, I'm not surprised. The bastard baby was very large. It's a shame ..."

"I think I need to go to the hospital. My breasts have turned rock hard, and I can't stop bleeding. Mother, I think I might be dying."

"Oh girl, you will not die. Your milk is coming in—it's a real shame there isn't a baby to feed. And blood ..." I saw the contempt and hatred ooze from every pore on her face. "That blood is God's reminder you can't be taking any man for a long time."

"Mother, it hurts."

"Well, you should've thought about that before you opened your legs. It's not an easy lesson, is it?"

"Oh, Mother, you're right. You've always been right. How do I get redemption? How do I make this pain go away?"

I watched Mother's face soften. It wasn't a lot, but it was there. It was enough to make her stop and study me.

"I'll get you some painkillers. They'll make you sleep. When you slept last time, I put on your new scarlet nightie. Do you like the way it squeezes your breasts together? Does it feel sexy? I bet your man would like it, too, wouldn't he? You're a scarlet woman, and you're but fifteen."

"Mother, I need you. I'm so sorry. I don't know how it happened." Instinctively, I knew I couldn't tell Mother about the other boys who took advantage of me. She already blamed me, but those boys weren't my fault. "I loved the daddy. We loved each other."

"Love." She spat. "You don't know what love is. It's a good thing that baby of yours is dead, otherwise, you'd never have a life. I don't know where I went so wrong."

"I'm sorry ... so sorry."

"I know you are, dear. I know." Mother ran her hand over my brow and down my cheek. "Here, take this. You'll feel better soon."

"Yes, Mother. I love you. I'm sorry, Mother."

Chapter Twenty-Eight

SELENA

Flashing blue and red lights bounced off everything and lit up the night. When I went back to the house, I thought the police would've come and gone already, but a crowd had gathered off to the side, by the alley, and watched as the police tied up yellow crime-scene tape. No one even saw me. I strode up the alley as though I owned it, and just before the house, I veered off the path so I could circle around back and get closer.

It had been great to see Mom sober this morning. She was smart and must've known what Gilbert did. Things were so different before he came into the picture. I wanted to say we were happier, but I couldn't. Money was always tight. Mom worked split shifts at the truck stop. I looked after the girls, even when they were babies, and soon after, Mom always had a whiskey bottle nearby.

Everything changed one morning about a year ago when

we woke to the smell of bacon frying. The girls and I found Gilbert standing in front of the stove in his underwear.

"Well, come on then. Come git yerself some bacon. Yer mama's sleeping. She never sleeps 'nough, but I'm here to change all that."

We were skeptical, but the lure of bacon was too much to ignore. We huddled around the table, silently eyeing this stranger in our kitchen as we savored the salty meat. Gilbert made us pancakes that day, too. The reins of suspicion and distrust loosened as he plied us with more.

"We's a family now." He stood there before us with his skinny, hairy legs and loose-fitting boxers. "Now you'd be Selena, yer Sofia, and this cutie here," he mussed her hair, "must be Victoria."

"Did you marry our mom?"

"I will if'n it kills me." He stood poised with the full frying pan. "Anyone want more bacon?"

"Yes, please." We held out our plates.

To this day, for me, the smell of bacon meant betrayal and ugliness. Lost in my memories, I didn't notice the light—it was a flashlight aimed straight into my eyes.

"Can I help you, miss?"

The deep voice surprised me so much I fell onto my butt and bit my tongue. The taste of blood infuriated me as the adrenaline gave me a sudden energy to leap to my feet and confront this unwelcome visitor. Before me was an enormous cop.

"Ah, no, I'm good, thanks." I brushed myself off as he towered over me with the bright light. "I'm fine. Is there a problem, Officer?"

"Problem? Well, you tell me. You're hiding here in the long grass at an active crime scene investigation. I think you have some explaining to do."

"Is hiding in the grass illegal?"

"No, sure isn't, unless you're scouting out a break-in or some such."

"Oh my God." I laughed. "Who would break into any of these dumps?"

"Then what're you doing?"

"That house." I pointed. "I lived there until a few days ago." Nothing was real anymore. The cop lowered the light and stepped closer.

"A few days ago? Did you move?"

"Not exactly. I've been staying with a friend."

"So why're you back now?"

"I, well, I visited my mom, and she ..." I paused and looked at his badge. It was real. The brushed metal was tangible—I wanted to reach out and touch it. I wanted this nightmare to end.

"What happened when you visited?"

"My mom ... I ... nothing happened. I visited my mom. That's all."

"Can you tell me what time of day you visited?"

"I don't know. Around eight or nine this morning—I don't know for sure."

"Why don't you come with me?" I knew his words weren't a simple request. "You can sit in the back of the car while I deal with this. You'll be warmer there, I guarantee it."

The heat in the squad car made my skin tingle. I rubbed my hands together and waited. The officer talked into the microphone clipped to the top of his bulletproof vest, then got in the front seat, pulled out a clipboard, and wrote something.

"Can you tell me who lived in the house?"

"My mom, Susanne Henderson—everyone called her Susie. And her boyfriend, Gilbert Kirkwood. There was also me, Selena, and my two sisters, Victoria and Sofia Henderson."

"Selena, is it?" he raised an eyebrow. "Do you have any identification?"

"Only my bus pass. It's in my backpack."

"Don't worry. We can get it later. When was the last time you spoke to your mom, or," he checked his notes, "Gilbert?"

"This morning. I told you I came to visit my mom."

Another police car rolled up beside the one I was in. The officers talked in muffled voices through the window. The crowd grew to include people on fold-up chairs smoking cigarettes, drinking beer, and videotaping with their phones. I lived here for two months, and I'd seen none of these people before now.

"I'll be right back." The officer exited the car.

A cold draft shot up the length of my body and startled me awake. The same officer I'd talked to returned to the front seat, closed the door behind him, and buckled his seatbelt.

"Sorry to wake you, but I'm going to take you to the station. Unless you have somewhere else you want to go."

"What happened?"

Everything was jumbled and out of place. The gum the officer chewed filled the car with peppermint scent. I wanted a piece, too, but I wanted answers more. "What's behind the yellow tape?"

The officer in the front had his back to me and wrote something in a notebook. His computer was on a sturdy swing arm attached to the dash. I scooted to the edge of the seat and looked over his shoulder. A thick piece of marked-up Plexiglas and bars separated the back and the front seats, but I saw Gilbert's picture on the computer. I guessed it was his mug shot. Maybe it was his record or something.

"Is he dead?"

"Do you have a picture of your mother? Or do you know if she had a record I can pull up? What's her full name and date of birth?"

I gave him the information and held my breath. There, before me, was Mom. I stared at the picture. It was probably five years old and taken after a night of drinking. It was a head-shot, face on, then a side view. Her eyes were half-closed, her skin sagged, and her mouth hung open, showing her missing teeth. Her hair, tangled and matted, had slivers of wood embedded into the wicked mess.

"Is this your mother?" He pointed toward the picture.

"Yes," I held my breath. His expression didn't change as he clicked off the computer and undid his seatbelt. "Did you find her? Do you know where she is? Wait, don't go. Is she alive?"

He left without answering. I closed my eyes and imagined her before me—it was as though I was there—then pop, pop, pop, pop—a brief pause and another pop. The cops didn't have to tell me. I knew the minute it happened.

A weakness overtook me. It was like someone pulled the plug on my body, and all energy ceased to exist. I flopped against the back seat. All I could do was wait. The car door opened, and a female officer slipped in beside me. She smelled of popcorn and peppermint. The uniform was tight on her and rode up her body as she sat down.

"Selena," she said as she yanked down on her protective vest. "I have something to tell you." She paused. "We believe your mom is one of the two deceased in the house. I'm so sorry for your loss."

A squeaky, scratchy sound escaped me as I doubled over.

"I'm sorry, Selena. I lost my mom too when I was about your age." The officer reached over to rub my shoulder. "I know it's hard. Crying is a good thing."

The warmth of her hand on my shoulder radiated deeply

and genuinely. All I could do was nod as snot ran over my lips and words backed up in my throat.

"Listen, I need to go, but we'll call Child Protection Services and get you somewhere safe and warm tonight, okay?" Fresh air wafted in to sting my tear-soaked face. The officer left the car and talked to a man wearing a suit and tie. I couldn't hear what they said, but a couple of times, they nodded toward the car.

"Do you have any family around here?" The first cop returned and started the car.

I thought about Mindy's apartment and shivered.

"Umm, I have a friend who lives close by. I'm sure she'd let me stay."

"It'll still need to be cleared by CPS, but what's her name and address? I need to record it because you're going to have to be available for a statement."

"Her name is Leslie... Leslie Smith." I lied. "I don't know her address, but I can show you where it is. I don't need CPS... I'm almost eighteen."

"Let's check out your friend, then. I'm sure you've had enough for tonight. I'm sorry it wasn't better news about your mother."

I locked eyes with the officer in the rearview mirror. He was young, and I could tell he meant what he said. I nodded and turned back to survey the scene as we drove away. Yellow tape fluttered in the breeze as bright floodlights lit the front porch and the dingy door. One neighbor lounged in his front yard on a discarded avocado green toilet with long tufts of grass shooting from the tank behind him. He crossed his legs and leaned forward as he drank a beer and watched the goings-on. I was about to turn back around when a little boy around age four, with a curly mop of red hair, came out and handed him another beer, taking away the empty. My heart broke for that kid.

Within a matter of minutes, the police pulled up in front of Leslie's townhouse. The officer left the flashing lights on as he blocked a lane of traffic. He went up and pushed the doorbell. I watched from the backseat—waiting for her to open the door.

He rang it again.

Nothing.

I said a silent prayer that Leslie would appear in the doorway right away. Please. Please. Please.

He rang once more, but didn't wait as he returned to the car.

"There's no one home. Is there anyone else?"

I thought of all the people in my life and wanted to laugh. Where can I go? I shook my head. "What now?"

"Well, if there's no one else, then I'll have to take you to family services, and they'll find a group home for you."

"I have a co-worker. She doesn't live far from here. She'll let me stay." I wanted to crawl into a ball and disappear, but anything was better than a group home. Mindy would let me in, the cops would leave, and I'd head out on my own.

The officer put on his seatbelt and checked his mirrors, then I saw a light go on over the front door.

"Stop! You need to stop. She just turned on a light—she must've been sleeping or something." I slapped the Plexiglas separating us as I watched Leslie's front door. "Stop. Please, turn around. Go back."

The cop acted quickly as he slammed on the brakes, turned on the flashing lights again, and reversed to the building. Adrenaline coursed through me, as it seemed like a movie stunt. There she was. Leslie. Everything gave way to a weepiness as I rocked back and forth. She stood in the open doorway, waiting. She looked disheveled and unsteady on her feet, but I didn't care. I wanted to rip the handle off and throw myself in her arms. I tried to open the door, but there were no door handles. The officer came around, opened the car door, and I bolted to the front door to throw my arms around Leslie. I'd never been so happy to see anyone in my whole life.

Leslie stood still and stiff for a few seconds—shocked to see me, I think—then she softened and pulled me in tight. I pushed my face against her and drank in the smells of burgers mingled with sweet fruity alcohol.

I closed my eyes. This ugly day could finally end.

Chapter Twenty-Nine

NOW

LESLIE

"Ma'am, I wanted to confirm it's all right to bring Miss Henderson to your residence."

"Yes, Officer, she's safe here." I held Selena close to me. "Is there anything else?"

"No, ma'am." He nodded and took a step back. "Well, yes, ma'am. I need your phone number and full address."

I gave him the requested information, then he returned to his squad car and drove off.

"What happened? What're you doing here?" I stepped back and held Selena at arms' length to make sure she was all right.

"I'll tell you in a minute, but right now, I need to use the bathroom."

"Up the stairs to the left."

She's here again. I spotted the mess around my chair and scurried to the drawer to grab a plastic grocery bag. I shoved all the fast-food containers into the bag and picked up the rest of the trash.

"You don't have to clean up for me."

"Oh, you startled me." I stooped over and picked up some french fries that had escaped the bag. "Not to worry. The mess needed to be picked up eventually." I surveyed the mayhem, and the heat of a blush rushed up my neck and into my face. "I, ah ... I ah, have a bit of a problem with food. Some people drink to forget. I shove crap in my face and wash it down with wine."

"You don't need to explain. Here, let me help you." Selena picked up all the candy bar wrappers and other garbage strewn through the area. "My Mom was a drinker. This is so much better—if one can be better than the other. At least you don't lose your license for eating and driving."

"You don't have to pick up after me. Seriously, leave it. I'll get it." I didn't want Selena to see how much I actually ate but the evidence was right there—the snack cakes, the french fries, the chips, burgers, all of it. "Selena, you don't have to. Let's go to the other room, and you can tell me what's going on."

Selena dropped to her knees, though, and crawled around the chair to pick up the trash. Her hair hung across her face. She was so young. I wasn't sure whether she'd heard me or was ignoring me because she didn't want to talk. I placed my hand on Selena's shoulder to get her attention.

"That's enough now." I smiled. "Come, and we'll have a chat."

It was a long night. Selena told me everything she'd learned about her mom, then collapsed in tears before succumbing to exhaustion.

"It's going to be okay." I rubbed circles on her back and

stroked her hair. "You can stay here, and we'll find your sisters. Shh, it's okay ..." My heart broke for the girl. Her entire family was gone. I took her to the spare room and tucked a blanket around her. She was asleep before I tiptoed from the room.

Selena's words buzzed through me as I returned to my chair by the window. It was from here that I'd first seen the girl. In one way, I felt I knew what she was all about, but finding out her mother was dead boggled my mind. I settled into the chair with my phone in hand and waited for the world to wake up.

"Max? It's me, Leslie." I said to the still air of the voicemail. "Are you there? I don't want to leave a message, so call me back as soon as you get this."

I watched as students shuffled onto the bus. I had learned a few of their stories last night as Selena poured her heart out. It pissed me off how the bus driver turned a blind eye to shit on the bus. How did the driver not know or care that kids vaped weed and gave blow jobs in the back of the bus?

All those kids across the street would never look the same to me ever again. I remembered my school days and how badly I wanted to be in the cool group—the ones who didn't appear to have a care in the world. Bastards.

The vibration of my phone made me jump.

"Hi, Max." I deliberately kept my voice low. "Thanks for getting back to me so quickly."

"No worries. You're sounding officious this morning. What can I do for you?"

"I need you to find a couple of little girls for me. Their names are Victoria and Sofia Henderson."

"And where would you suggest I find these two little girls?"

I told him the whole story. It sounded incredulous in my ears. "I want you to locate them. Don't do anything."

"What is it you're planning? Don't get sucked in by some streetwise teen with a sad story. LES, you know better, right?"

"Of course, I do. I'm not stupid. I'm concerned, that's all. Oh, and if you can find out the rules for a seventeen-year-old escaping state care, I'd appreciate it."

"I'll see what I can find out, and in the meantime, I need you to finish up the paperwork from Phillip's fiasco."

"I'll sign and send them over by courier today."

"Works for me."

I hung up the phone and went back to the window. The school bus left, and the park was empty. Was I being played like Max suggested? I didn't get that sense at all. I searched the news on my phone.

The headline screamed: Murder-Suicide! The Area, Best Known for Drugs 'n Hookers Now Adds Murder!

"Disgusting tabloid journalism." I shook my head. "The editor who allowed that to go to print should be fired, and the reporter should be ashamed. Don't they realize these are real people? I seriously wonder sometimes."

I hit the escape button and checked on Selena, still sleeping. There was a renewed fire in my gut to jump back onto the wagon of life. Whether it was this connection fostered with Selena, or something else, I didn't care. Though I'd kept writing and taking care of my basic business needs, the renewed energy convinced me to check my email. There were 1033 unread messages.

"Ugh, I guess it's been a while."

I scrolled from the top and found the one I wanted. A three-book deal I pitched to the editor. Let's see what she says. I took a deep breath and clicked.

Hi Leslie. Hope all is well. We're happy to ...

That was all I needed to know. The deal was still on the table. My self-imposed nervous breakdown hadn't ruined everything. In fact, I knew most of it was in my head. Hell, I didn't get to be a bestselling romance writer without fantasizing about life, love, and the dreams upon which they're built. I'm not stupid, but the brain goes where it wants to. Sometimes it takes more energy to wrangle it in. Like Johnny... where would we be now if we'd let love lead us. Perhaps if we'd been a bit older... And Phillip. Oh how I worshiped that man and his love for me. Writing romance fulfills my fantasy to someday be the lucky one that has that special, forever, and deep to the very center of my bones knowing that there is no one else who could possibly satisfy my heart.

Great! Can't wait to get started.

I punched out my reply, then headed to the shower.

Selena continued to sleep as I methodically plowed through emails.

The doorbell chimed. The security monitor on the phone showed two uniformed cops standing at the front door.

"I'll be right there," I said through the intercom. The cops relaxed their shoulders and took a step back from the door.

"Hello, Officers. What can I do for you today?"

"Leslie Smith?"

"Smith?" I frowned, then realized Selena didn't know my last name. "Actually, it's Leslie Richter. I used to go by Smith but not anymore, and well, it's kind of a standing joke." I bit my bottom lip to curtail the rambling and reground myself. "Anyway, what can I do for you?"

"We're actually here to see Selena Henderson. She's a witness in a murder-suicide that happened in the neighborhood."

"You mean she saw it happen? Oh my God, that's terrible." I grabbed the door to steady myself. My poor Selena. Shit, I'm going to pass out right on the cop's shiny boots. The thought of her seeing such horror...

"We won't know for sure until we speak to her." The officer removed his cap. "We need to determine what she saw."

"I'm sorry, ma'am." The other officer stepped forward. "What my partner is trying to say is that we need to talk to Selena and take her statement." He glared at his partner. "We apologize for the misunderstanding."

"You scared me there for a second." I sighed and pulled the door open. "Please, come in."

"Thank you, ma'am. We appreciate your cooperation."

"Yes, well, of course. Come this way."

I came around the corner to find Selena in the kitchen. She wore the same clothes she'd slept in and had pulled her long hair into a knot at the base of her neck. She looked all of twelve years old.

"Well, good morning. I was going to wake you up."

"I heard the doorbell and voices."

The police followed me into the kitchen. I stood beside Selena, who leaned against a kitchen bar stool.

"It's okay, hun." I forced a smile and rubbed her arm. "The officers want to ask a few questions."

"Good morning, Selena." The older officer stepped forward. "I hope you had a good sleep. Do you feel up to answering some questions?" The officers who'd appeared like oafish idiots on the front step turned into caring, sensitive people. A part of me relaxed—they were not the enemy.

Selena had already told me everything, but I stayed close, like a hovering parent who wasn't ready to go too far in case she needed me. Should I put on a pot of coffee? I've never had cops in my home asking about a murder-suicide. What is the etiquette? My fingers twitched with the need to be busy, but I balled them into soft fists and opted not to make the coffee. I listened in case I needed to intervene. It came at the end. I knew it would.

"Do you have questions for us?"

Selena shook her head. The knotted hair had come undone.

"Officer, if I may?" I asked.

"Yes, of course." He nodded. "Do you have a question, ma'am?"

"I do. Selena and I," I glanced over to her, "well, we were talking, and we'd like to know the procedure of what happens next."

"Next? Well, it's an active investigation," the officer said, "but I'm sure the evidence will speak for itself. We'll file Selena's statement with the district attorney and coroner's office, and they'll make the final decisions." The officer shifted his weight, glanced at Selena, then back at me. "We'll still need Selena to make a positive identification, and you can make arrangements if she wants to spend any time with either of the deceased."

"Oh, wow." I sidled closer to Selena. "Can I go with her?"

"Oh, yes, ma'am. I'm sure that'll be fine."

"Will there be a funeral?"

"I believe that'll be your decision." He wrote a number on the back of a business card. "If you call this number, they'll answer your questions much better than I can. I don't want to steer you wrong."

"Thank you." I took the card. "How do we, ah ..." I looked over to Selena again. "How do we find out where Selena's sisters are?"

"The people at that number should be able to help you. I imagine the sisters would be under the jurisdiction of Child Protective Services, but they'll know." He closed his notebook. "If there's nothing else, we'll be on our way. Thank you for your cooperation, and Selena, I'm very sorry for your loss."

Selena stood and shook the officers' hands. A lump formed at the base of my throat. She handled it with such grace and maturity. I wanted to hug her and never let her go.

"I'll walk you to the door." I led the officers out, then waited and composed myself before going back upstairs.

"Selena, would you like to stay with me? You can home-school if you want and get away from that cesspool of students at the school."

"Leslie, I need to find my sisters." She buried her face in her hands. "I don't know how, but I need to take care of them. They need me."

"Listen, you still need to have a place to stay, and besides, I can help you find them. I sincerely believe everything in our lives happens for a reason. You're here, in my home, because that's where you're supposed to be. I think you know that, too, otherwise, you wouldn't have come here last night."

I meant every word I said. From the depths of my soul, I knew this girl needed me. A force beyond my understanding connected us. Something in the universe had deemed us to be together. Selena didn't speak—she didn't have to—she let out an anguished cry and fell into my lap. I knew she felt it, too.

"We'll do it together. I promise we'll find them."

The week flew by. Selena officially moved into the guest room across the hall from my bedroom on the third floor. Max and I discussed the legalities. She'd age out of the foster system at eighteen, which was only a few months away. With Selena's blessing, Max would request emancipation through the courts on her behalf, so she'd be released from the system altogether.

He tracked the sisters down to a middle-class neighborhood across town. They were together with an older couple who'd never had children. It took another two days for Max to arrange a visit in a public area so Selena could tell the girls what had happened.

We agreed to meet at a family restaurant. Selena leaped from the car before it came to a full stop. Immediately, two young girls bolted across the parking lot and attached themselves to her. They held each other and wouldn't let go. Even when we ate lunch, they held hands and stroked each other's arms. Selena told them what had happened to their mother, but I wasn't sure the gravity of it actually hit home. They all wept and wiped each other tears.

The foster parents stood back with me and observed.

"They're lovely girls. It's such a shame, isn't it?" The foster mother said.

"Is it okay if Selena calls them every once in a while? It'll take time for everything to settle down."

"Oh my, of course. I'll give you the number. Those bureaucrats at the family services have their own rules and sometimes frown on that kind of thing, but these are sisters, and I'd be willing to bend the rules so they can talk." The lady twisted the handle of her purse back and forth. "I have two sisters—one's dead now. I sure wish I'd talked to her more."

The girls chatted quietly amongst themselves as they ate ice cream. The change in Selena astounded me. She glowed from within, and her cheeks had shone a rosy color as her face stretched in a never-ending smile. Gone was the strain and worry.

The meeting was the first of many, thanks to the willingness of the foster family. The system moved slowly. For the next two months, Selena and I drove across town once a week for a visit. Nothing was easy, though, as the tears and separation tugged on everyone.

"Did you enjoy seeing the girls?" I asked as I cranked the heat in the car and rubbed my hands together.

"Yeah, they're great." Selena stared out the side window.

"You all right?" A tickle in my brain sensed her distant tone and faraway look. Did I piss her off? What have I done? Mother always said I didn't make a good friend. Was she right?

I bit my lip as fear filled me. Once I asked, my mouth wouldn't stop.

"You've been off these last few days? Is it about the girls?" Am I ready to hear the truth? I live in fantasy land—I know that. Harsh reality sucks. My brain went to the darkest place. She's leaving. I know it. "I sure hope we can do an overnight visit soon, don't you? I'm sure the paperwork will be approved soon..." I recognized the desperate reach in my voice and forced myself to stop talking.

"I think I'm pregnant."

Chapter Thirty

THEN

LESLIE

"Pregnant? How the hell can you be pregnant?" Johnny waved his hand in front of my face and stared at me as we sat together on the cold concrete step of the fire escape. "We only did it like a dozen times. How do I know it's mine?"

"Sorry," I lowered my head. A small fissure crept down the center of my body until my heart cracked right in half. He couldn't hide the sneer of disbelief and complete disgust. It radiated from him. If I needed to, I'd get on my knees. "Johnny, I don't know what to do."

While I didn't expect any huge excitement for this new reality, I dreamed he'd take me in his arms and promise to take care of me. In my fantasy, I'd be the perfect wife and mother. But now, I studied the lines on my hands and tried not to think about his sudden aversion to even glancing in my direction. We could be a family, and while he finished school, I'd clean the house and feed the baby, but any hope faded with his words.

"What're you going to do?" He bounced from one foot to the other. "My mom's going to fuckin' kill me." He fished a cigarette out of his shirt pocket, lit it, and tossed the match over the open railing.

The smoke from his cigarette wafted across the two of us as I reached for his hand.

"Don't touch me." He leaped back as though I zapped him. "Leave me alone. This is your fault. I never wanted to touch you—you're always wanting to touch. It's not normal."

"I might need to leave town." My heart grew heavy. Every word formed slowly in my head as my energy fell away like water sucked down the drain. "My mother really will kill me when she finds out—and not the way your mom will kill you. It'll be the end for me."

"I didn't think ... you said we ..." He threw his cigarette over the side and lit another. "Jesus, Leslie, we're barely fifteen. We can't have a kid."

"No, I guess you're right."

"You should get a scrape. I heard my brother talking about some girl in his grade, and she got herself all knocked up. My brother said you pay some doctor, and they scrape it away. I don't know what they're scraping, but it means no kid."

I watched his lips move up and down, but his words hung in the air, inaudible and veiled in selfishness. It didn't seem real, and this was not what I'd pictured as I lay in my bed the night before, imagining his acceptance and blessings—his love.

"I will not get a scrape. That sounds horrid."

"Are you sure? I could try to get some money." He moved closer. "I know I have eleven dollars in my room, and I bet my brother would help." He was right next to me again, and I could feel the warmth of his leg against mine. "I feel better now. We have a plan." His eyes danced with relief and self-satisfaction as though he hadn't heard a word I said. He reached over and pulled at my breast through my thin jacket. My nipples reacted immediately, and he could see his handiwork through my cotton blouse. "We can still do it, right? Because you're—well, you know—I can see your tits want me. It's okay, right?"

"Yeah, I guess, but don't you think there are too many people around here?"

"Nah, come farther back. No one can see." He pulled me away from the stairs and laid me on the concrete landing. He swung his leg over my lap and laid on top of me. I'd worn my prettiest panties—they had an ivory-colored silk bow sewn at the top center waistband, and soft lace bordered the leg openings—I'd worn them in hopes of us sealing our love forever. He leaned to one side, yanked up my skirt, and pushed my panties to one side with his chubby hand. The elastic dug into my leg as he leaned on top of me.

"I wore new panties for you today." I tried to get his attention. "Do you like them?"

"What?"

"Nothing, I just said I love you. Do you love me, Johnny?"

"Yeah. You're sure it's okay, right? My dick isn't going to like hit a foot or anything, right?"

The cool breeze blew against my bare skin, and the rough concrete dug into the back of my legs and butt. Delusions of a happily-ever-after faded as Johnny finished, stood, and left without a word.

The next day, I clutched my books close to my chest and strode down the hall toward him. I wanted to feel him brush against me. Tell me in our secret code, everything was going to be okay. As he got closer, he averted his gaze, and I knew that in his eyes, I no longer existed.

Chapter Thirty-One

NOW

LESLIE

"I think I might be pregnant," Selena repeated. "I'm thinking of an abortion. All I've ever wanted to do is finish school and get a full-time job. I can't do that with a baby. Fuck, I'm having enough trouble doing it without a kid in tow."

The unexpected announcement threw me into a tailspin down a dark, twisted rabbit hole of secrets, despair, and horrors. I'd spent years trying to reconcile the supposed death of my baby, and it all flooded back in an instant. I was so alone through the entire ordeal—there was no support or tenderness. I'd met with Mother's flailing fists and vile words as they sliced to the core of my soul. Abortion? My head split with the right versus the reality.

Selena stayed silent as I tried to absorb the information.

"Wow, I'm ... I'm ..." I turned the heat in the car down. "Phew. It's warm in here. Sorry. Um, I'm surprised, is all. Can we talk about it tomorrow? That'll give me some time to get used to this idea."

Selena nodded. It wasn't until the next afternoon when I studied the young girl curled up in the nesting chair that I recognized the innocence of youth, and the blossoming of a young woman who'd seen far too much in her short lifetime.

"Listen." I kneeled by the chair and held Selena's hand. "I meant what I said before—I believe you're here for a reason." I lowered my head when I saw the bright sheen of Selena's eyes. "I talked to Max, and he said I can petition for guardianship with a clause to independence." I pushed up from the floor and joined Selena on the chair.

"Are you going to take my baby?" Selena stiffened beside me.

"No, no. It's about you, not your baby. This will allow you access to my medical benefits, and if either of us doesn't want to continue the relationship, then we sever it immediately and without question. The baby, well, that's ultimately your decision."

"Leslie, you've done so much already. I appreciate it, but it's too much. This is my problem. I haven't even decided whether I want this baby."

"It's a huge decision, and I'll support you in whatever you choose to do. Use my laptop if you'd like to do some research. It's good to make an informed decision. How about the father of the baby?"

"More like sperm donor. Asshole. He doesn't deserve anything. Besides, no use getting so stressed about something that might not even be happening."

"You're right, let's make a doctor's appointment and have you checked out first." I studied Selena before I continued.

"Scoot over and share the blanket. I want to tell you a story about a young girl with a crazy-ass mother."

Selena made room and snuggled beside me. With a glance toward the window, I realized the outside world now sat beside me. Somehow, the fantasy viewed through the binoculars—meant to stay safe and distant—was real as it reverberated into the essence of who I always wanted to be.

Chapter Thirty-Two

SELENA

Even without confirmation, I knew I was pregnant. I couldn't explain it other than the development of an intrinsic warmth and self-protectiveness within me like I'd never experienced before. Abortion flitted through my mind, but I already loved this baby.

I had no regrets about Chad. The entire relationship had been full-on intense from the beginning. So much fun, connection, and bullshit all rolled into one. It both terrified and excited me to think of a baby growing inside me. Once, I heard a story of a baby born with a hole in its back because the mom didn't take vitamins. I wanted to take vitamins. I didn't want my baby to be born dead or broken.

I sat with Leslie in the doctor's office, waiting to be called to discuss the results of the sonogram and examination. I couldn't remember the last time I'd been to the doctor.

"Can you come in with me?" I asked Leslie. "The doctor is going to tell me stuff, and I'm afraid I'll forget everything."

"Yes, I'll come in if you want me to." Leslie lowered the magazine she was reading, and I slipped my hand into hers, holding it tight. I couldn't look at her, or I'd cry. My mom loved babies. She wouldn't have celebrated about the circumstances and timing, but she'd have smiled her near toothless grin and been excited. Losing Mom the way I did wasn't fair, but to have Leslie beside me was like Mom making things happen from Heaven.

"Selena Henderson," the nurse read from a clipboard.

"That's me." I leaped up and pulled Leslie along with me. We followed the nurse down a wide hallway, where she stopped and waited for us.

"You can have a seat in here." She gestured to an office with a solid wooden desk set before a large window and two solid straight-backed wooden chairs in front. In the far corner, the leaves of a towering palm tree extended into the room providing balance and calm. "The doctor will be with you shortly."

We took our seats in front of his desk and waited. I didn't know where to look. There were charts and diagrams everywhere. I'm way too young to be a mom. What am I going to do? I reached blindly for Leslie's hand and took it in mine.

"No matter what happens, we'll be fine," Leslie whispered, and squeezed my hand.

"Hello ladies," the doctor said as he entered seconds later. "Or should I say congratulations?"

Though I wasn't surprised, a breath escaped me as Leslie rubbed my back. An image of Mom popped into my head, then I realized just how much I missed her. Oh, Mom. Did you feel this way when you found out you were pregnant with me?

Tears stung my eyes, but fear gripped my heart. *I'll take such good care of myself and my baby. I promise.*

"You're approximately twelve weeks pregnant, with an estimated date of delivery being mid to late July. Are you continuing with this pregnancy, or should I schedule a D and C?"

I had done my research and was thankful to live in a place where I had a choice, but I wanted this baby.

"I'll definitely continue with this pregnancy," I said. I sensed Leslie release her breath in relief as she squeezed my hand again and moved closer—like a mama bear moving in to protect her young.

"Okay. I'm going to prescribe some prenatal vitamins then."

"Oh, yes, please." I nodded to him. "I want vitamins."

"Good." He smiled as he studied me over his glasses. "It sounds like you're going to be a model patient. We did a sonogram today. Are you interested in knowing the sex of your fetus?"

"No, I don't think so." Then I shrugged and glanced toward Leslie. "Yes. I want to know." A giggle bubbled up within me, and I couldn't sit still.

"Which is it?" The doctor raised his eyebrows in question.

"I'd like to know the gender, please." I reached back for Leslie's hand.

"You're having a boy." He smiled. "Do you have any questions for me?"

"Are there any things I should avoid?"

"No alcohol, tobacco, or THC in any form until after the baby's born, and longer if breastfeeding. Is that going to be an issue?"

"No problem."

"I'll have my nurse give you some reading material. You're young, healthy, and considered a low prenatal and/or postnatal risk. I'll see you after your next sonogram in about a month's time, then monthly until we get closer to delivery, at which time I'll see you weekly. Please make your next appointment on the way out."

We followed the doctor from the room and continued to Reception. Everything was so ordinary. There was no harassment or judgment. This was alien territory for me. It was like watching a sitcom from the sidelines. As he handed me the script for vitamins, I couldn't quite shake the feeling it was all too good to be true.

Chapter Thirty-Three

NOW

LESLIE

Right after the first doctor's appointment, we drove to the high school to withdraw Selena from classes.

"It'll be weird not going to school," Selena said, adjusting her seatbelt. "I've always liked school, but my senior year got complicated fast."

"Well, it's a reminder that we don't have control over things." I glanced at her. "It'll work out. We need to concentrate on you now—you and that precious baby you're carrying—that's the priority."

I pulled the car into a visitor parking spot and studied the impressive arched brick entrance framing the extra high glass doors. Massive cedar trees, casting swathes of shade and providing shelter for birds and squirrels, appeared to stand

guard over the area. Above the doors, it said Washington
Heights High School established 1984. The building itself was
relatively new and worked hard on maintaining an image that
screamed upper-middle class. And, though I'd spent more than
a few hours in the school vicinity, this would be my first time
going inside the school.

Selena swung the door open, and we stepped into the wide
corridor with shiny polished floors flanked by closed rainbow-
colored classroom doors, and several rows of indistinguishable
lockers.

"Come on, the office is this way." Selena stepped through a
door that closed quickly behind her. She stuck out her foot to
hold it open. "Leslie, are you coming?"

"Sorry." I scrambled over to the door and followed Selena
to the administrative area. This was my first time back in a high
school in years, and voices from my past gnawed at me. Memories of being swept along with the crowds when the bell rang,
the taunting, and the shoulder shove into the wall. Even
without ever being in this building, the essence of the unspoken
hierarchy clung to every wall, every fixture, and to every
molecule of air that dared float through the hallowed halls. It
devoured me whole as the memories and nightmares roared like
raging seas through the corridor.

"Can I help you with something?" An older woman behind
the counter approached us.

"My name is Leslie Richter, and I'm here to withdraw
Selena Henderson."

"All right," she nodded. "I'll need your documents to start."
The lady explained the procedure. "You can have a seat if you
like. This will only take a few minutes."

I looked past the woman and saw the man who'd
approached my car when I peed my pants. The door said Mr.
Freeman, Principal. He was on the phone, deep in conversa-

tion. Heat rose in my face as I spied Selena already seated across the room. The last person I wanted to run into was the principal.

"Selena? Is that you?" A voice called across the counter, then a blur of a woman opened the door and marched toward the girl. "I've been worried about you. It's been weeks since you've been to school, and I heard the horrible news about your parents—"

"It wasn't my parents." Selena frowned. "It was my mom."

"I stand corrected. I'm sorry for your loss." The woman patted Selena on the hand, and turned to study me.

"Hi, my name is Leslie Richter." I stuck out my hand. "How do you know Selena?"

"It's nice to meet you, Ms. Richter." The woman stood to the side of Selena. "I'm Mrs. Bonder, the school nurse. Selena and I had some wonderful talks at the beginning of the school year, but I've missed her these last couple of months. I'm happy to see she's all right." She turned back to Selena. "Are you back at school, then?"

"No," Selena answered without looking up.

"We came to withdraw her, actually." I stepped closer to Selena. "She's being homeschooled and will continue to prepare for graduation." It was then I sensed another presence, and my blood froze.

Selena glanced up with a frown and studied my face. I dared not move. In my head, I was already in my car, driving away from this very fear. This man with the geometric tie was too close. I turned to introduce myself and saw he was actually still in his office. He'd never been there. The walls of the school lied to me. But the whispered truth within me spoke loud and clear. I needed to tell Selena about my stalking. My brain was in a void. Words vibrated through the air, and the air was thin.

"All the best to you, Selena," Mrs. Bonder said as she walked away.

It had already been three months since Selena moved in permanently. The child welfare department didn't put up much of a fight. They didn't need another kid in foster care, and after a quick court appearance, she was emancipated from the system.

Initially, the adjustment was difficult. I often returned home to find Selena twisted up in a ball on the floor, weeping and inconsolable. There was nothing I could do except wrap myself around the young girl and hold her through the rocking sobs. Curled together, I shared her pain as my body absorbed her trauma and offered unconditional peace and acceptance in return. The entire process, though necessary, was stressful.

Today, when we returned from withdrawing her from high school, Selena showered, climbed into bed, and fell right to sleep. At one point, I watched her sleep. To see the rhythmic rise and fall of her breathing reassured me of her well-being.

I returned to the living room and stared at the computer. I had lived my entire life with so much denial and pain. In adulthood, I'd blocked out most of my childhood. The survival instincts of the brain to compartmentalize the pain always amazed me. Selena was the only person, besides Phillip and Max, to whom I'd ever told my truths, and I'd been much more honest and open with Selena—at least about most things.

During the in-vitro, so many doctors examined me and said the scarring was beyond what they'd seen from a normal delivery. They asked about the birth and what tools were used, but I had no memory. I had no answers. All I knew was that he was born, then gone.

I stared at the computer and knew I needed to do it before I lost my nerve. I typed Johnny White into the search bar above my Facebook page and pushed enter.

I held my breath as the page loaded, and in seconds, a list appeared. The top one was a picture of a young, tattooed, muscular guy wearing a ball cap. I scrolled down to examine the other profile pictures, and there he was—the twelfth one; the sidebar showed Pine Hills High School, currently living in Omaha.

I leaned back and stared at it. Now what? Oh, my god. This is him. I clicked on the link, and a page full of smiling people appeared before me. There he was. He had his arm around a buxom blonde woman with enormous hips. To the side were two children, a boy and a girl. All four of them wore matching red plaid shirts, blue jeans, and huge put-on smiles. Johnny's other hand bore a gold band and held a beer bottle resting casually against his leg.

A ping raced through my heart and stung my eyes. For a split second, I was in his arms and could hear him breathe. My gut convulsed at the reality—I still felt something for him ... love wasn't the right word. He was nearly bald now, his belly puffed over the top of his belt, but his smile was still that of a fifteen-year-old boy. But he also looked tired around the eyes, and I could see gaps of missing teeth. He was still handsome. A tightness in my lower gut stirred as I studied his eyes. What would I do if he were here now? He acted like a piece of shit who walked away when I needed him most. Would I fall on my knees and weep with joy at his feet? Or was he just another Phillip?

I carefully backed out of his page. The last thing I'd ever want to do is push the wrong button and let him know I searched for his name. He had the perfect all-American family, and I was a nasty secret locked somewhere deep in the past. Did he ever wonder about our baby or me? I'd disappeared from school once Mother discovered my pregnancy. I prayed and prayed for hours that he'd come to beg forgiveness. To marry me. To save me.

The memories overwhelmed me, and I wanted to get in the car, drive to the nearest drive-thru, and stuff myself with food and drinks until I couldn't move. I stood before the computer, debating with myself.

"Fuck it." I grabbed my purse and slung it over my shoulder. In my haste, it swung and hit the chair. I was about to go, but froze when I saw Selena standing and rubbing her eyes at the top of the stairs. I skipped up the few steps and embraced her. She was warm and flush from her nap, and smelled like baby powder.

"Thank you for all your help today." She hugged me. "I love you."

I drank in the words and let them wash over me. Never had anyone ever clung to me and imparted such raw and unbridled truth. A switch clicked audibly in my brain—like a snap of an elastic band against my skin. A jolt slapped me into sudden awareness—why was I still running? What I needed stood before me, right here, right now. I drew Selena closer and allowed a tear to fall onto her mussed-up hair.

"I'll always protect you, I promise," I said, my throat tight with emotion. With a deep breath, I let my truth fall from me. "I love you, too, and I have something I want to tell you." We snuggled close, and I told her of my spying and watching.

"Did you go to the school?"

"Yes, the principal knocked on my window. That was the day I threw up in the car. Do you remember?"

"How could I forget?" Selena nodded. "Can I ask why?"

"Yes, an excellent question. I got it in my head that you needed my protection. As you stood out there at the bus stop, it reminded me of myself as a young girl. You appeared to be vulnerable and alone."

"Don't tell me any more, okay? I don't want to know. We're here together, and you're not crazy any more than I am. Maybe it was you who was vulnerable and alone. Let's be happy."

Selena cozied in even closer, and for the first time in my life, I understood unconditional love.

Chapter Thirty-Four

SELENA

"Do you want to feel him kick?" I took Leslie's hand and put it to my swollen belly. "There! Did you feel that?"

"He's going to be a soccer player for sure," Leslie said, laughing. "He's strong. It brings back a lot of memories."

"Oh, Les, I'm sorry." I sat up and reached for her hand. "I didn't mean to make you sad."

"Don't be silly, I'm fine. Besides, it's a miracle what's happening inside your body, and we should celebrate it." She grabbed my hand. "Don't ever be sorry."

"Okay." I caressed my belly in a circular motion. It felt magical knowing my son. My son. Just thinking the words overwhelmed me. Knowing he was a part of me was not only mind-blowing, but other-worldly. They say it's hormones that cause the tears, but for me, it was the awe of the entire miracle.

"I think I hear them." Leslie jumped up and looked out the window. "A square white sedan pulled up to the curb, and a woman got out. "Yup, they're here. I'll go get them. You keep your beautiful Buddha belly right here."

I couldn't stay on the couch, though, so I moved to the top landing as Leslie rushed down to open the door.

"Oh, Auntie Leslie, I missed you so much. I have so much to tell you." Sofia threw herself against Leslie and clung to her. Victoria, though, walked right past her with a mumbled greeting.

"Hi guys, how about me? I've missed you, too." Both girls squealed as they darted toward me.

"You're fat." Sofia hugged me.

"She's not fat, you idiot. She's pregnant." Victoria stood beside me. "You're such a baby. You know nothing about sex and stuff."

"I do, too. I know lots about sex."

"Well, little sisters, both of you know way too much for your own good. Come on, let's go have a chat."

"Selena, I was kidding about knowing stuff. I'm not in trouble, am I?" Sofia asked.

"See, Sof, you're like so immature."

"Whoa, Vic." I stepped back and eyed my younger sister. "Lay off, okay? You seem pretty intense today, but now would be the time to chill. You and I can talk privately later, okay?" I waited until I saw the slight nod. "Okay, good, you guys take your stuff upstairs, and I'll get some popcorn."

The girls clamored up the stairs, and I walked over to the window to see Leslie talking to the social worker. I looked forward to finally getting some answers about the girls. We had applied for Leslie to foster, with a plan to adopt, almost four months ago. The home visits, one planned and one a surprise, were completed, and now it was a waiting game. Leslie nodded at the woman, then jogged back to the front door.

I kept my fingers crossed as I filled bowls with snacks. The girls came running down and leaped onto the couch.

"Come on, Selena," they called in unison. "Come sit with us."

I waddled over to where they were, and squeezed in between them. Having them next to me was like regaining the rest of my heart. We weren't meant to be apart. Mom would want to know we were together, and at this place, this minute, I could feel her with us.

"Why're you crying?" Sofia smudged my tear away with her chubby hand. "Are you sad?"

"I was thinking how happy Mom would be that we're here together." I smiled and let the love flood from me.

"I didn't want to come here," Victoria mumbled. "It's stupid to come here, then have to go back."

"Hey, listen to me." I grabbed her arm. "We need to stick together. Family is all we have. It's the four of us now—me, you, Sofia, and Leslie."

I turned at the loud crash in the kitchen. Leslie stood there with a broken bowl at her feet and tears streaming down her face.

My belly stretched more every day. Sometimes I thought my skin would tear and the baby would fall into my lap. He loved to kick me and swirl around—already active and carefree. I'd watched my mom go through two pregnancies, but I was too young to understand any actual physiology. The doctor had been helpful, but my real teacher ended up being Leslie.

Together we watched videos and read books. She insisted we go to prenatal classes when I didn't even want to be seen. I learned about the birth, but also the bond. For me, it was such a relief to find out that the strong protective feelings I had were normal. I couldn't stop rubbing my belly to calm him or to say good morning. We were one. Connected in ways I never imagined existed. I often thought of Mom. I knew how much she loved us, but her demons interfered. I recognized she did her best as we struggled every day to survive, and I now understood how much it must've hurt her to see us going without.

Tears came easily. I missed her, but I was also thankful and content to be with Leslie—warm and cozy without a care in the world.

"Hey, little mommy, how're you doing there?"

"Oh, Leslie, I'm ready to meet this guy. I swear he's growing bigger every day, and I seriously don't think there's enough room."

"You look beautiful." Leslie extended her hand to pull me to a standing position. "Stop right there, I'm going to take a quick picture for the scrapbook."

I stopped as she reached for her phone and clicked off several pictures. "You're making a scrapbook? You're such a grandma."

"Um, yeah." Leslie laughed as she turned on her phone. "I'm videoing now. What do you want to say to that little man of yours?"

"Ugh, I look terrible." I covered my face with my hands. "I don't want to be videoed."

"Oh, come on, you're stunning. Say hello so we can show him later how he started out."

"Okay." I stroked my belly as a lump formed in my throat and heat built behind my eyes, threatening tears. "Um, hi, I'm your mommy, and I can't wait to meet you. I'll miss having you close, but I look forward to kissing your little toes." I pushed my hair back and looked straight into the camera. "You've been my reason for living, and you've given me so much hope for the future, and I'm naming you Von."

"His name is Von? Such a wonderful name. When did you decide?"

"A couple of weeks ago—it means hope. I kind of thought I'd surprise everyone, but," I paused and shrugged, "now you know. Do you like it?"

"Like it? I love it! Von is a lucky boy to have you as his mommy."

"You don't think the name is too weird?"

"It's not weird at all. It's unique and special. Von will come into this world knowing he's loved and wanted. He's already given us all hope to continue on this journey of life, and he exemplifies all that's right in this world. I can't wait to meet him either." Leslie turned the phone around to face herself. "You, Von, are already loved, but I need to take your mommy out to a concert. Okay, Selena," she said as she turned the camera back toward me, "we better get going, or we'll be late. Say bye-bye."

"I can't say bye," I said, though I waved at Leslie as she turned off her phone and I waddled toward her. "I'll bring him along with me. Can you help me get my shoes on?"

"Yeah, we better get going before we're too late and can't find parking."

"The girls will be excited to see us. I told them I probably wouldn't be able to go. Their little faces had such big pouts on." I looked up at Leslie. "Victoria's ... getting quite the attitude, and I can see she's going to be a real handful. I remember when I was twelve—oh man—that's when I got into boys, which worries me. When she was here last time, she told me she and her boyfriend were getting pretty serious."

"What exactly does serious mean?"

"It means they're gearing up for sex."

"Oh my God, no! They're still babies."

"I know, right? Vic developed and matured early. Her boobs were bigger than mine by the time she was in grade five.

She got her period, and all hell broke loose. I talked to her many times. I used to go to the nurse at school. The one you met when I withdrew from school." I put my foot up on the table, and Leslie tied my shoe. "She'd give us pads and stuff."

"I didn't know that. It sounds like you had some good people around you."

"Yes, there were some. Anyway, Vic has always had a pouty, sultry look to her. She was the one who caught the eye of Gilbert—my mom's boyfriend. Vic says he didn't touch her, but I'm not sure. She has such an attitude and tells me to mind my own business most of the time."

"We need to get the paperwork pushed through, don't we? I think the sooner we have them here with us, the better. That way, we can at least keep an eye on them and get her some counseling if she needs it. The fact they're still in foster care and across town makes little sense. They need to be here with us—with you." Leslie plucked her keys from the hook and tucked her phone into her purse. "Remind me to call Max tonight."

"You've got to be kidding me." I raised my eyebrow in disbelief. "You're asking me to remind you. That's funny because I can't even remember if I put socks on, and Lord knows I can't see my feet, so I can't even check."

"You are too funny. Come on, let's go."

We arrived at the girl's school for the June assembly at the same time as every other parent, or so it seemed, as several cars circled the packed parking lot in search of a spot.

"I'm going to drop you at the door." Leslie pulled the car over to the sidewalk. "I may have to park quite a ways away. I'll be back as quick as I can."

I hoisted myself from my seat and went to stand beside the door as parents rushed in to get their seats. No one paid much attention to me as I waited and watched. All different sizes, shapes, and colors bobbed toward me like a faceless sea of strangers. The chatting masses passed me by in everything from flip-flops to designer high heels. People smiled at me, while others raised an eyebrow or tossed what I thought of as a knowing look. My heart raced a million miles a minute as sweat pooled under each breast and trickled down the taut skin of my belly. Baby Von kicked up a storm as I stood waiting for Leslie.

"Phew, I parked a mile away, so I definitely got my steps in today," Leslie said, emerging from the crowd. "Are you ready to go in?"

"I don't think I can."

"Why not? Are you all right?" Leslie came closer. "Is it the baby? What's wrong?"

"I'm not sure. I'm feeling anxious with all these people around. Give me a minute, and I'll be fine."

"Okay, take a deep breath and try to relax. We'll sit near the back so we can slip out any time."

We entered the gym, and I scanned the room. Chad entered my mind, and a warm tingling flush crept over me. The passion and hunger I'd felt for him stirred. Here I am at an elementary school assembly. I'm as big as a house and horny as hell. I fanned my face with my hand and wiggled in the chair. I stifled a giggle, but it came out as a snort. The whole thing was absurd. I thought back to meeting Chad's mom in the hallway, when all I wore was his T-shirt. Mortified, I still went back to his room, and we had sex again. I stroked my jiggling belly as I tried to suppress the laughter.

"Selena? What's so funny?"

"I can't stop ... can't stop laughing."

"Well, that's better than tears, I guess."

I drew in a deep breath to calm myself, but the baby reacted with a sharp kick right in the bladder.

"I need a bathroom, or I'm going to pee my pants," I snickered, but the mirth had passed. I shuffled to the end of the row and asked an older, heavier-set lady to point out the nearest restroom.

"Oh my, look at you." She eyed me up and down. "The closest is right around the corner, on the left."

Yeah, look at me. If I could, I would. Why not tell me I'm as big as a fucking elephant? Jesus Christ, some people. I waddled down the hall where school children lined up by grade. The oldest were into the gym first and out last. The excitement in the air was palpable. I spotted Victoria, and we locked eyes. A deep frown creased the middle of her forehead as she shook her head ever so slightly.

I squinted my eyes and cocked my head, but soon discovered Victoria stood close enough to a boy to have their arms touching. I peered closer and saw their pinkie fingers hooked together.

Suddenly, having to pee could wait.

"Hi, Victoria." I stopped, so my belly brushed up against her. "I can't wait to hear your class sing."

The entire class turned and gawked at me and my enormous belly, then shifted their gaze to Victoria. She rolled her eyes back in her head and stepped back from me. A blush inched up her neck toward her face.

"Hey Victoria, is this your boyfriend? We haven't met yet. Maybe you could do the introductions now." I glared at her. Victoria set her lips in a firm line, and her eyes were mere slits. The boy slinked off a bit and stood with another student.

The older lady who'd given me directions at the door signaled for the students to enter the gym. I stood back and let them pass. I watched as Victoria tried to take the boy's hand again. He pulled away as he kept his head averted, but his eye on me. We'd all been through way too much, and the last thing I wanted was for Victoria to find herself in a situation like mine.

I shook my head and scrambled to find the restroom.

"Selena, I think we can safely say you'll be ready to deliver in the next ten to fourteen days. Have you noticed anything unusual? Less movement? Spotting? Anything?"

"Um, mostly everything is the same. It's just ... this is embarrassing. I'm horny as hell," I blurted out.

"That's normal." The doctor smiled. "For some women, it's a signal to entertain coitus to start the labor, and for others, it's pressure pushing down hard. When you're in a certain position, the clitoris is engaged."

"Okay, so long as it's normal." The giggles overtook me, and I couldn't wait to tell Leslie about the engaged clitoris—she's waiting for her wedding night, you know. Oh my God. The image of a clitoris wearing a diamond engagement ring overtook my brain. I stifled a chuckle.

"I'll see you in a week."

I followed the doctor out and turned to the waiting room. Leslie sat with a magazine in her lap, talking to someone. As I got closer, the hair on the back of my neck tickled, then I saw who it was—Chad's mother.

I spun myself and walked in the opposite direction. I didn't know where I was going, but I knew there was no way I'd go back to the waiting room.

"Do you need the restroom, dear?" the receptionist asked.

"Yes, the restroom." I nodded. "Thank you. Where is it?"

I pulled out my phone as I hid in the stall.

Leslie. I'm in the restroom, I texted. Come meet me.

b there in a minute

"Selena? Are you in here?" The bathroom door creaked as it opened.

"I'm over here." I peeked out from behind the bathroom door.

"What are you doing? Is everything okay? What did the doctor say?"

"I'm fine. That lady you were talking to—do you know who she is?"

"No, I don't. Should I? Is something wrong?"

"She's Chad's mother."

"Who's Chad?"

"Chad is Von's father."

"Shit."

There had never been any discussion about Chad. I hadn't told him about the baby and had no intention of doing so. This was my baby—end of story. Chad used and humiliated me, and he didn't deserve any part of this.

"The decision is yours," Leslie said. "Don't you think he has a right to know, though?"

"He's an asshole." I paced back and forth. "He two-timed me. He already had a girlfriend before he started up with me."

"None of it makes any sense to me."

"I met Chad at a party in my old neighborhood. He said nothing about having a girlfriend, so we hooked up. Then I transferred here, and we hung out at school. Scottie was on some extended trip with her family or something, but eventually, she came back and found out about us, and all hell broke loose. Asshole. I thought we were exclusive, but apparently, you're supposed to discuss that stuff."

"Disgusting, but I don't think high school has changed much over the years. Why would anyone treat someone that way?"

"Believe me, that was probably one of the easier things I had to deal with." I stroked my belly then pulled my long hair into a ponytail. "Do you think I should tell him?"

"I won't say what you should or shouldn't do. He's the father. He has rights and responsibilities. It's up to you to decide."

"I'll tell him after the baby's born, or at least I'll think about it. You know, Chad's a decent guy, and I fell for him. How stupid is that, huh?"

"Not stupid at all. It's lovely, and you'll always know you conceived Von at a special time when you were otherwise alone."

"Yeah, I suppose. Hey, I need to tell you about the engaged clitoris ..."

"I'm not stupid enough to get pregnant. So you don't have to worry."

"Listen, Victoria, I didn't set out to get pregnant either. Believe me, shit happens, and I want you to learn from my mistake."

"You're such a fucking hypocrite. You go out and do whatever you want whenever you want and don't give a damn about anyone else. That day when the social workers came and took Sofia and me from our classes, I knew it was your fault. You ruined everything."

"What did I ruin, Vic? Tell me. Gilbert was grooming you for his own. Did you know that?"

"You don't know what you're talking about, Selena. I'm smarter than you give me credit for. You left all the time. You don't know."

"I was there when I needed to be."

"Selena, you're such a selfish bitch. You had a job back in Dayton, and that weird boyfriend, too. You'd sneak out to see him, and he'd sneak in. You two would cuddle and whisper, but I wasn't stupid. I heard you. I know."

A blast of reality slammed into my chest and knocked me back into the couch.

"What, wha ..."

"You don't have a clue what went on." Victoria waved her arms in my face. "You were as clueless as Mom."

"No. I ..."

"It's okay." She lowered her voice and looked at me with weary eyes. "I don't blame you. I saved Sofia. Gilbert and I had a deal." Victoria used air quotes to emphasize the word deal.

"What?" My throat went suddenly dry and seized up as the harsh reality slammed me. I didn't do enough. Fuck. My baby sister ... Mom must've known. "Oh my God, Victoria, why didn't you tell me?" I opened my arms and waved toward her. "Come here, come. I'm too big to go to you. Come here."

Victoria finally climbed onto the couch beside me, and I stroked her hair as we cried together.

"I'm sorry all that happened to you. I should've been there for you. That's what big sisters are for."

"Yeah, I know, 'cause I'm Sofia's big sister, and I knew I needed to protect her." Victoria pushed herself away to sit cross-legged beside me. "I'm glad he's dead. I'm glad Mom is, too."

"Did you know it was mom who killed him?"

"No, I thought it was the other way around. I heard it was a murder-suicide. No one said who did what. No one ever talked about it. Even you. You seemed so far away."

"I'm sorry. I'll never be that far away ever again. I'm always with you."

"Hmm, maybe I'll change my mind about Mom."

"Yeah, I got a report after the investigation was complete, but the pregnancy took over my priorities, and I sort of forgot about it. I'm sorry. Please forgive me for not telling you sooner." I reached for her hand. "The autopsy said Mom had stage four liver cancer. I suspect her signing over her rights was her way of making sure none of us got left with him. She shot him four times, then herself once." I studied Victoria's face. "My concern at this point is you, though. Are you okay? I don't want you having sex and having to deal with all that shit."

"I know, and I'm not." Victoria stared off. "I like Leslie."

"Me too. I have a lot of respect for her and what she's done for us. She said the paperwork came through, so hopefully, we'll all be together again soon." I reached to bring Victoria closer, and a whoosh of warm fluid rushed from me.

"I think my water broke. Oh my God, I'm not ready. What do I do? Vic, go get Leslie. I think she's upstairs having a bath. Hurry!"

Chapter Thirty-Five

NOW

LESLIE

I leaned my head back and stretched my legs to let the hot steamy water loosen the sore, tense muscles. It was all getting real. Max told me yesterday the courts had approved me as a permanent guardian for the girls. They'd be coming to live here next week. I hadn't told them yet.

The whole last year was still catching up with me. Last month Phillip's baby had his first birthday, and apparently, they were pregnant with twins. Max also informed me he'd heard someone spotted Phillip at a fancy restaurant with his female junior partner, and it didn't appear to be all business. This information gave me a sliver of satisfaction, though the blame would always be on Phillip. He broke the vows and the sanctity of our marriage. Jerk. And yet here I am with a family of my own, despite him.

I jostled the water to redistribute the warmth in the tub. Selena's words kept playing through my mind.

"He made me feel special at that moment, you know? I remember thinking that I could fall for this guy. How stupid is that, huh?"

I wanted to cry for her. I thought the same about Johnny and my baby. Even if I tried, I couldn't have loved him more. My baby, like Selena's, was conceived through love. Life would've been so different. I dreamed about what could have been for far too long. The picture of Johnny and his family on Facebook jolted me more than I cared to admit.

When Mother discovered my pregnancy she locked me in the house, and I knew I'd never see him again. No one from school cared or reached out. I became yesterday's trash thrown far enough away so as not to interfere with others' lives.

Johnny. He never came to see me.

I knew it was a dark path to venture down when I typed his name in the search bar. Choice and power now belonged to me. I wasn't a fifteen-year-old girl anymore. I needed to concentrate on the present and not the past.

"The baby! He's coming!" Victoria burst into the bathroom. "The baby's coming!"

"What the—" My hands flew up to cover myself as I sat upright in the tub.

"Selena needs to go to the hospital. Come on."

"Okay," I stood and grabbed my towel, "Victoria, you go get the hospital bag and tell Sofia to get ready. We're having a baby!"

Victoria dashed from the room, and I pulled the plug from the tub. I couldn't make myself move fast enough. I dropped the towel and picked it up, only to have it fall again.

"Jeez, I hope I hold the baby better than I do a towel." A sense of jubilation overtook me as a tipsy-drunk giddiness emerged. "A baby, we're having a baby ..." I sang as I danced naked around the bathroom. Within minutes, I bounced down the stairs, ready to whisk Selena off to the hospital, but there she sat on a tea towel, propped against a bar stool, scrolling through her phone.

"Selena? Are you okay? You should sit down?"

"I'm fine—just watching YouTube. I'll wait for you guys."

"Have you had any contractions?"

"Not yet, but the doctor told me it could be a long labor because it's my first. No worries. I'm ready when you are. Oh, and sorry about the chair." She nodded toward the nesting chair. "I cleaned it up with paper towels. I'm not sure how well I did, though."

I couldn't believe this was the same girl the police brought here in a frenzied panic, and now she was this restful presence in the room. I took Selena in my arms.

"I love you so much." I hugged her tight. "I'm so proud of the beautiful young woman you've become." I pulled back and gazed into her eyes. "You're going to be a phenomenal mother, and I'll do anything in my power to help and support you."

"Why can't we stay? She's our sister."

"I promise I'll come get you as soon as I can." I told the girls.

"No, we want to stay," Victoria insisted, and Sofia nodded. "We won't be in the way, and besides, it's not every day we become aunties. That should be worth something."

"Oh, you two drive a hard bargain." I shook my head, and couldn't help but smile. "Okay, you can stay, but babies take their time, and it could be a long night."

The maternity ward felt alien, like something I'd only ever seen on television.

As a teen, I'd given birth at home, then as a wife, I'd fought to get to the maternity unit, only to be disappointed. Today was beyond my wildest dreams. Surrounded by pastel pink and powder blue, I leaned against the wall, closed my eyes, and said a prayer of thanks as the girls stood yawning beside me.

"What are they doing?"

"The doctor is doing an examination." I smoothed Victoria's hair, pleased that she didn't cringe or step away. "It's still going to take a while for the baby to come."

A nurse poked her head outside the door. "You can come back in now."

The three of us tiptoed into the room.

"She's almost fully dilated. It shouldn't be too long now." The doctor stood at the end of the bed, tapping his finger on a tablet. "It's been a long night for her, but she's young and strong. I don't expect any complications."

"Thank you, Doctor." I turned to Selena, whose long hair hung in every direction and was developing a huge bird's nest at the nape. "You're my hero. You're doing awesome, and it won't be long before you meet Von."

"I can't wait to meet him." She took a deep breath and held it as she grimaced through the pain.

"Selena, you need to breathe. Look at me." I bent close to the bed and lifted Selena's chin. "Breathe, blow, breathe, blow, as we practiced. In ... out ... in ... good girl."

It took another four hours before she was fully dilated and ready to push. The doctor strolled in at regular intervals to check on the progress. Victoria held vigil on the other side of the bed and followed my lead, while Sofia anxiously sat on a puffy pink chair in the corner. Flashbacks to my own birthing experience lurked on the edge of my consciousness, but I shoved them away. That was then. This is now. This is my future. My family.

"Here's your boy," the doctor finally announced as he held the baby in the air, then laid him on Selena's chest, where the nurse rubbed him vigorously with a blanket.

"Look at his long fingers." I watched as Selena counted his fingers and toes.

"Here you go, Grandma." The nurse held a pair of scissors before her. "Time to cut the cord." I accepted the scissors.

"Sofia and Victoria, you need to help me with this." I wiped the tears from my cheeks. "Let's do this together. One, two, three ..." The three of us cut between the two clamps and hugged each other. The nurse immediately scooped the baby up to weigh and clean him while at the same time the doctor attended to Selena.

"You're my hero." I touched my forehead to Selena's. "Such an amazing job. You're a mommy now. Von's such a lucky little boy to have you."

The nurse brought Von back and placed him on top of Selena. He sported a tiny white beanie on his head with his name embroidered across the front.

"Come on, girls, let me get a picture of you with Selena and Von." The girls scampered to opposite sides of the bed to smile, pose, and touch his cheek as I snapped pictures on my phone from every angle. Selena, with her hair tied up, was an exquisite mess as she beamed at Von and the camera. The camera captured the moments ranging from the tender to thoughtful to silly. The infectious energy of love and elation filled the room as everyone cooed over the baby.

"Smile, everybody—our first family picture." I flipped the

lens and extended my arm to angle the phone down to include myself within our small family.

"Les ... I can't ... catch my br ..."

I stepped forward as the girls backed away. Selena's eyes bulged as she gulped for air. "Nurse!" I screamed. "Something's wrong. Selena? Oh my God, what the hell is going on?"

The nurse glanced at a monitor, scooped up the baby, lowered Selena's bed, and pushed a button. A high-pitched screeching alarm filled the air. Selena's eyes rolled back in her head as her back curled toward the ceiling. Victoria and Sofia stood in the corner, frozen in place.

"I need the family out of here," the doctor shouted as he entered the room. "Now!"

"You'll have to wait out here." The nurse's calm voice echoed in my head. "Take the girls and have a seat in the waiting room. Don't worry, she's in excellent hands."

"No, no, no ..." I pushed against the weight of the voice. "I can't leave. You don't understand ..."

"Auntie Leslie, I'm scared." Sofia plucked at my hand.

"What?" I stopped and considered the situation. "Come on, girls, we need to let the doctor work." The three of us huddled along the wall near Selena's room. My mind raced as the frenzy unfolded behind a closed door. They whisked baby Von from the room in a clear bassinet as doctors and nurses came from every direction. Some pushed carts, while others darted in, then immediately back out. Pressed against the wall, I knew we were invisible. I pulled the girls as close to me as possible. The alarm, now silenced, left a clawing calm reverberating between my ears.

"Hit her again!" I heard someone bark when the door swung open to let someone in.

I lowered my head and rocked my upper body to will it all to stop. I prayed. In the last several months, I had prayed for anything and everything, but this—this was palpable. The last time I genuinely prayed was immediately following the birth of my own child. This time felt even more urgent. Fear gripped me as my entire body churned with a litany of pleas and whispered promises.

"Leslie?" The weight and warmth of someone's hand rested on my arm. I ignored it as I continued my vigil. "Leslie, we need to talk. Selena ..."

"No, get away from me!" A scream ripped through my entire body, taking every ounce of energy left. "My baby, my Selena. No, no, no ..." My body slackened and slid down the wall into a jumbled heap. My lips continued to move in prayer as I wept through closed eyes.

Chapter Thirty-Six

THEN

LESLIE

It had been a week since my baby left me. I missed him beyond anything I'd ever felt. Emptiness reached beyond my belly and right into my shattered heart. The twinges of physical discomfort meant nothing compared to the unsatisfied yearning I felt to hold my baby—to see for myself the tiny feet and hands on the person I'd created.

"I don't know why you're moping around." Mother wiped the table in front of me. "I'm your family. Babies are nothing but trouble, if you ask me. God smiled down on you when he took your baby. Now you can actually have a future."

"I want my baby," I said as I sat at the kitchen table, stirring my oatmeal in circles. "Mother, I felt him in my belly." Tears rolled unchecked down my face. "I know he was a happy baby."

"Devil lust spawned that so-called happy baby of yours, and it's a blessing it's gone."

I wanted Johnny—to feel his arms around me and beg forgiveness for my stupidity. Mother said the baby died because I put myself under too much stress. I choked off the oxygen to the baby. My fault...

It was right to love him and stroke him through my belly. I loved Johnny, too. It was pure and unselfish love, and I needed him to forgive me. It wasn't his fault that I was stupid. I wanted to start fresh and go back to the way it was before.

"We're moving back to Lincoln tomorrow." A sneer covered Mother's face as she dared me to question or disagree. "There's nothing wrong with you except you like to slut around, and I won't let that happen again. No one needs to know about this baby. It's over and done with—ancient history. You'll thank me one day, mark my words. Your selfishness is uprooting our home, but you've left me no choice. You've burned every bridge there is. Nothing but a town harlot—the county laughingstock." She reached toward me and lifted my chin. "You need to look at me when I talk to you. It's this sort of disrespect and brazenness that got you into this trouble."

"Yes, Mother." The spongy warmth of her finger on my chin lingered, making me want to vanish and break free. "I'm sorry, Mother."

"You best be sorry." She pinched the soft flesh of my cheek. "You're a marked woman, and I'm the only one who can save you."

"Yes, Mother," I recited as I stared at the chair's dull, worn finish next to me. "Thank you, Mother."

"And dry up those tears. You can't cry over something that wasn't meant to be." She released my cheek as though flicking a dry piece of snot off the end of her finger. "The pain you felt," she leaned toward me, her face mere inches away, "that pain is God's reminder of your sins—don't you ever forget that." The pungent stench of boiled turnips assaulted my nostrils, but I didn't flinch. "Do you hear me?"

"Yes, Mother," I said. "I won't forget."

Chapter Thirty-Seven

NOW

LESLIE

"It was an amniotic-fluid embolism," the doctor had said. "Sometimes, during delivery, the amniotic fluid enters the mother's bloodstream and causes an extreme, allergic-like reaction. It's rare, but there's no way to predict anything like this. She was a low-risk pregnancy. There was nothing we could do."

I watched his lips move, but didn't hear a thing he said. She was just another patient to him. He didn't know Selena—he didn't love her or lose anyone. He could explain everything away, and it made no difference because no matter what, it wasn't fair, and it shouldn't have happened. Selena, a healthy and vibrant young woman with her whole life ahead of her, was stolen from her new family—it wasn't right.

Each day blurred into the next as I had Max complete the required paperwork in order to get baby Von released into my custody.

"Leslie, you have legal custody of the girls, and Selena listed you as her next of kin," Max told me over the phone. "The legalities are taken care of, but you need to complete the hospital paperwork for his live birth and a birth certificate."

"Oh, Max, I just want to take him home with us," the sob escaped from me. "I feel like someone keeps slamming a bulldozer into my chest. It's not real."

Platitudes of sympathy given by strangers meant nothing as I struggled to find the strength to stand and function. I studied the forms on the clipboard as I filled in the required information. Name of Father: I lifted my pen, paused, then scribbled unknown in the allotted space. Without glancing up, I thrust the forms across the desk at the nurse and returned to the baby.

That afternoon, I took him home.

"Twinkle, twinkle little star ..." I gently bounced and swayed back and forth in front of the bassinet to soothe baby Von. "Shh, shh, it's going to be okay. I won't let anything happen to you, I promise. I promised your mommy..."

I jiggled him in my arms as I walked around the small bedroom that once belonged to Selena. On the dresser sat pictures of Selena and the baby. In one, Von lay across her chest as she gazed down at him with an expression of wonder and awe. I touched the picture as it tugged on my heart. It was a wonderful day, while also undeniably one of the worst days of my life.

The high school nurse called the day after I took the baby home. I had run into her at the Java Jenny's, where Selena used to work. Dazed, I didn't even remember stopping, let alone going into the coffee shop. The school nurse nudged me and asked about Selena. Straight babble fell from me about the baby, Selena's death, and my own baby. With a sudden rush of realization, I tucked my head down and dashed for the Jeep. A voicemail came a couple of days later.

"Hello, this is Karen Bonder, the school nurse from Selena's high school," the voice boomed through the silent house. "I don't know if you remember me, but I saw you at the coffee shop the other day, and you were upset. I now understand why and wanted to offer my condolences. Selena was a lovely girl. If there's anything I can do, please call me."

The next day, she left another message.

"Hello, Ms. Richter. I don't mean to bother you at this difficult time, but I may have some information about the father of Selena's baby. If you could give me a call... Thank you."

"No. No. No." I screamed at the phone as my entire body shook.

I rushed up the stairs to where Von laid swaddled in a blanket Selena had embroidered. His chubby cheeks and swath of dark hair drew me closer. He was safe, and I'd make sure he stayed that way. No one could take him—ever. He belonged to me.

"Your aunties will move in this week, and we'll be a complete family," I said as I stroked the baby's cheek as he slept. "I'll always protect you."

With renewed fortitude, I went downstairs to check on the world. The new school year started a week ago. Everything was the same out there, while inside, my entire world had collapsed and shattered, and nothing could fix the hollowness within me.

The sharp, jagged torment tightened in my chest and swelled in my throat. It was the same one that made me want to curl up in a corner to allow the deterioration and putrid reality of my world to starve me further. Living in this unrelenting misery had become synonymous with my life, and I wanted out. Despite being broken, I still longed for peace.

The world went on around me even when I wanted to stop it. The death of Selena left me powerless and directionless.

But the baby needed me.

I padded back up the stairs, picked him up, and went to the rocking chair. He crinkled his brow as he let out a small cry at being disturbed.

Tears spilled down my face for Selena and for my own loss all those years ago. For me, it was a mourning coming full circle to start once again. The deep-seated pain begged for answers that I didn't have. The warm room, bathed in the scent of baby powder and fresh linens, cocooned me against the reality of the world.

"Together, we'll take on the world," I whispered to the sleeping baby. "Your mommy was stolen from you like my baby was stolen from me—we're a perfect pair, and I'll never, ever leave you."

Part Two

Chapter Thirty-Eight

NOW

LESLIE

It's funny what happens when you're not given a choice between life and death. The stronger of the two reinforces the quiet confidence we don't realize exists within us, until all the fear and doubt suddenly gives way to laughter that brings back life. It happened one day as the girls cuddled the baby on the newly cleaned nesting chair.

"Eww ..." Victoria pinched her nose and turned away. "He let off a huge fart, and he sttaaah-inks." She waved the air in front of her.

"Hmm, I think that's more than a fart." I checked him.

"You mean he pooped as he sat on my lap? Gross."

"Yes, babies pee and poop when and where necessary." I picked him up. "Come help me change him."

Victoria scrunched up her face as we changed the diaper. Suddenly, a tall, narrow stream of pee flew up to soak everything in its path, including the front of Victoria's T-shirt.

"Eww ... gross."

She jumped back and gawked at me as baby Von cooed where he lay.

"He seems pretty pleased with himself." I raised an eyebrow but couldn't keep a straight face as a giggle pushed up from my gut.

"It's not funny. He just peed all over me." Victoria held her hand up as though in surrender.

"Oh my God, the look on your face."

It was a gift at that moment, as life concentrated on the levity and folly of the situation. I welcomed the moment, and hugged Victoria from behind as we both shook with laughter.

Life fell into a semblance of order as the girls adjusted to living with me full time.

"Are you sure you want to do all of this? Taking custody of and adopting three kids is quite a handful." Max strode across the kitchen and refilled his coffee.

"I've never been so sure of anything in my life. See this mess?" I gestured widely with my arm. "We call this living. This clutter and treasures spread all over the house are a sign that real people live here."

"Doesn't it bother you, though? You were single and used to being on your own."

"Oh, Max, this is like a dream come true. The girls are both seeing a counselor, and I think we caught Victoria before she went off the deep end. They're excited about school and being back with all their old friends."

"You let them go back to their old school, then?"

"Yes." I peeked at the video monitor that showed the baby sleeping in his crib. "The teachers were supportive, and though the surrounding area isn't perfect, the staff are amazing, and it's where the girls wanted to be."

"It's been a hell of a year for you. The whole Phillip thing, then all this, but you seem determined to make this work."

"I'm getting used to the whole three instant kids thing." I stopped and examined my fingernails. "It should be four. Damn, I miss Selena."

"Hey there, don't get all emotional. It won't solve anything, and besides, I'm here to give you a court date for the final adoptions."

"Thank you for making it happen so quickly." I swiped at the edges of my eyes. "I want the kids to know they've found their forever home."

"Let me tell you, Les, these things usually take months of interviews and home visits, but you're lucky because Children's Services already completed their due diligence with the girls' adoption."

"Max. I don't know what I'd have done without you."

"I wanted to tell you, too, that the wrongful death lawsuit for Selena may be a hard one to win. She received top-notch prenatal care, and they see her death as being an Act of God and no one's fault. No one could have predicted what happened. I'll meet with the hospital lawyer later this week and may come to some sort of settlement. I don't want you to be disappointed, just realistic."

"I want Von to have a trust fund so he can do something later in life. It's a travesty that he won't know his mother. A real travesty."

. . .

The milestone of Von turning one month old came swiftly and with celebration. It pressed on me that the day was also the anniversary of Selena's death. A day they'd always share.

"Careful when you hold him. You need to support his head." I put the baby in Victoria's arms. "Sit in the big chair with him, then you don't have to worry."

"You mean then you don't have to worry."

"You, my Victoria, can read me like a book."

The doorbell rang. Biiinnng Booonnng ...

I bounced down the stairs and opened the door. Even with his back turned, I recognized him immediately. A part of me froze while another leaped into action to slam the door, and turn all the locks into place. This couldn't be happening. Everything had been going so well. Happiness was within my grasp, and I couldn't let anything ruin that.

I leaned against the door and slid to the floor. The doorbell rang again. Victoria was standing with baby Von in her arms on the landing at the top of the stairs.

"Leslie? Are you okay? Who's at the door?"

I saw Victoria's feet and recognized how close she was to the edge. Her grip on the baby looked fragile and uncertain as she readjusted her stance. My heart skipped.

"It's no one," I breathed. "Victoria, step back from the stairs."

Victoria stared at me and didn't move.

"I said, get away from the stairs!" Even to me, I sounded like a crazy woman. Victoria's eyes grew large and her body stiffened. Shit. Sweat broke out all over my body, and my damp hands slipped against the floor.

Biiinnng Booonnng ...

Chapter Thirty-Nine

THEN

LESLIE

My still swollen belly ached for the baby's kick. I'd named my son Joseph. It made me smile when I thought of how I'd talked to him, and he'd responded from inside. We were one for so many months, but Mother expected me to forget and simply move on. How could I do that? I sensed his spirit around me, warm and protective. My heart and body longed for a stolen glance—a kiss, a touch. I didn't want to leave town and the only home I'd ever known. I didn't want to forget, but Mother said we must.

"Someone will find out and brand you a dirty slut," she spat. "Now we have to leave the only home I've known for my whole adult life—all because of you."

"We don't need to go, Mother. I want to go back to school

when I'm better. Everything still hurts, but I'll be fine. I promise." The tears wouldn't stop, especially since the birth was just
days before. I had no control. Even when I fought with all my
might, the tears flowed, and sobs tore through me. "Please,
Mother. I don't want to move."

"You lost any, and all, rights to decide anything in this
family. You've shown your true colors, and you'll do as I say
when I say."

I could barely move. Since the birth, I'd either been on the
couch in the front room or propped up in my bed. Any movement shot severe pains from my groin to my chest, then down
my legs. Mother took care of me. She wiped me down, carried
me from room to room, and changed my diaper every couple of
hours.

"I did well on those stitches, huh?" she said when she
changed me. "That baby of yours was huge—ripped you stem to
stern."

The only one who'd seen or touched me down there,
besides me, was Johnny. The thought of Mother examining and
wiping me filled me with burning shame and embarrassment. I
hid my face behind my hands.

I thought about the times with him and the tenderness he'd
shown me—especially in the beginning. My baby boy probably
would've looked like him. I squeezed my eyes shut and imagined his touch. He'd been rough at first, but it was because he
was excited. Other times, he was gentle and affectionate. We
had long talks, and he told me how he wanted to own his own
mechanic shop when he was older.

"We'll leave tomorrow. I've already told the landlord. Stop
blubbering and think about praying for some redemption. You
offered yourself to some boy when you should've been offering
yourself to God. I'm not sure you're worthy of his forgiveness,
so you best pray real hard."

I didn't hear her. I wanted to die and be with my baby, Joseph.

Mother helped me into the car's front seat the following day. She draped thin, ragged towels over the woven tan fabric of the seat on my side. Mother said it was to sop up leakage. The lap belt cut into my tender belly, and every time the car jerked, the towels slid and took me along. With each bounce, I lurched for the door handle to avoid slipping toward the floor. Blasts of blinding blue and white light slashed through my body at every turn.

I didn't know where we were going, but we drove for hours. Mother went through the drive-thru and ordered me a vanilla milkshake. I sucked on the straw for miles. The cool richness coated my belly for a while. Then, it boiled and rumbled until a sour stench wafted up and made me turn and hold my breath.

"Did you mess your diaper again? You're nothing but a baby yourself, aren't you? Well, we're not stopping, so you'll have to sit in your own filth until we get to where we're going."

I wept silently as I clung to the armrest. I desperately willed myself to die. I wanted to be with Joseph—to lie beside him and comfort him if he cried. I wanted to keep him warm and safe. I wanted to tell Johnny we'd had a baby boy. That our baby died. That we could try again. That I learned my lesson. Over and over, I prayed.

Mother turned into the driveway of a small older house on a side street lined with trees and parked cars. My butt lifted a couple of inches off the seat with the dip at the end of the driveway, but Mother didn't slow down. The neighborhood resembled something from an old-fashioned TV show, and I expected the perfect family to stroll across our path at any minute.

"Come on, girl. This is our new home. I don't want you being too loud, though, because the front part of the house has foreigners living in there. The house is a duplex but not side by side—it's front and back. We'll keep to ourselves, and everything'll be fine."

I lowered my feet to the ground and tried to stand, but my legs wouldn't hold me. There was no strength in my muscles, and there was no will in my being. As I waited in the car, Mother opened the front door of our new home and turned on a light. I saw the enormous whites of eyes peeking around the curtains at the front part of the property.

Mother returned to the open passenger door and yanked me from the car. My stomach heaved at the sudden movement, and my neck was like rubber—unable to hold up my heavy head. I leaned toward the car, opened my mouth, and a long slimy stream of white cream spilled from me as a brown pulpy liquid, tinged with brilliant red, ran down the inside of my leg and puddled at the top of my sock. I stared at it for a minute—what was it? I tried to touch it, but my hand wouldn't move. The watery fibrous flow tickled my skin. I wanted to scratch. I watched the furrowed brow on Mother's face. She kept fading away as her face squeezed tight, and though her lips moved, I couldn't hear her. Mother made no sense. I closed my eyes and floated back. Baby Joseph smiled at me, but he moved as soon as I reached for him.

I realized someone had heard my prayers as everything went black.

Chapter Forty

NOW

LESLIE

My resolve crumbled the morning the doorbell summoned me to the front door. After I slammed and locked it, I sat on the cold tiles with my back against the door. I couldn't move until I saw Victoria at the top of the stairs with the baby.

Damn it, I shouldn't have yelled, but Vic knew better, and the rule was no holding the baby near the stairs. One wrong step and ... I shook my head as my imagination took me to the darkest places. The doorbell rang again and pushed me to action. I scurried up the stairs and steered Victoria into the other room.

"Who's at the door?" Sofia asked as tears pooled near the edge of her eyes, ready to fall. "Is it a bad man?"

"Shut up, you idiot." Victoria kicked her sister's leg, but glanced up at me with raised eyebrows.

"No, it's not a bad man." I took the baby and softly bounced in one spot as he fussed. "It's a guy I saw once before and wasn't expecting to see again. It's nothing to worry about, I promise. Now, you guys go get cleaned up. Do not, I repeat, do not answer the door under any circumstances."

The girls went upstairs, and I thought about the man's face —it still swam before me as I tried to figure out why he rang my doorbell. I cradled the baby in my arms as I called Max.

"Hey, Leslie, what's up?"

"Max, something's going on." The words rushed from me. "Someone's after me, I know it."

"Whoa, slow down and tell me what happened."

"Someone tried to serve me today. It was the same guy as last time." The memory started my heart racing. "He was at my door less than a minute ago."

"Who's trying to subpoena you? We wrapped up the Phillip issue, and I haven't received anything on your behalf."

"Well, it must be someone who doesn't know you're my lawyer." I bounce-walked with Von tucked against me. "I need you to find out what's going on."

"Okay, give me a couple of hours, and I'll call you back. In the meantime, I suggest not answering the door."

"Gee, thanks." I peeked out the window to see the car still sitting there. "Hurry, okay? I have a bad feeling."

I grabbed a bottle from the half dozen the girls and I had made earlier. I warmed it and drew baby Von close. His mouth searched for the nipple, and once he found it, he drank greedily. "Your mommy loves you so much." I held the bottle and stroked his cheek. "I love you, too."

. . .

"Someone named Chad Spenser wants a DNA test for the baby," Max said. "That's what the subpoena is all about. You're being ordered to take the baby to a licensed physician to have blood drawn in order to complete the test."

"What? Max, that can't be right." I held the counter for fear of falling. "I'll never let it happen—I can't. He's mine. Selena would want him to be with me!"

"Les, you don't have a choice in this matter. Apparently, someone is claiming to be the father, and parental rights are first and foremost in importance when it comes to the welfare of the child. You know that."

"Max, they can't." I searched my brain for words. Nothing made any sense. "She was here for her entire pregnancy, and there wasn't one phone call or visit. What makes anyone think they can stroll in and take my baby?"

"Les, the baby isn't yours. The adoption papers aren't complete, and you don't have a choice. Chances are it's going to be negative, anyway. Don't start worrying about it now."

"They're going to take my baby."

"Leslie, if there's something you need to tell me, do it now. You know I don't like surprises."

"Oh. Max." I gripped the phone until my knuckles turned white. "Selena told me Chad is Von's father."

I thought about buying plane tickets to somewhere where they'd never find us. I'd take all three kids and disappear into the wilds of Chile or to the back streets of Italy. Even the vaguest thought of losing baby Von made my stomach drop. It would kill me, simple as that. I'd die. I spoke with the doctor, who diagnosed panic attacks and gave me a prescription to combat the anxiety. A year ago, I would've filled it immediately and gone straight to bed for a month for a first-class pity party. That was then. I shredded the prescription and did deep breathing exercises to the best of my ability.

I tiptoed up the stairs to where the girls watched a movie on Netflix. They were both stretched out on the floor. Von laid between them. He grabbed Victoria's finger as he cooed and drooled, watched closely by his young aunties. I winked at Victoria, backed out of the room, and pulled the door closed as quietly as I could.

With a deep breath, I attempted to control my racing pulse and walked to my bedroom. I tucked myself around the corner of the bedroom door, scrolled through my phone, and finally, after another deep breath, pushed a button. He answered immediately.

"Max, I need to talk to you privately. It's about ... about everything."

I hung up and crawled into bed. With my knees drawn up to my chest, I buried my face into the pillow to stifle a cry. My entire body heaved with my sobs.

The next morning, I woke to the baby's cries.

"Oh, my little man, you are soaked, aren't you? I think that's the longest you've slept. Such a good little guy, aren't you?"

"Leslie?"

I turned to see Sofia standing at the door. She wore the same clothes as yesterday, and her hair resembled the beginnings of a rat's nest.

"Good morning, sweetie." I smiled. "I'll be right down to make you some breakfast as soon as I finish up with Von."

"It's okay. You don't have to." She swiped her hand clumsily across her face to move the straggly hair. "We came and checked on you last night, but you were fast asleep, so we made our own dinner." She smiled proudly.

"Really? What did you make?"

"We made cereal, then had ketchup sandwiches for a

bedtime snack. But we're out of milk, so we wanted to make toast but couldn't find the toaster."

I closed my eyes as I listened. A heavy blanket of guilt wrapped around me as I shook my head.

"I'm sorry. You guys have been so patient with me, haven't you? I need to get my act together and start cooking and taking care of you."

"Vic said I shouldn't bother you because then you might not like us enough to keep us."

I laid the baby in the crib and kneeled to gaze into Sofia's eyes.

"It's not a matter of me liking you to keep you." I took her hand in mine. "We're a family. I'd never, ever send you, or your sister, away—never. I should've made you dinner last night—and breakfast this morning. I'm sorry. I guess I've been pretty down lately."

"You don't need to be sorry." Sofia patted my shoulder. "We love you."

"Oh, my baby girl, I love you, too. Come, give me a hug."

I went downstairs to make the girls' lunches, tucked Von into his snuggly, and walked them to school.

"It's parent-teacher interviews next week," Victoria said. "We had to make a special display envelope to hang up. Will you go, even though you're not our parent? It's okay if you don't. I can still bring the envelope home for you to see. It's no big deal. It's my last year of elementary, anyway."

"Are you kidding me? Like hell-o! I can't wait. I hope you can think of me as a parent, too, one day."

"I hope you can think of me as your kid," Sofia whispered.

"I'm here for you, and I do think of you as my kids." I made sure each girl heard me. "I'm learning things as I go, but I love you guys with all my heart. I'll meet you right here after school, okay?"

The girls raced across the field, and I watched until they were with the other kids. The baby nestling against me felt right as I stroked his back with long sweeping motions. He was mine—there was no doubt in my mind, but the girls needed me even more. They'd been through enough already. They needed my attention and constant validation every day. As I turned one last time to look at the girls, I realized how much I needed them, too.

"Come on, little man, we've got an appointment."

I drove to where Max kept an executive office. Polished and professional men and women carried leather briefcases as they strolled, scrolled, or chatted on their phones. I swung the Jeep into a spot where a willow tree cast a long shadow over the nearby vehicles, and I thought back to the first time I'd come here. At twenty-three, I'd ceased to function on a normal daily level within the world. My mother's darkness and vile nature severely hampered the simplest of tasks. I told a priest I needed an exorcism, which led to counseling, and finally, here. It was the priest who recommended Max. He said Max was a lawyer with a degree in common sense, and I'd need that to deal with all the fallout. Taking back the control meant everything. I strapped Von into the snuggly against my chest and made my way into the building.

"Leslie, good to see you," Max said as he came out to greet me. "Come on in. I'm curious what we couldn't talk about on the phone."

"Nice to hear you cut right to the heart of the matter." The words came out sounding harsh when I meant them to be teasing. "Sorry, I didn't mean to sound like such a bitch." I took a deep breath. "Max, you're my best friend. You've seen me through the darkest crap in my life, and you're the only one I trust. I need help before I do something stupid."

"Well, let's look at this little guy." He stepped toward me. I wasn't even sure he'd heard what I said. He sounded calm. "He sure is getting big."

"Yes." I glanced down and stroked his head as he slept against me. Safe. "The father wants to steal him."

"Come on, Les, let's sit down. What else is going on?" He took the chair opposite me and crossed his long legs.

"He's mine," I blurted out. "I'm the only one he knows, and strangers want to take him away." It was the first time I'd said it aloud. The reality choked the breath from me and made my pulse race. I wanted to run and never stop. "Max," I said, sliding to the edge of my seat. "I need your help." My mind raced in loops as all of my caged energy fought to be heard. I didn't know where to start as my forced semblance of contrived restraint shattered.

"Is this why you're here?"

"Selena told me how Chad used her and hurt her." I ignored his question as I stood and paced before him. "My head's so jumbled, it's not even funny. Von deserves to know his real father, but ... and then there're the girls ... oh God, Max, I'm not even sure I feel anything anymore. Does that make sense? Every step, every decision, takes another piece of me. When I close my eyes, I hear my mother telling me I'm a selfish whore." I paused directly in front of him. My hands shook as I rubbed the baby's back. "Max, I need help."

"Les, I'm glad you're here. Together, I think we can make some sense of all of this, okay?"

"I can't hand him over to strangers and walk away. He'd never be the same."

"Are you sure it's all about the baby?" He motioned for me to sit back down, and I did. "You've already lost so much in your life. Is this more about you?"

"Fuck you." I jumped to my feet and walked toward the door. I stopped and spun on my heel. "Who the hell do you think you are? This isn't about me, it's about this tiny person left to me by his mother. He belongs to me, with me—" I wiped my damp brow, not knowing whether to go or stay.

"Leslie, I'm sorry, but it needs to be considered. You're still grieving the loss of your own baby all those years ago. Is baby Von a replacement, or does he belong to someone else?"

"I've relived the nightmare every single night since Selena gave birth." I peeked down at Von's sleeping face snuggled close to my chest. "She died right in front of me." My voice cracked. "She was smiling and laughing one minute, then ..." I shook my head to clear the image. "I stood there like an idiot. Why didn't I do something? I should've done something—anything."

"Are you talking about Selena or your own baby?"

"Selena." I drifted back to the leather chair. "My baby, too. Yeah, both, I guess. I don't know."

"Leslie, why did you call me?"

"I need help. I need—"

"Okay, fair enough." He leaned forward, resting his elbows on his knees. "Do you remember what you told me the first time we met?"

"Yes," I said, nodding. "I have PTSD like a wounded soldier who'd forgotten to push the reset button." I closed my eyes. "This is different, though," I whispered. "It's about the baby."

"Think about it, Leslie. Is his birth family violent? Will Von be in danger? Leslie, is it about the baby?"

A heavy silence hung over the room as I considered Max's

words. A sharp, throbbing truth undulated in the bottom of my gut. I pushed it down to squelch any validity beyond my own. Knowledge. Conjecture. I didn't want any of it, but each breath brought the inside closer to the outside.

"No," I murmured quietly. Max nodded toward me, and I turned away. The truth released itself but offered me no answers, relief, or plan of action. My thoughts filled me as the cloak of silence shielded my fears and doubts.

"Max," my voice sliced through the thick, stifling air, "I'm tired of being the good one. The one who always does the right thing for everyone else. Maybe this time I'll pack up and move to Central America."

"Is that who you are or want to be?"

I studied the floor. I had no words.

"It won't be easy." He reached for my hand. "You're a survivor. You'll come through this. We'll negotiate visitation and ensure you impact this little fellow's life." He smiled. "Also, don't forget you're the legal guardian to the baby's two aunts, which is very special. It's not like you're leaving him on a doorstep and walking away."

I'd gone through it all in my mind repeatedly.

"That little guy is a beautiful gift from a girl who loved you like a mother."

"I miss her so much ..."

"Les, I can help you reset everything and get back on track, but I have something to show you. I'm not sure this is the right moment, but it's probably time you take this and deal with it." Max walked across the carpeted office to the filing cabinet in the far corner. He used a key to open the top drawer, then flipped through the files. "This," he held up a thick golden brown manilla, "has been left undone for far too long now."

I knew what it was. It was the past, and I didn't want it. Adrenaline surged again, and Von wiggled. He probably sensed my heart rate double. Max took both my hands and placed the package in them. It had softened with age, smelled musty, and made me sneeze. Another envelope was inside. CONFIDEN-TIAL in big red letters caught my sight. My eyes welled up, and I glanced at Max.

"Listen, this was sent here at your request so we could open it together. Leslie, it's past due. We need to deal with this."

"Seriously, I can't, Max. I'm not ready. It doesn't matter anymore. Life has changed, and I don't care about the past anymore. I just can't."

Chapter Forty-One

THEN

LESLIE

The bright lights on the ceiling flicked by like fireflies going in the opposite direction as fast as they could. I had wings as the air whooshed over me, cooling my damp skin.

"Leslie, can you hear me?" It was a woman with short, cropped brown hair. The woman's hair and chubby cheeks bounced with her physical effort as she jogged somewhere alongside me. I wanted to tell her to slow down—not to worry. "We're taking you to the operating room." She talked as though she had a wad of bubblegum in her mouth. I tried to understand, but it made no sense. The sudden stop of forward motion made my gut jump as everything continued to move and spin around me. My eyelids grew heavy as a group of people came and talked to me in their secret coded language. I felt no fear as they slipped a needle into my arm. A warmth spread, and a heaviness forced all thought from me ... I was ready to die.

"Leslie. Sweetie, it's time to wake up." Someone slapped my hand. "Come on, it's time to come back. I'm your nurse, Niki. The doctor fixed you all up, and you're going to be fine." Her voice trailed off as her moist, soft hands ran down the length of my arms.

My body didn't work. My mouth, my eyes, my arms. A warm, thick pool of drool oozed down my chin toward my neck. It was like melting ice cream as it crept and tickled ever so slowly over the flesh to leave a slimy trail of evidence.

"There you go." The nurse swabbed at the drool. "Don't you worry now. You'll be able to talk soon enough."

"Baba," I moaned.

"You want some water? Okay, I'll get you some ice chips that you can suck on."

My head fogged up, and I wanted to sleep—to slip away forever. I didn't want water; I wanted my baby.

Chapter Forty-Two

NOW

LESLIE

I donned a pair of oversized sunglasses to cover my red, swollen eyes. Makeup had worked wonders to conceal the broken blood vessels in my cheek—crying for twenty-four hours straight wasn't great for the skin. The slightest notion of losing Von sent me reeling. Each time I moved or reached for something, my abs screamed and my head constantly ached from blowing my nose, and I had chapped and raw lips from biting down to stifle a sob. I avoided as many people as I could as I clung to the fray of life surrounding me. My daily walks to and from school with the girls were the only time I went out, unless deemed necessary.

Meeting with Max had brought me back down to earth.

Sometimes, I wondered how he could gaze straight into my soul and understand me better than I did myself.

I waited by the chain-link fence on the edge of the school field. Normally, I met the girls in the triangle park, but today they wanted me to come to the school to meet them.

"I don't enjoy going all the way in either," a voice beside me said. "Some moms in there are cliquey. I'm not very good at that stuff. It's much safer to wait here."

I turned to find Limpy-Mommy standing right beside me. Her voice sounded mature and articulate. Over time, I'd imagined she'd talked with a lisp and twang—sort of thick and slow.

"Yeah, I didn't want to have to make small talk either." I nodded. "I don't know any of them, and I'm not really interested."

"Are you the foster mom for Victoria and Sofia?" She stepped back and covered her mouth with her hand. Her long, elegant fingers wrapped around her face. "I'm so sorry," she mumbled through her hand. "That was terribly rude of me, and again, I apologize. It's none of my business."

"It's all right." I forced a weak smile. "I'm actually adopting them both."

"That's wonderful. My Emmy, she's in the same grade with Sofia. I guess the principal discussed the ... you know ... the tragedy with the students. It was awful what happened to the parents, but it's those little girls I worried about most."

I studied this young woman for a moment, as though reassessing her entire existence.

"My name is Leslie." I stuck out my hand.

"Hi," she said as she wiped her hand on her shirt and took mine. "I'm Autumn. It's nice to meet you. I thought about you when I heard the news."

"What do you mean, you thought about me?"

"The school parents are pretty gossipy, which is why I'm

not over there." She cocked her head to where a group of mothers gathered around the playground as they waited for their kids to get out of school. "Someone said you lived in the ritzy townhouses on the other side of the highway, and you'd taken the girls in. They said you planned to send the girls away to some preppy private school."

"I do live in those townhouses, but I didn't know they were ritzy. I have to get closer to the gossip, so I know what's going on."

"I hope I didn't offend you."

"No, not at all. I'm glad you told me because it gives me some insight into what the girls are going through with the other students."

"I like you. You're smart."

"Well, thank you. I try."

"You know, Leslie, I've been studying those townhouses for the last few months, wondering which one was yours. I didn't think I'd ever actually meet you."

I was taken aback. She'd been studying my neighborhood? Looking for me? Every morning for months, I'd sat in my enormous chair and watched Limpy-Mommy make her way over the horizon and off to wherever. I realized how in-my-head I was for so long. Heck, I'd forgotten other people had lives and curiosities, too.

"And yet here we are." I wanted to pull those words back. It sounded sanctimonious. "I'm thrilled to meet you. You're the first mom in the school I've met."

The bell rang, and minutes later, the playground was full of kids.

I saw the girls right away. They walked with another little girl, and as soon as they saw me, they broke into a full-out race. I held up my hand to slow them down for fear of being knocked right over.

"Whoa, girls, remember I have Von under here." I flapped the excess material of my oversized poncho.

"You have a baby?" Autumn raised her eyebrows.

I heard Max in my head. "It's not your baby. You had a baby, but this is not the one. This baby has a father who wants a relationship with him. This is not your baby."

"He's not my baby. I'm just taking care of him."

The girls gathered around and lifted the tasseled edge to see the sleeping infant. He hadn't stirred, and even with the cooler air getting in, he was content to snuggle close.

"He's my nephew, isn't he, Mommy Leslie?" Sofia asked.

"Yes, Sofia, he sure is. He's lucky to have aunties like you and Victoria. He's surrounded by women that love him."

"Well, it was nice to meet you, Leslie. I hope we'll see each other here again. This is my daughter, Emmy," Autumn said.

I watched as the younger version of her mother tucked in behind the stroller and hid from view.

"It's nice to meet you, Emmy. We'll have to get you over for a playdate with Sofia. We'll see you again soon." I looked at Autumn. "It was a pleasure. Thank you for letting me in on all the goings-on around here. I appreciate it." I turned. "Come on, girls, it's time to go home."

With all the goodbyes said, we trudged up the path toward the highway. The last few days had been turbulent and had left a lot of skeletons rattling in my brain. When I thought back to how Mother treated me, I wanted to scream. I was a kid who didn't know any better—my younger self deserved much more. I also considered Phillip's betrayal during our marriage. He knew my entire past, and still, he screwed with my brain—asshole. The only redeeming thing of this day was meeting and chatting with Limpy-Mommy. Meeting such a pleasant young woman was a real pleasure. Autumn, her name is Autumn.

"Did you mean what you said?" Sofia tugged on my hand as we walked.

"Which part?"

"You said I could have Emmy over for a playdate?"

"Yes, of course, I meant it. Would you like that?"

"I don't know. I've never done it before. Mama wouldn't let us have friends over, and no one ever invited me. I think they were afraid of Gilbert."

I smiled down at the little girl, glad I still had my sunglasses on. I'd allowed myself to get wrapped up in the baby and Selena, and had totally forgotten that these two little souls not only lost their sister, but their mother, too. God, how selfish could I be? I kept in step beside the girls as I pulled Sofia's hair back and stroked her head.

"We'll do it as soon as possible, okay?"

My heart swelled at the innocent glance and eager nod. These two girls were brimming with love, and I realized it was about time I opened my heart to receive their generous, untainted gift.

It was time to sit down with the girls and have a straightforward conversation about what was going on. It would not be easy.

"I don't want Von to go live anywhere else. He belongs here with us."

"I know, Vic. I don't want him to go either. But he has a daddy who wants to get to know him, too. Imagine if someone tried to keep you from your mom. That wouldn't seem fair, would it?"

"No." I saw Victoria contemplating the situation. "Could the dad come live here with us? I don't want Von to leave."

"Here's the thing. Chad, that's the baby's daddy, has his

own home and family, and he wants Von to live with him there. Chad's mom and dad live there, so he'd have lots of help, and Von wouldn't be alone. I know we'll miss him terribly, but his daddy will love him, too. Does that make sense?"

"Could he come visit?"

"Oh my goodness, yes!" I jumped up and clapped my hands to turn the doom and gloom into something positive and upbeat. "Von would visit on holidays, and any time he wanted to. Did you know you and Sofia have a powerful role to play, and that's the cool auntie!"

"What's a cool auntie?"

"It's just about the best thing in the world. You're not Von's mom, you don't have to worry about feeding him or saving for his college. And you're not his sister, so you don't have to worry about him bugging you when you're trying to talk to your boyfriend." I winked. "You'd be the cool auntie. He could tell you his secrets and confide his deepest wishes to you. It's a special relationship. Then, you send him home and let other people, like his dad, take care of the big serious stuff. How does that sound?"

"Sounds okay." Victoria wasn't totally convinced. "I'm going to have to think about this."

"I want to be honest with you and Sofia. The choice is out of our hands. Von will go to live with his dad. It's just a matter of time. It doesn't mean we love him any less. In fact, I think it shows him how much we love him, because letting someone go is much harder than holding them close."

"I miss Selena."

It was the first time Victoria had opened up even a crack with me.

"Come here." I pulled Victoria close. I felt the stiffness, but as I held her, she softened into the hug. "I miss her, too."

Chapter Forty-Three

THEN

LESLIE

My eyelids were heavy, and didn't want to open. A curious beeping in the background called to me, though, as I forced my lids to flutter. There, at the end of my bed, Mother sat ramrod straight and unsmiling. I nearly laughed because the bizarreness of Mother's nearness was so foreign.

The signals from a monitor kept dinging softly in the background. The pale green curtains that framed the window enhanced the stark white walls, but couldn't compete with the scent of disinfectant and floor cleaner.

I kept my eyes near closed as I imagined Mother lying unconscious on the shiny floor after being surprised by a powerful kick to the head. A giggle tickled my brain, a poof of air escaped my lips, and my foot moved.

"Leslie?" She jumped off the bed and leaned over me. "Can you hear me?"

Her dank breath swirled over my face. The smell of sour egg salad and coffee caused an involuntary recoil on my part. I didn't want to answer her. I wanted to feign death and have her disappear from my life forever, but I knew better. I nodded.

"Remember what I told you?" Her teeth, caked with gunk, sneered and threatened. "Remember when you had the baby, and the doctor came? You remember the doctor, don't you?"

I couldn't think. Why was she in my face? The pushing and the pain—oh, the intense pain—I remembered that, but I didn't remember anyone except Mother and me. She gave me a needle that made me sleepy. The entire experience was full of dark shadows—sometimes, I wasn't sure it had happened at all.

"You let me do the talking." Mother pinched my arm. "Is that clear?"

I held my breath against her stench and shifted my face away.

"Mother," the words croaked out my dry throat. "Mother, I want ... I want my baby."

"Shut up, you silly, stupid girl," she hissed in my ear. "There is no baby."

Mother stood back from the bed, her face flushed a bright crimson, her mouth a tight line. She wore her Sunday best. A full-length, dark gray wool coat-dress buttoned tight to her throat. It hung like a heavy shroud, obscuring the vile reality beneath. The door to the room swung open with a sudden whoosh. A dark man in a white coat with a stethoscope draped around his neck entered, with four others dressed exactly the same.

"Hi, Leslie." He passed right by Mother and came to my bedside. "I'm Dr. Anders, and I'm glad to see you're awake. You had us worried for a while there. How're you feeling?"

"Tired, I guess." I peeked over at Mother, who stood by the window and out of the doctor's way. She stared straight ahead with her hands clutched before her.

"Yes, well, you have a right to be tired." He checked the chart. "Case history, Dr. Stewart."

"Yes, sir, a clipped young voice said. "Miss Leslie Matheson, aged fifteen, presented at ER eight days ago. She was four to seven days postpartum and suffering from an infection due to fourth-degree tears of the perineum. The skin, muscles, and anus—all compromised. Patient was placed on heavy sedation and antibiotics for three days to reduce fever and infection, at which time she underwent reconstructive surgery for the torn perineum."

I listened in disbelief. I didn't remember any of it. If I closed my eyes, I could hear Mother and a faraway siren, but I could also hear Johnny telling me he'd love me forever.

"Prognosis?" the senior doctor asked.

"A full recovery with no ongoing musculoskeletal pain expected after all healing is complete." I watched as the young doctor continued to speak robotically about me, as though he'd memorized everything. He glanced over at me before continuing. "The patient's uterine scarring caused by the infection may decrease the overall health of the endometrial lining and cause infertility in later years." I squeezed my eyes shut as tight as I could. I wanted them all to go away and end this nightmare. I pictured myself with my books clenched tightly against my chest as I meandered down the hall, hoping to see Johnny. My heart raced when I saw him and our paths merged. We'd bump into each other. The fire would start.

My reverie ended when a tear escaped from the corner of my eye and sped into my ear. I wanted to die. To be left alone with my dreams and skewed memories, but the doctor wanted answers.

"Leslie, could you tell us about the birth and the baby?" he asked with a silken voice that stroked the air between us. "Where's the baby?"

My eyes flew open, and I searched the room for Mother. She still stood by the window, now with her hands shoved deep into the pockets of her bulky dress. I felt, rather than saw, the fury in her eyes, so I spun my head back as fast as I could.

"The baby was born dead." Mother's voice boomed through the room. I wondered if she meant to say it so loud. Her declaration sounded like an accusation, and it filled every available crevice.

I wept silently. I couldn't help it. The thought of my kicking, active baby being yanked so violently from my body that it tore the muscles and flesh reinforced my will to die. I wanted to be with my baby.

"There ... there was a doctor," Mother continued. "I don't know his name. We don't have a lot of money. The fact she got herself pregnant in the first place was an atrocity, then I had to pay a doctor good hard-earned money to birth a dead baby."

I didn't move or speak. Mother was lying, and I knew it. I wondered if this doctor could tell. I opened my eyes and glared at her. Mother stared back. The unspoken threat was mine alone to see, and I knew better than to question her.

"Why didn't you go to the hospital for the birth?" the doctor demanded, his silky voice gone.

"We didn't have the money," Mother sneered at him. "I don't know if you realize it, but going to a hospital costs money." She waved her hand toward me. "Besides, she's otherwise a healthy young woman, and I didn't foresee any issues."

I heard a rustle amongst the medical students as they murmured to each other and shuffled their feet.

"Hmm—we don't see a problem until it's set before us," the doctor said, with his arms crossed in front of him. "Your daughter will recover fully from her physical wounds, but there are serious consequences that could arise from the infection." He shook his head and gawked at Mother. "Your daughter's emotional scars are a different story, and I would recommend she talk to the hospital psychologist prior to discharge."

"Is it a requirement of her treatment here?" Mother crossed her arms.

"It is not a requirement." I watched the doctor take a deep breath before he continued. "It is merely a suggestion in order to best serve your daughter's mental health."

"Well, then, I'll tell you I don't believe in that sort of doctoring and can tell you it's unnecessary. Leslie will be fine with me." She shot me a glance that warned me to keep my mouth shut. "The girl had an infection, is all, and it's done now."

"Actually, the problem is that your daughter gave birth to what appears to be a full-term fetus." He shook his head as his fingers gripped tighter on the chart. The vein in his temple throbbed as though it were trying to break free. "Your daughter had no prenatal care, no medical support, and gave birth in an unsterile environment." He scowled at Mother. "And that, madam, is the problem."

"Doctor, women have babies every day in the fields and continue to work the rest of the day." Mother stepped closer to the doctor. "Don't tell me you need a doctor to have a baby."

"Madam, you are completely correct, but Leslie wasn't in a field and had access to a hospital and trained medical personnel who could've prevented her injuries and saved her baby."

"You don't know that."

I glared at Mother.

"Could a doctor have saved my baby? I remember hearing him cry. Mother, my baby cried, I know he did."

"You know nothing," she spat as she swung around and

bore her eyes into mine. "There was nothing anyone could've done. He was born dead. He'd probably been dead for weeks."

I stopped listening. My baby was alive—he kicked and danced through the whole thing. I wanted to stand up and spit in her face.

Chapter Forty-Four

NOW

LESLIE

Today was the day Max had scheduled a meeting with Chad's family.

I followed him reluctantly down the hallway. The baby slept in his car seat, and as I entered, all eyes swung in my direction. If I turned now, they'd notice. Shit. Opportunity missed. With shaking hands, I hoisted the car seat up onto the boardroom table. I concentrated on the glossy finish reflecting the lights in wavy movements. I wished I could disappear from existence. *Who the hell are these people, anyway? Oh, no.*

I snuck a glance at Max. His face was serious and gave nothing away. I wrinkled my nose at the foreign smells of these strangers. I already despised them. A bubble of darkness surrounded me, and I couldn't move. Max's hand lightly touched my shoulder. It reminded me I wasn't alone.

"Hello, everyone. We're all here in the best interest of Von. It's been legally determined that Chad," Max nodded toward him, "is the biological father. In order to bring about a peaceful and amenable transfer of the baby from one home to another, we must discuss logistics."

"Max, stop," I blurted out. "I can't do this. Selena—"

"We're here to discuss the situation." He inched closer to me. "This will be a slow process as we work together in the best interest of this child." Max strode to his desk, where he shuffled some papers. "Today, we'll discuss visitation and the documentation required to avoid any conflict or confusion in the future." Max cleared his throat and scanned the room. "Leslie, let's start with you. Do you have anything you want to say?"

I assessed the family across the table. The mother wore a white dress covered by a simple tailored jacket. She fingered her long silver heart necklace. Von would love to play with that. The woman's blonde curls hung loosely and framed her slim face. She was probably the same age as me, and appeared healthy enough to still have the energy for a youngster. She'd probably end up being Von's primary caregiver. I wasn't stupid enough to believe any teenage boy would do it all. I wondered if the woman remembered chatting with me at the doctor's office. I liked her then. That was before I knew who she was, though.

The husband stood well over six feet, with a muscular build and dark tan. He had his hand on his wife's chair in, what I considered, a protective stance. It was hard to tell if he was all-in with this idea of taking on another baby.

Beside the dad was a young girl—probably Victoria's age. Her phone was face down in front of her on the table, and she checked it every minute. At one point, the mom reached over, took the phone, and placed it out of reach. The girl shot her mother a scathing look, but didn't act out.

Then, at the end of the long table, there was a man in a suit —the family lawyer, I assumed—and finally, Chad.

I understood what Selena saw in him. He had a puppy dog look about him. His soft curls and full lips gave him a look of innocence, but I knew better.

"Why are you here, Chad?" I stared straight at him as he fidgeted in his chair.

"How come you gave me a fat lip outside of Java Jenny's that day?"

He was challenging me, and I wanted to wipe the arrogant smugness right off his face. His bravado was fragile, though, as he hung his head to avoid seeing me. I recognized the immaturity, but also the strength behind his words. He'll never forget that fat lip as long as he lives.

"Chad, that's enough," the mother interjected. The room went still. "I didn't make him come here, if that's what you're implying. This is something he wants to do."

"I'm talking to Chad." My eyes caught the quick glance between mother and son, and I heard his mumbled apology. "I don't want to be rude, but I need to hear it from him."

"Actually, it was all me," he said. "When I found out Selena had a baby, I knew it had to be mine, and I wanted to step up. My family supports me."

"Are you still dating that horrid Scottie girl?"

"No, she was actually jealous of Selena. After Selena and I, ah ..." He blushed and glanced at his mom. "After we started dating, I meant to break up with Scottie, but I ... I was stupid. I didn't think Scottie was coming back."

"Did Selena dump you?"

"Yes. We dated for over a couple of months, but I, ah, forgot to break it off with Scottie. I wasn't expecting Selena to come to our school. Everything was good until Scottie came back. Then one night at Java Jenny's, Scottie wanted to call Selena out, but I ah," he looked into my eyes, "um, I injured my knee and fought with Scottie. Both dumped me that night, I guess."

"What did you see in Selena that was special?"

"You know, she pretended to be tough, but she was the gentlest person I knew." He blushed a deeper red. "I'm not saying that because we, ah ... like, had sex and stuff. We talked, too. She had dreams and wanted to do well in school."

"How did you find out about the baby?"

"Mrs. Bonder told me."

"Yes." I nodded. "Selena told me this baby," I peeked down at Von, who stirred in his car seat, "was conceived through a mutual need to be together. It was a time in her life where she needed to feel love, and you were put before her." My throat got dry, and my voice broke. "She cared for you. This baby is a part of both of you, and he deserves your full and unconditional love. Do you understand what I'm saying?"

Chad got out of his chair and walked around the table to where I stood. He came closer, and I thought he was about to take the baby, but instead, he embraced me. His tears fell to my shoulder, and I wanted to kick and punch him for the pain he'd caused, but I put my arms around him and soothed the boy, who was all too soon made a man.

I needed to step back and look at the entire situation. Von wasn't mine. The talk with Max had set me straight. The girls, however, were mine, but not this precious and final piece of Selena.

"I think it's time you held your son." I picked up the baby and put him in his arms. "There you go. Hold him tight."

Oh, how many times had I wished to hear those same words? For someone to hand over my son—to recognize the need for parent and child to be together. Tears burned behind my eyes, and I fought them off as I stepped back. Everyone stood at once. His sister rushed to his side and stroked the baby's chubby fingers.

"I understand your reluctance to give him up." Chad's mother stood by my side. "Thank you for being tenacious and strong for those who can't speak for themselves. I admire your devotion to Selena and to the baby."

"To be honest, I'm terrified to let him out of my sight—out of my control—but ..."

Chad's mother pulled me into a firm embrace before I could stop her. Through the hug, I felt the gratitude and tender yearning of someone who wasn't a threat, but an ally.

"Go." I broke from the hug and stepped back. "Go meet your grandson."

The family appeared to be in awe of baby Von as he cooed and waved his arms.

Initially, I wanted to fight—to make Chad admit how much he hurt Selena. I was ready to dig in and fight like hell, until I told Max.

"Is that what you want, Les?" He sat across from me as I mapped out my strategy.

"What do you mean? Of course, it's what I want." I shook my head, trying to grasp Max's question. "Chad totally blind-sided Selena. He used her and threw her away like a piece of trash. I want him to answer to the courts—to me."

"Leslie, if we go to trial on this, you'll also be open for cross-examination."

"I have done nothing wrong. I took Selena in when she was all alone. I cared for her and gave her a home."

"Yes, that's all well and good." He reached for a pen. "I'm more concerned regarding questions about your past. The defense will dig up any, and all, dirt on you they can find. They'll ask why your marriage ended and what happened when you were young."

"They couldn't ask that. No one knows about the baby."

"Come on, Les. Think about it. They'll put Phillip on the stand, and I'm sure he'll have a lot to say. A woman with an eating disorder refuses to leave the house and stalks young girls. They can spin it any way they want." He scribbled something on a piece of paper. "Leslie, they'll crucify you."

The flood of my past shames choked me. The fact that things outside of my control could affect my life, or the lives of the children, sickened me. It all made me want to fight for vindication.

"The adoption for the girls isn't final yet," he continued. "That needs to be the priority. They don't need to be dragged through a trial that you're bound to lose. Remember, Chad is the biological father, and his family is standing behind him."

"I won't lose. Selena would've wanted me to have the baby." I stared at a paperclip that was on the floor near my foot.

"I'm sorry, but it doesn't matter what Selena wanted." Max stood and walked toward my chair. "Les, Selena is dead, and Von has a biological father and family who want him. You're never going to win."

As I studied the family around baby Von, my heart ached for Selena. The overwhelming grief I'd pushed aside in order to care for Von stirred within me, and I trusted Max had been correct in his assessment. It nearly killed me to stay back and allow Chad to get to know his son. I knew Selena was nearby. Watching. Loving. It was the right thing to do.

After the meeting, I left with Von and drove straight to the girls' school. I didn't want them at this first meeting. I needed to get a handle on myself first. There'd be plenty of time and opportunity for the girls to meet Chad and make up their own minds. Today was the first step.

I parked the Jeep at the school, carried Von in his car seat into the office, and had the girls paged. Both came down and were excited to see me at first, but then fear filled their eyes. I realized the last time someone pulled them from class, their mother was dead, and social workers took them into custody.

"Hey, Victoria. Hey, Sofia," I kept my voice light. "Von and I came to sneak you out early so we could go for ice cream." I whispered it like a special secret for only their ears.

"Really?" Sofia's large eyes stared up at me. "Won't my teacher get mad when I don't come back?" She glanced toward her sister.

"The principal will tell her. I made arrangements."

"I don't want to go," Victoria declared loudly. "I want to stay here and be with my friends. Ice cream is stupid."

"Okay, Vic. That's fine." I realized my mistake. "Tell you what, we'll go another time, okay? It's not a big deal." Sofia heaved a sigh of relief. "You guys go back to class, and I'll be in the same spot to pick you up like always, okay?" I gave them both a kiss and sent them back to their classrooms.

As I watched them walk down the hallway, I realized how young they were and how much they'd already been through. Baby Von wouldn't live with us forever, but we'd still all be a family. Halfway down the hall, Sofia smiled and waved. I blew her a kiss and watched until I could no longer see them.

These two girls were mine to raise and educate into

productive citizens. We'd have Von to always link us back to Selena. I'd never let them forget their sister.

I checked my phone and saw I had three hours to kill before school ended. I could go home for a nap or get some shopping done. Instead, I picked up the car seat, and sprinted for the car. I knew exactly what I needed to do.

Chapter Forty-Five

THEN

LESLIE

"Come on, Leslie, don't lollygag. It's taken you all day to clean the kitchen. What's wrong with you today?"

I couldn't even look at Mother. Every time I did, the lies and betrayal stung like razor-sharp thorns pushed into my flesh. A burning hatred gurgled up from my gut and threatened to spill out as I struggled to keep it in check. My baby would've turned one-year-old today. He'd be a chubby, healthy baby who jabbered and stumbled over his own feet as he drooled and giggled. The searing pain tore through my heart as much as the physical pain had torn at my body exactly one year before.

No one knew.

No one cared.

Sometimes, I'd babysit for the people down the street, and

pretended the little boy was mine. I'd put on an apron and be a wife and mother for a few hours. The two-year-old loved to play Drop It and Pick It Up. For hours he'd drop a toy, and I dutifully picked it up—together, we laughed. I stroked his soft hair and traced my finger down the side of his face.

Around babies, it was like my feet got stuck deep in gumbo mud that sucked me down and trapped me beneath a thick crust of melancholy. I tried not to pay attention to the world because, when I did, all I saw were baby boys and pregnant women.

After they'd released me from the hospital, Mother and I returned to the rental house, where the eyes of strangers peeked out from behind the curtain. I understood because I, too, hid behind a barrier as a foreigner in the normal world. The memories didn't fade. I returned to a new school after my recovery. Nothing helped. Mother kept an eagle-eyed watch, but I bided my time.

"Leslie?" I shook myself back to reality from the close vicinity of her voice. "What in the world are you doing? You need to answer when I call. I tell you, you're going to be the death of me."

"Sorry, Mother." I tried to sound sincere, but even to my ears, my voice sounded flip. "I was just thinking."

"Well, stop the nonsense and get on with the cleaning."

"Today, my baby would've turned one." I allowed the words to escape from me. "He'd be calling me mama by now."

Mother stopped in her tracks, then returned to loom over me. She swung her arm around and slapped me across the face. Like a clap of thunder, the blow rumbled across the room. I slumped to the floor. The sting prickled through my cheek, and I tasted blood in my mouth. I stayed down.

"There. Was. No. Baby." She clenched her teeth as she stooped over me. "Is that clear? If you want a reputation as a slut, then you go ahead and continue, but it won't be in my home. There was no baby. Period. It's something you dreamed up in a state of fever-induced hallucinations. Do you understand?"

From the corner of my eye, I saw froth had formed at the corners of her mouth, and her eyes glazed over in madness. It brought back the memory of when she discovered I was pregnant, and she'd kicked me over and over again as I cupped my belly to protect myself. This time, she used the broom. She batted at me with the bristles as I pulled my legs up and tucked my head into my chest. There was no place for me to go and no place to hide. Finally, Mother tired and threw the broom on top of me, stomping her feet.

"Sweep this house, then you go kneel on the bottom step and do penance for that foul mouth of yours. You need to pray for forgiveness. There's no supper for you tonight." She gawked at me. "Well, what're you waiting for?" She kicked my side. "Move."

To fight was futile, but to forget was not an option.

Mother never hit me again. I became the perfect daughter and model student. Graduation couldn't come fast enough. I worked hard and secured a full scholarship to the University of Washington State. In my last act of attrition, I, in my cap and gown, stood beside Mother for pictures for the newspaper. Winning the top scholarships had a price, but I dutifully smiled and stood where I was told. Soon I'd be free of her forever.

The next day, I packed my bag and left, vowing never to speak to that woman ever again.

Chapter Forty-Six

NOW

LESLIE

Today, Von would go to live with the Spenser family. It came all too fast. I woke with a knot in my gut as I got the girls up. We'd all go to Max's office to deliver baby Von to his new family. I came to realize the girls took their cue from me, so I fought hard to stay calm and positive. I wanted the girls to know and understand that this was the right thing to do.

"Did you bring his blanket?" Victoria asked, as she handed over a bag of his clothes.

"I was going to, but decided he needed his favorite blanket here. So, I didn't pack it."

"Good thinking." Victoria said. She checked around the baby's room and made a beeline to the picture of him lying with Selena right after his birth. "She's pretty, don't you think?"

"I sure do. She also has a beautiful spirit that surrounds us every day. Do you feel her with you?"

"Sometimes, I guess. Last week, a boy wanted me to sneak off the playground with him and go to his house." Oh, my God. I held my breath and let Victoria continue. "I thought about it, but I could hear Selena whispering in my ear that it wasn't a good idea." She looked up at me. "Is that what you mean by spirit?"

Shocked that Victoria even told me this story, I was careful not to overreact. I let my breath go and gingerly placed my hand on her shoulder.

"Yes. That's exactly what I mean. You know, Victoria, I believe your older sister was protecting you. What makes me so happy is that your heart is open, so you can hear those warnings. I'm so proud of you."

"Really?"

"Yes, really." I smiled. "You made a mature and grown-up decision. That's very cool."

Victoria pulled her shoulders back and stood taller as she smiled up at me.

I made a mental note to talk to Victoria about going to boys' homes and stuff. I wasn't much older myself when I got pregnant. The memories flooded back and filled me with remorse, guilt, and loss. If I could go back with the knowledge I had today, I would've escaped from Mother and told a teacher. My baby didn't have to die in a secret home birth planned by a maniac who had no sense of reality or morality.

"Victoria, I love you." The words were out of my mouth before I realized it. A bright pink crept into the girl's cheeks, and her eyes widened for a moment.

"I love you, too." She shot across the room and clung to me as she wiped her tears and snotty nose on my shirt.

I'd never seen such a hard little girl. But the shell, now

cracked, let the promise of goodness seep through. I knew it was going to be an uphill battle, but the foundation was taking hold.

"What do you say we go get Sofia and Von? We need to pack and get ready to go. You two will have to decide whether one of you wants to move into Selena's bedroom. We can paint it and change it if you like."

"I think me and Sofia need to sleep in the same room for a while. She drives me nuts, but I'm used to her. I don't think she'd do well without me."

"See, there it is again. You care so much. I hadn't even thought of that, but I can see how you're so right."

Victoria beamed, and I smiled.

Over the last month, baby Von had overnight visits with Chad's family and even one weekend. He was close to seven months old, and I knew I needed to let him go, or it would become more difficult. Von went easily with Chad and settled back here with no problem.

On the first overnight visit, my heart ached. An emptiness filled me as I paced and worried. I re-downloaded the app for GrubHub on my phone, and came close to ordering from a bunch of different fast-food restaurants in order to numb my brain, but I thought of Victoria and the spirit of Selena saying stop, be safe. Instead, I scrubbed the entire house from top to bottom. Every tile, surface, and wall—scoured, buffed, and sanitized. It kept me from thinking of Von—it was the only way to get through the night, and the house had never been this clean.

"Today's the day," Max announced.

The energy was palpable as I stood near Max's desk with Von. The Spenser family was ready to move forward, and so was I.

"Hey girls," I said, "come give your nephew a kiss, then he's going with his daddy for a couple of weeks."

"Don't worry, I got this." Chad took Von in his arms. Over the last month, Chad had cut his hair, renovated his bedroom to fit the crib, and got a part-time job to help with expenses. "Hey, son, let's go home."

I didn't want my tears to upset anyone, so I studied the sky through the window. I wiped my face and gave Von another kiss. I squeezed Max's hand to convey my thanks then followed the Spenser family outside. The mood was one on anticipation, but also transition. Life was moving forward at warp speed and acceptance was paramount. We waved and blew kisses to baby Von, then the girls and I climbed in the Jeep and drove away from the office building.

"You missed our turn," Sofia said as she twisted in her seat to point at the road sign.

"I did, didn't I?"

"Where are we going? Are we going to go visit someone? Or are we going to drive by Chad's house like we did before, when he had the baby?"

"No, no." I rolled my eyes in exaggeration and perhaps some embarrassment that the girls figured it all out. "I actually have a surprise for you guys."

"What is it?"

"Wow. Please contain your excitement. You two look skeptical."

"I don't like surprises," Victoria said.

"Okay, Victoria. I'll give you a hint. Let's see—where in the world would you most like to go if you could?"

"Disneyland," the girls answered in unison.

"What? I thought it was the cleaning store."

"It would be Disneyland for me. You know that, Mommy Leslie."

"Yes, I do. I've always known, so guess where we're going?"

"The cleaning store?"

"No! We're going to the airport, and we're going to go to Disneyland for three whole days. I already told your teachers you wouldn't be there on Monday and Tuesday."

"Our teachers know?"

"Yes, I told them last week."

"You planned this? For us?" Victoria whimpered as tears rolled down her cheeks.

I checked the traffic, and when it was clear, I pulled over.

"Victoria, why're you crying? You don't want to go to Disney?"

"I ... I ..." She sobbed so hard that she hiccupped.

"Whaa ..." Sofia cried. "Why's Victoria unhappy? I don't wanna go ..." She rubbed her eyes with her tiny fists as huge tears fell onto her lap.

Oh my God, what have I done? The day I tried to take the girls out of school to get ice cream, I left and booked the trip. I was positive the girls would be over the moon.

"Oh, my goodness." I studied the two crying girls. "I'm sorry. I screwed up again, didn't I? Disneyland was my idea of making a new beginning for the three of us. I thought it could be our first adventure as a family unit. I've obviously made a big mistake. We'll go home."

"N ... n ... no." Victoria stammered.

"Should we go to Disneyland?"

Victoria nodded.

Sofia looked at her big sister then nodded, too.

"Sweetie, we don't have to go." I reached over to touch her face. "Can you tell me why you're crying?"

"I don't know," she sniffed. "I miss my mom."

Neither of the girls wanted to talk about their mom, Gilbert, or what happened. The psychologist told me the girls would speak when they were ready, and I should be prepared. This was a true blindside, though, and it reminded me of their vulnerability.

"You know, girls, I never met your mom, but I know she was a special lady. Selena used to tell me stories about how your mom would bring home leftovers from the restaurant. Do you remember? She also told me that every Christmas, she'd always make sure there was a tree, and a gift for each of you."

"I miss her, too ..." Sofia wailed in time with her sister.

I checked the mirrors for traffic, then got out and climbed in the back seat between the girls. They each snuggled under the weight of my arm and cried. Their tiny bodies shook in tandem with the ragged breaths of their sobs. I undid their seatbelts and pulled them as close as I could. I wanted to shelter them from the world. We melted into each other like gold bullion in a molten pot. The girls clutched my hands, and a seamlessness emerged as I felt we'd become one. It had been an emotional day with the handover of the baby—the last tangible connection to Selena. Feverish in my grasp, I wondered if I'd miscalculated the level of bond that had formed between myself and the girls.

Finally, Victoria calmed her tears and relaxed her head on my chest. Her face, stained with tears, searched mine as I pulled her tight to me. On my other side, Sofia did the same.

"Can I call you Mom instead of Mommy Leslie?"

My breath caught in my throat. Boom—another blindside.

"Yes, of course you can if you want."

"I don't like calling you Leslie," Victoria confessed. "People get confused, and besides, you're like our mom now, right?"

"You bet. I totally get it, and I consider it an honor."

"I want to call you Mommy, too," Sofia chimed in.

"Then you shall."

A sense of calm settled over the three of us, and I wanted nothing to change. These two beautiful girls accepted me with all my craziness and horrid past. We were a family. My first real one in my life. These two were now my daughters. My entire body swelled with gratitude and hope. I was their mother.

The three days in Disneyland was magical. Together, we experienced and explored the enchantment of fireworks, castles, and adventures. Filled with wonder, all three of us walked for miles, experienced the magic, and met people who made us giggle and grow memories as a family. When we got home, a new routine of life fell into place.

"I'll meet you here after school." I let the girls continue on to the school grounds.

They blew kisses, and I returned home to call my editor. Every day, I worked until two, then walked over to meet the girls.

"Hi again," Autumn said, as she stopped beside me.

"Oh hey, I was hoping to run into you."

"You were? Why?"

"No reason." I shrugged. "I enjoyed our talk the last time. Our girls are the same age, and I'm pretty new at all this. I thought we could go for lunch or something sometime. You could probably teach me a thing or two."

"I'd like that." Autumn smiled.

For the first time in my life, I felt I had made a true friend.

Chapter Forty-Seven

NOW

LESLIE

"Leslie, you need to come in and see me." It was Max on my voicemail.

After the handover to the Spenser family at the office, we'd drawn up a visitation schedule and, with no snags, I hadn't talked to Max in months.

Everything was wonderful, and I didn't want to throw off the balance. The girls had made the honor roll last term. Autumn and I went for coffee regularly, and I didn't want to talk about the past anymore. I was happy.

"Les, come on," the message continued. "We need to talk. You have to face it sooner or later."

Reluctantly, I picked up the phone and dialed his number

Chapter Forty-Eight

THEN

LESLIE

After graduation, I left and went as far as I could, as fast as I could. The college scholarship covered my tuition and partial rent, so I ended up with two part-time jobs, then I studied all night. Lots of people, my school counselor being one of them, thought I took too much on, but to me, it all spelled freedom. I'd leave nothing to chance. This was my shot at an independent life, and nothing, and I mean nothing, would stop me.

The dorms were quiet. No one stayed around on a Friday night. That is, no one except me and the other studious nerds. This had been my first night off in over two weeks, and I enjoyed the room's stillness. I sat down at my desk to write out a list of what needed to be done, when a sharp rap on the door reminded me I wasn't completely alone.

"Who is it?"

"Les, there's a telegram for you," a boy said through the door.

"Slip it under the door."

Mother in hospital. Stop. Not expected to make it past tomorrow. Stop. Request to come immediately. Stop. Lincoln Memorial Hospital. Stop.

I stared at the words until they blurred into one another. My fingers released the paper and let it flutter to the floor. It burned with the reminder of her existence. I preferred to think of her as dead and gone, but once again, the ugly reality had reared its head. I sat on my small bed and considered my options.

Did I have to go? I'm not after any daughter of the year award, so what did it matter? I could ignore the telegram and pretend it never arrived, but the boy who delivered it knew—and, of course, I knew. It had been two years since I'd seen or talked to her, and those were the best two years of my life as I liberated myself from the dark cloak of secrecy and tyranny.

Breaking away from Mother had been the healthiest thing for me. I soon learned people didn't care about anything I did. Everyone was busy and focused on their own issues—not on my shortcomings. All the fears drilled into me over the years were lies. I didn't want to breathe the same air as her. My life was mine, and I had choices. I pushed myself up from the side of my bed and found the piece of paper.

I paid the cab driver, grabbed my bag, and stood on the concrete stairs that led to the hospital's main entrance. I felt rooted there. Nearby puddles, formed by a recent rain, glistened red as ambulances sped off with their lights flashing. My chest tightened, and a dull, steady throb took hold of my head. I forced my feet into a shuffle, climbed the stairs, and pushed through the swinging door.

"Excuse me." I spoke through a hole in the Plexiglas. "I'm here to see my mother. Her name is Marion Matheson."

"She's on the tenth floor." The young woman pointed toward the elevators. "East wing, room 1062."

I slung my bag over my shoulder and set off to find the room. My damp shoes squeaked on the waxed floor with every step, like a squeegee cleaning a window. I knew if I hesitated for even a minute, I'd turn and bolt.

The sterile smell of pine-scented cleaner and bleach filled the air until I entered her room. As I got closer to the bed, a fetid bouquet of urine and sour body odor enveloped me and caused my throat to constrict and my eyes to water.

"Leslie? Did you come to see your old mother? You don't need to cry."

Hearing the voice, I cringed and took a deep breath through my mouth, which was a mistake, as I could then taste the stench. I wiped my wet eyes with the back of my hand. Weep for her? Never.

"Yes, Mother, I came." I held my hand in front of my face. "I received word you were apparently going to die."

"Is that what college teaches you? To be disrespectful to your mother? Such a hideous tone you're using, young lady."

"Well, this tone can leave anytime. What is it you want to tell me? I suppose you should inform me where the family fortune is." I watched her gnarled fingers reach for me. I'd fallen for such tricks before and ended up with a fist in my face or a gob of phlegm dripping from my hair—never again.

"Come, I won't hurt you. Grant a dying woman her last wish."

"Are you dying, Mother?"

"Stay and talk to the doctor if you like. The cancer has consumed me. They say you get strong at the end in order to deal with unfinished business, and that's what I'm trying to do."

I poked my head out the door for a sanitized breath of air, but also to see if a nearby doctor or nurse could confirm Mother's story. I returned to the bedside and studied her. Her hair, thin and stringy, barely covered her freckled and uneven skull beneath. Her face looked old and sunken as the excess skin fell to the side with gravity as she lay on the bed. She was a wisp of a thing and appeared innocent—like someone's granny who was sick in bed. But I knew she was a wolf and would bite my head off, given the chance. I got too close, and suddenly there was an iron-clad grasp on my wrist. Her fingers were freezing cold, but surprisingly strong. A small yelp escaped me as I tried to pull away. I was five years old again and trapped in the clutches of a monster.

"Come here, Leslie." Mother tugged on me.

My gut constricted as I squelched a scream. I wanted to run. I tried to pull away to escape, but Mother's whole body came with me. I was afraid if I pulled too hard, she'd spill to the floor, and I'd be responsible.

"Let go of me." Sweat ran down my back as my heart banged violently in my chest. "I knew I shouldn't have come."

"I'm your mother," she hissed. The strength she possessed was incredible as she tugged me closer to her. It was a magnetic force beyond my control. I closed my eyes as tight as I could as she brought her face close to mine.

"There, that's better."

The stink of decay emanated from Mother's breath. I gagged and tried to yank my hand away, but some unknown force rendered me feeble and small—any power I came in with had vanished.

"Now, Mother's going to tell you a story, and you're not to ask questions. It's your job to listen."

I knew I didn't have a choice.

I couldn't breathe. My legs wobbled and threatened to give out, and a chill skipped down my spine as her words filled my head. It was a confessional—a cleansing of her soul. Nowhere did she apologize or beg forgiveness. As she finished, she eased her grip on my wrist and fell back onto her pillow, into what looked like a peaceful slumber. I rubbed my wrist and scrutinized the evil before me. I drew back and spat in her face. Unworthy of my time or sympathy, I spun on my heel and left her.

Chapter Forty-Nine

NOW

LESLIE

The day dawned bright and sunny. The rays came through the window and bounced off the mirrors, sending colorful prisms dancing on the ceiling. I wanted to stay in bed. Life was peaceful and smooth, and I didn't want to upset the order of things, but I padded downstairs and put the coffee on. It was so quiet.

It had been months since I had the house to myself. I climbed into my chair and considered the park across the street. It was still the same small, city green space at a bus stop that allowed some to rest, while others passed by without even noticing it.

It differed from the first time I saw it, though. There was no Selena, and the girls were now family. Last night, they stayed overnight with Autumn and her family. It had been over three months, and the kids went back and forth. It terrified me at first, especially since it was in such proximity to where the girls had lived with their mom, but after a discussion, it was clear the girls were fine. Autumn and her family became extended family by default.

I watched the Saturday morning traffic and sipped my hot coffee. The stillness in the house was foreign now. The girls had been with me since baby Von was born, and he was almost a year old. Chad and his family were coming here for a birthday celebration next month. The girls planned it, made decorations, and were excited to host a party.

I glanced over and saw Prince. He dug through the garbage and picked out the cans I placed there before going to bed. I'd been negligent for a while, but was finally back on a normal schedule.

I'd told Autumn what I did, and she laughed at me.

"Why are you laughing? It gives me pleasure to see him happy with all those cans."

"That so-called Prince is Derek Dobster. He was a used-car salesman, until he sold one too many clunkers and got sued. Do you know he takes all those cans, turns them in, then heads straight for the market to get his vodka?"

"So I'm feeding his habit, is what you're saying?"

"Pretty much. I usually see him sleeping it off late in the evening down on Sixth Avenue. There's a bench that he likes there."

"Is he violent or nasty?"

"Nope, he scours for cans all night, then gets his booze and sleeps it off. Pretty harmless, I think."

"Hmm—well, you know he'll still be my Prince. He's probably the most reliable man I've never met."

We laughed, but I contemplated the situation for a long

time. Was I feeding his addiction? I thought back to when I'd stuff twinkies in my mouth three at a time and wash them down with wine to make room for three more. I always had the means to purchase my drug of choice, and no one ever questioned me. He's going to drink regardless of what I do, and if I can make his life easier or satisfying, then who am I to judge? I continued to stuff the cans in the trash when I could, and enjoyed watching him discover the cache.

I finished my coffee, and Prince rolled his cart up the street. I had to go. There was no way to avoid the inevitable. I returned to my bedroom to get showered and dressed. Today was as good a day as any to put my past to rest.

With my hand on the doorknob, I paused. I'm strong now. I can do this. All the demons have been exorcised, and blessings surround me at every turn. With a deep breath, I pushed open the door.

"Hey Les, come on in." Max sat behind his huge desk. "It's been too long. You look good."

"Thanks, Max." I spied the envelope on his desk. "I'm in a good place."

"It shows. Sorry I've been such a pest, but not only am I your lawyer and confidant; I'm your friend." He waved me to the couch to sit. "I knew you needed time, but I also know this needs to be done."

"I appreciate it. I do. The girls always ask about Uncle Max." I smiled. "I'm good now, Max. Do I need to know something that can ruin it all?"

Max went back to his desk and grabbed the envelope. All I could see was CONFIDENTIAL in bold, red letters.

"I think it's time." He walked over and once again placed the envelope in my hands.

I took it gingerly by the edges and set it on the table beside me. I didn't want to look. Digging up things was not necessarily good for the soul. I studied him and tried to determine his agenda.

"Do you remember the last time you saw your mother?" He leaned back in his chair and crossed his legs.

"I try to forget, not remember it."

"You're being difficult."

"Okay. Okay. Yes, I remember it. She was in the hospital."

"And?" He raised his brow and waited.

"Okay." I sighed. "She made me listen to a story, and I spit in her face. She was an evil, vile woman who hid behind the Bible and used it to torture me for years."

"What did she tell you?"

"Max, why are you doing this?" I closed my eyes and sighed.

"I need you to say it out loud and acknowledge the things she left you with. Before she died, she piled on the fear and expectation, and you've lived with that for years."

"Okay, okay. She told me my baby was actually a girl, not a boy, as I always thought. She was born healthy, and Mother gave her away."

"What else?"

"She told me my baby was still alive, and I'd never find her."

"Is that the first time you've said that aloud since you told me all those years ago?"

I nodded. Even now, the stench of her filled my nose, and I wanted to claw her eyes out.

"She said she sold her in order to pay the rent. She thanked me." My chest constricted as a sob escaped me. I rocked back and forth where I sat. It was like being fifteen again. "I spit in her face," I said as I gulped at the air. "I fled the room and heard her cackle. She laughed at me."

"Her actions had a huge effect on your life, didn't they?" Max asked.

"For years, every little girl I saw had Johnny's smile or my eyes. I searched every little face. Never forgetting..."

"You know, don't you? Can you tell me, Les?"

"The priest sent me here, and you hired an investigator for me, but he couldn't find her." I wiped my nose and cleared my throat. The investigation had stalled before it even began. I could hear Max breathing across from me. "Max, did you find my baby? Is my baby alive?" I pulled my feet up onto the couch, and hugged them close before I allowed him to answer.

"I know it took a long time for the investigation to come full circle," Max said, "There were a lot of loose ends, but this report was delivered over three years ago now. It's been here waiting for you."

I couldn't breathe. I placed my hand on my belly and recalled the movements—the kicks, the somersaults, the life—my baby.

Max crossed the room, sat beside me, and took my hands between his.

"Les, I know this is hard, but there is no little girl..." he said. "Your mother played with your emotions and your psyche for years. She manipulated the truth in her favor and drove your self-esteem down until it was nonexistent." He stirred in his seat before continuing. "Les, the investigator found the skeleton of a newborn baby boy, buried in the backyard of the house where you gave birth."

"No! He's alive. I heard him cry. Please. He's alive. I know he's out there somewhere."

"There were stains on the blanket he was wrapped in, so they conducted DNA tests and the lab confirmed that it was your baby. They weren't able to tell whether it was a live birth."

Leslie, I'm sorry. I know it wasn't the news you wanted. All the documentation is in the envelope."

I'd always known she wouldn't let my baby live, but I harbored the faintest of hopes. My heart squeezed in my chest as a sharp yelp escaped from the depths of my soul.

"The mourning can finally begin for you, Leslie. They sealed the baby's remains for when you're ready to have a proper burial."

"Thank you," I squeaked and blew my nose. "My poor little baby—my poor little Joseph." I blew my nose a second time. "When I saw the envelope, I knew it was the investigator's report. I hoped for a miracle, I won't lie, but I couldn't open it. I've grown a lot in these last few years."

"There's something else in the envelope that may interest you." Max reached over and retrieved it.

"What?"

My baby was dead. All those years of studying faces and wondering. Oh, how I loathed that woman.

"Well, the private investigator did some background work and found your father." Max pulled a paper from the package. "They ran your DNA through a genetics-testing center database, and it matched up with your father and his family."

"What? My father is dead." I shook my head. "Mother told me he died before I was even born."

"Unfortunately, you were misinformed. He knew nothing about you. He said he and your mother had a brief relationship, then she left town, and he never heard from her again."

This can't be real. My baby is dead, and my father is alive—what?

"The DNA doesn't lie. And not only is he your biological father, but you also have three half-sisters."

"No." I took the sheet from Max's hand and studied it. "I don't believe you."

"When we told him about you, he wanted to meet you immediately. I tried to get you to talk to me, but you were dealing with Phillip and Selena and everything else. It's been a hell of a few years for you, but I knew you'd face it when you were ready."

"Oh my God, I've wasted so much time." I scanned the report. Three sisters? "So much time."

I opened the envelope and pulled out a picture. A balding man with large hazel eyes smiled back at me from behind thick glasses. My hands shook as I studied every line of his face. He appeared to be sixty, with laugh lines and an open, welcoming smile. What did he see in that evil bitch? This was a piece of my puzzle I didn't even know I was missing.

"Thank you, Max." I clung to him. "I should have trusted you, but thank you for not giving up on me. I'm going home. I need to absorb all this new information and get it straight in my head."

"I'm here for you whenever you need. We'll move at your pace."

I stood, took the envelope, and left the office.

Chapter Fifty

TWO MONTHS LATER

LESLIE

I stood on the sidewalk and watched my father play with the girls. He welcomed all of us into his life, as did the rest of his family.

I have three half-sisters, which is surreal. I'm the oldest. The next one is only two years younger than me, and the similarities in facial features, body type, and personality are out of this world. If we did our hair and makeup the same, we could easily pass as twins. To say I'm overwhelmed would be an understatement. How does one explain the satisfying pleasure of fullness—of spirit and of self—if you've never lived it? I can truly say I'm satiated beyond belief.

Meeting family proved to be more significant than I ever

thought. As soon as he saw me, my biological father pulled me into his embrace, and it was a perfect fit.

"I wish I'd known," he whispered through his tears. "I'd have come right away."

"We're here now." I wiped his tears away. "I didn't even know until now how much I missed you."

It took me a long time to share the story of my baby. The grieving process and accepting new truths meant dealing with all the lies. Max recommended a fully accredited counselor, and I finally gave in and went. Max had been my steadfast friend and confidant for years. I knew he needed a break, too. I planned a private memorial service for my baby. The only person I wanted at my side through it all was Max.

We stood by the tiny white coffin. "Thank you for putting up with me over the years," I said, "and I'm grateful you're with me today."

That afternoon, I mourned my baby boy as I embraced a new beginning. With my friend's hand tucked tightly into mine, I finally stood in my new truth.

AUTHORS' NOTE

AUTHORS' NOTE

INSIDE OUTSIDE is a work of fiction. All of the characters and incidents within the story are the imagination of the author. If you, however, find yourself in any situation similar to Leslie or Selena please speak to your family physician and/or social service providers in your area. You can also talk to a teacher, the police, your pastor, a friend... someone...and keep telling until you are heard.

Acknowledgments

Thank you to you the reader. I share your passion for reading and like you, appreciate a good story with a few twists along the way.

To those who've waited all this time for my book to finally be published, a huge thank you for your patience and dedication.

I'd also like to thank and acknowledge my family. Michael and Parker have believed in me (and been so patient) right from the very beginning. Much love to you both.

Thank you to Kara Antifeau, Leesa Immelmann, Tacia Topham... all nieces who constantly cheer me on. Advance readers for **INSIDE OUTSIDE:** Kara Antifeau, Leesa Immelmann, Sam Cutts, Carol Bentley, and Sally Quon. Your feedback was invaluable. Thank you.

Huge kudos to fellow writers, teachers, and mentors Jonas Saul, Lorna Schultz Nicholson, and Carol Rose GoldenEagle who constantly give back so much of themselves to writers, creatives, poets, storytellers and authors. You're not only inspirations, but leaders within the writing community as a whole. Thank you for that.

Thank you also to author Steena Holmes who pushed me and said I *had* to publish my book and wouldn't take no for an answer.

And, last but certainly not least, a huge shout out to my late sister Maureen, who was herself a gifted writer, educator and mentor. Maureen was instrumental in igniting the creative spark within me and I believe it is her spirit that continues to light the way as I move forward~~she is, and always has been~~on this journey with me. ♡

About the Author

Faye Arcand has been writing for her
entire life. This is her debut novel.

Watch for her second novel
CAN YOU SEE ME in 2025.

Faye lives in British Columbia, Canada with her family.

Follow her on Goodreads and Instagram
Sign up for Faye Arcand's Newsletter to get first hand news on
current projects and opportunities to participate in draws and
polls.

www.fayearcand.com

Manufactured by Amazon.ca
Bolton, ON

41533041R00181